BLACK
KARMA

Also by Thatcher Robinson

White Ginger

THATCHER ROBINSON

BLACK KARMA

A WHITE GINGER NOVEL

SEVENTH STREET BOOKS®

AN IMPRINT OF PROMETHEUS BOOKS

59 JOHN GLENN DRIVE • AMHERST, NY 14228
www.seventhstreetbooks.com

Published 2014 by Seventh Street Books®, an imprint of Prometheus Books

Cover design by Nicole Sommer-Lecht
Cover image © Maciej Toporowicz/Arcangel Images

Inquiries should be addressed to
Seventh Street Books
59 John Glenn Drive
Amherst, New York 14228
VOICE: 716–691–0133
FAX: 716–691–0137
WWW.SEVENTHSTREETBOOKS.COM

18 17 16 15 14   5 4 3 2 1

Library of Congress Cataloging-in-Publication Data

Robinson, Thatcher, 1952-
    Black karma : a White Ginger novel / by Thatcher Robinson.
        pages cm
    ISBN 978-1-61614-003-8 (paperback) — ISBN 978-1-61614-006-9 (ebook)
    1. Buddhist women—Fiction. 2. Women private investigators—Fiction.
3. Missing persons—Investigation—Fiction. 4. Chinatown (San Francisco,
Calif.)—Fiction. I. Title.

PS3618.O33376B57 2014
813'.6—dc23

                                                        2014023932

Printed in the United States of America

To my wife, Susan Noguchi

chapter 1

"I need friends," Bai declared.

The knife flicked into the air to arc gracefully before falling into her outstretched palm. She tossed the blade again—a slow, repetitive ritual, like a silent chant.

Exhaust fumes, along with the scent of five-spice, wafted through the open window. On Grant Avenue below, horns blared as traffic came to a standstill. Voices clamored for attention over the bustling din.

"You have friends," Lee replied. Tall, lean, and muscular, he wore tan slacks and a blue cashmere sweater. His long torso reclined on a red leather couch as he read a magazine. Looking up, he added, "You have me."

"Friends—as in plural, meaning more than one," she said. "I lack the ability to make friends. There's definitely something wrong with me."

He put down his scientific journal and turned to look at her. "You dress like an undertaker. You're surly, impatient, and sarcastic. You scare people."

She leaned back in her chair to reflect. "Are you sure you're my friend? Don't you want to mention any of my good qualities?"

"Friends tell you the ugly truth whether you want to hear it or not."

"If that were true, my bathroom scale would be my best friend."

An alarm buzzed in the adjoining lobby to let them know someone had entered their offices. Lee stood to confirm the identity of their caller while Bai slipped her knife into the sheath sewn into the sleeve of her black leather jacket. When the door opened again, Inspector Kelly of the San Francisco City Police Department stood in the entry.

Grizzled, fat, and over fifty, Kelly nearly filled the doorway. Eyes hollowed by dark rings stared blurrily from a pale, round face. A veined nose bearing a striking resemblance to a baby squash dominated his features. In one hand, Kelly held a four-pack of coffee; in the other, a grease-stained paper bag. He spoke in a graveled voice. "Am I inter-rupting anything?"

"Nothing important," she said. "I was just being insulted."

He walked across the room to place the tray of coffees and the bag on her desk. Picking up one of the large paper cups, he said, "Have a doughnut and get over it."

What might have once been a tan raincoat covered his bulky frame while rumpled tweed pants with high-water cuffs exposed white socks tucked into a pair of scuffed brogues big enough to require parking permits. Without further fanfare, he walked around her desk to plop down on the couch with a thump. A shudder ran through the floor-boards as leather cushions screeched in protest.

Lee closed the door to the lobby to lean with his back against the frame and silently observe.

"Make yourself at home," Bai belatedly suggested as she uncapped a coffee and rummaged in the bag to find a chocolate-glazed sinker. "To what do we owe the pleasure of your company?"

"This is just a friendly visit."

Kelly pulled a pint of Jameson's from inside his coat. Trembling fingers twisted off the cap while a fat, splotchy tongue slid over his lips. His eyes fastened greedily on the bottle as he poured a healthy shot into his coffee.

Bai watched him with a wary expression. "A friendly visit suggests we're friends. I was just telling Lee I have *way too many* friends."

San Francisco's finest didn't make a habit of policing Chinatown. Black-and-whites cruised the streets should a perpetrator get a sudden, inexplicable urge to surrender. But, for the most part, they left the Chinese community alone. The arrangement seemed to work well for everyone, which left Bai to wonder what the inspector wanted.

He ignored her remark and held out the bottle. "Care for a taste?"

"I'm good," she replied, waving him off with a doughnut.

The inspector shook the bottle at Lee, who declined the offer with a curt shake of his head.

Kelly put the pint carefully back inside his coat before taking a sip.

"Ahh . . ." A smile spread across his face. "Nothing like a little Irish to start your day."

Her brows lifted. "I can only assume you're referring to the whiskey."

His eyes narrowed as his face squeezed into a jaundiced grin. "Either one would put a smile on your face."

She frowned. "It's really sad when you can't tell the difference between a smile and a grimace."

He stared at her a moment before shrugging off the comment. "I'd rather have a bottle in front of me than a frontal lobotomy."

"Seems a little late to change your mind," Lee observed.

Kelly turned to squint at Lee before shaking his head and turning away again. He leaned back into the cushions to sip his morning cocktail, his eyelids slowly unfurling.

"Why are you here?" Lee asked.

Kelly opened his eyes slowly as a scowl pulled at the corners of his mouth. He turned to Bai while making a point of ignoring Lee. "There's nothing I enjoy more than having a morning libation with a beautiful woman. But, truth be told, that's not entirely why I'm here."

He leaned slowly back into the sofa cushions again to drink his coffee with a look of trepidation.

"If you have something to say, Kelly, just say it," she said.

"What happened to that Oriental patience you people are famous for?"

She spoke slowly, as if addressing a child. "A rug might be Oriental, or a lamp, but not a person. I'm Chinese, and I have little tolerance for racists. So unless you have something to tell me, our time together, though memorable, has come to an end."

Kelly appeared perplexed by her indignation and raised a hand defensively. "Give me a chance to explain," he said gruffly. "I'm here on official business. That's to say, I'm here to ask for your help on behalf of the City of San Francisco. But if anyone were ever to ask, I was never here."

"Would that be too much to ask?" she said impatiently as she leaned back into her chair.

Kelly's eyes darted around the room. He took another gulp of coffee and seemed to draw courage from it. "You heard about that little altercation in the SOMA yesterday?"

The SOMA, an area wedged between the Business District on the north and the Tenderloin and Mission Districts on the south, had once served as a warehouse district. Warehouses gave way to the building of a new stadium in a dramatic transformation that made South of Market a trendy district showcasing stylish nightclubs, restaurants, and high-priced condos.

She offered a guarded response. "Are you referring to the *little* altercation that left three dead, one of them a policeman?"

"That would be the one. And," the inspector raised his index finger for emphasis, "let's not forget about the wounded. The papers dubbed it 'THE SOMA SHOOT-OUT.' Reporters love to lay it on thick, don't they? The truth isn't nearly so dramatic. Only a dozen shots were fired, and it was just pure dumb luck some of them proved fatal." The inspector let out a sigh and seemed to reflect. "But that's beside the point."

"What does any of this have to do with me?"

"I'm getting to that," he said, taking another sip from his cup. "The bust was a sting operation. Our officers were there to buy drugs. Shots were fired, and when the smoke cleared, the drugs were gone and so was the bag of money our officers carried. Three stiffs were on their way to the morgue, and another half-dozen injured were on the way to City General. The mayor is fit to be tied, and the chief is looking for someone to blame. On top of that, the relatives of the perps are threatening to sue, claiming the cops executed their dearly deceased. It's a clusterfuck of massive proportions."

Bai shrugged. "I still don't see how that's my problem."

"There's more," Kelly stated while raising the cup to his lips. His eyes lidded as he drank. "A Chinese by the name of Daniel Chen, at least that's the name he uses, was involved. It seems he might be an illegal. Our best guess is he's hiding here in Chinatown."

"We don't work for the police," Lee interjected.

The inspector's somber gaze fixed on Bai. "You're a *souxun*, aren't you? Finding lost people is what you do. We have an officer down, and the reputation of the department is at stake. We want you to find Chen. There's a ten percent finder's fee for any money recovered."

She studied the inspector while he stared back at her with dulled eyes. "I really don't think I can help you."

Kelly shrugged. "If SFPD brings Chen in, it might be in a body bag. A cop has been killed. Tempers are running hot. You'd probably be saving a life if you were to get this guy into lockup before SFPD can find him."

Bai looked at the inspector for a clue to his motives. She wondered why Kelly wanted her involved. The more she thought about the situation, the less she liked it. Still, if she could save a life, the selfless act would boost her karma, which currently flushed in a counter-clockwise direction. She'd taken two lives while rescuing a girl from slavery. As a Buddhist, her prospects for advancement on the astral plane had taken a sudden and precipitous nosedive.

"Do you have a picture of Chen?"

Kelly rummaged inside his raincoat to pull out a piece of paper. The sheet held a grainy image of a man standing on the street, a candid shot showing only his profile. The face in the picture appealed to her. She'd guess him to be in his late twenties or early thirties with a strong, straight nose and full lips.

"It's not much of picture, but it's all we've got," Kelly said. "The picture was taken in the Mission District where Chen's been making a name for himself on the local fight circuit." Pulling a piece of paper out of his pocket, he held it out before him. "This is the address of the gym where he trains."

Kelly turned his attention to Lee. "I understand you used to be something of a legend in the fight clubs."

Lee stepped forward to take the paper from Kelly's outstretched hand but didn't respond to his comment.

"Pretty face like yours," Kelly observed, "it's a cinch you didn't lose many fights. Me, on the other hand," he said, reaching up to feel his misshapen nose, "well, it's pretty obvious my talents lie in other areas."

"Hidden talents, no doubt," Lee said.

Comprehension seemed to elude the inspector as he stared at Lee with pursed lips.

Bai drew Kelly's attention away. "How much money was in the bag? What kinds of drugs were being sold?"

He hesitated as if ordering his thoughts before replying. "A million dollars in pure China White—at least, that's what I've been told. The same in cash."

She looked up to meet Lee's gaze. If heroin from Asia traded hands in San Francisco, *Sun Yee On*, the resident triad, would know about it.

"All right, Kelly," she conceded. "We'll look into the matter."

"Your assistance will be greatly appreciated," Kelly noted. The inspector stood, wadded up his empty paper cup, and tossed his garbage out the open window. He dropped one of his business cards on Bai's desk in passing. "I look forward to hearing from you."

As he lumbered toward the door, Bai addressed his back. "Sure. What are friends for?"

chapter 2

"I have seen the enemy, and it is tasty," Bai said as she sipped her coffee while staring balefully at the half-eaten doughnut in her hand.

Lee stood at the window with his back to her and watched the street below. "I'm willing to bet there's more involved than Kelly's telling us."

Bai's lips fell into a frown. "Kelly has a dark aura. I can feel it, a black karma that pursues him."

Lee chuckled. "It's not karma following him. It's a girl, and a pretty one. Do you want me to follow them?"

"No. At this point, I'm not even sure I want anything to do with Inspector Kelly. I want to check out his story before getting involved. The article in the paper didn't mention money or drugs. Something doesn't feel right."

Lee walked over to sit on the edge of her desk. "I'll make some calls. The fight circuit is a small, close-knit culture. Someone is certain to know Chen. I'm somewhat familiar with the gym where he trained."

"While you're doing that, I think I'll pay a visit to Uncle Tommy and see if he's missing any China White."

Uncle Tommy was Bai's godfather. He was also *Shan Chu*, head of the dragon, overlord of *Sun Yee On* triad. When her grandfather had been alive, Tommy had been *Fu Shan Chu*, underboss. After the death of Bai's parents, Tommy practically raised her; he was the only father she'd ever known.

"Give him my regards," Lee said derisively.

Lee had also been close to Tommy—family. When Lee had come out as *tongzhi*, their relationship ended. Rabidly homophobic, the Brotherhood enforced strict prohibitions against associating with gays. Tommy had never spoken to Lee again.

Bai didn't spout a witty reply. She wouldn't make light of Lee's pain. Instead, she stood and hugged him before turning to walk out of the office.

As she stepped out onto the busy sidewalk, she fumbled her dark glasses out of her pocket and onto her face. Bright sunlight made her squint. Her eyes adjusted to take in fluffy white clouds floating in a pale blue sky. A whiff of salt and the subtle tang of decay teased her nose as a chill breeze blew in from the harbor.

She turned to walk north on Grant Avenue, avoiding pedestrians, mostly tourists whom the natives referred to as *gwailos*. Sightseers with cameras, maps, and bags stuffed with trinkets crowded the sidewalks on both sides of the narrow street. She dodged between herds of shoppers and tables piled high with brightly colored souvenirs. The *gwailos* stared at her as she sidestepped through the crowd. Tall, agile, and beautiful, she turned heads like a breaking wave as she passed by.

Sun Yee On headquartered in the Businessman's Association Building, an eight-story gray monolith built in the early seventies. The exterior of the building possessed all the charm of a charcoal briquette. The interior of the building fared much better with finishes in light woods and polished brass. Despite its lack of architectural character, the building retained intrinsic value: its location in the heart of San Francisco's Chinatown made it prime real estate.

She took the elevator to the eighth-floor penthouse offices. As she stepped out of the lift and into an airy atrium-style lobby, the scent of fresh lilies greeted her. Large white blooms placed in tall Chinese vases bracketed a circular receptionist's desk. Overstuffed armchairs covered in brown leather hugged the walls. A petite Chinese woman in a chic black suit stood behind the desk with a wireless headphone inserted in her ear.

Bai walked across the room to stand before the receptionist and wait.

"How may I help you, Ms. Jiang?"

The receptionist recognized Bai as a familiar face. It also helped that Bai owned the building.

"Is Tommy available? I only need a few minutes of his time."

"I'm sorry. Mr. Hu is in Hong Kong. Would you like to leave a message?"

She paused to consider the offer as the receptionist's eyes shifted. Bai turned, instinctively, to find Jason walking toward her with a welcoming smile on his face.

Jason, her ex and the father of her thirteen-year-old daughter, served as *Hung Kwan* of *Sun Yee On*. *Hung Kwan* translated to "red pole" and signified the position as second in line for succession after the *Fu Shan Chu*. Jason managed the organization's strike teams, which meant he commanded a small army of triad soldiers. He'd earned his position at a relatively young age by being very, very good at his job. He killed people.

To look at him, one wouldn't think him an assassin. A handsome face with chiseled features and a lean, muscular body made people, especially women, take note. When he smiled, which was often, white teeth dazzled. The fashionable tailored suits he wore cost a small fortune. From all outward appearances, he looked like a successful, sophisticated businessman. His striking appearance served as just one of the many reasons Bai had such difficulty getting over him.

"Is there something I can help you with, Bai?"

"Can you make me stop eating potato chips and doughnuts?"

"I could, but you wouldn't like me afterward."

"Maybe we should talk in your office, then—if you have a minute?"

"I have more than a minute," he assured her, gesturing toward the glass doors leading to the executive offices.

He ushered her into his office where they took seats in massive armchairs facing each other. She suspected the oversized chairs were designed to make the occupants feel smaller by comparison.

Jason seemed to read her mind. "I could join you over there if you're feeling lost."

"Stay where you are. The last time I sat next to you, I ended up naked."

"I remember vividly," he replied with a smile. "You forget. I have a pornographic memory."

Despite every attempt not to, she smiled.

"That's better," he said. "Now, what can I do for you?"

"The killings in SOMA yesterday. Was *Sun Yee On* involved?"

"No."

Her forehead furrowed. His accommodating response baffled her. She'd anticipated having to ply him with favors to get what she wanted. "That was too easy."

"Had *Sun Yee On* been involved, my answer would have been much more oblique."

"'Oblique'?" Her voice showed dismay. "You've been spending too much time with your attorneys. You should get out more."

"I've been thinking the same thing. How about joining me for dinner tonight?"

"No, thank you. We're finished. I'm over you."

"That's what you said the last time when you ended up naked. Remember?"

"I find it difficult to forget when you keep reminding me. Let's talk about something else. You're sure *Sun Yee On* isn't missing a million dollars' worth of China White?"

"I'm pretty sure I'd know if that were the case," he stated as he leaned forward. "What makes you think the Brotherhood is involved?"

"I've been told a million dollars in cash and the equivalent value of China White went missing yesterday during the shootout in the SOMA. I assumed if China White traded hands in San Francisco, *Sun Yee On* would be involved."

"There's nothing wrong with your logic," Jason assured her. "It's your facts that are wrong. First, if the Brotherhood were to broker a large sale, we'd make sure the transaction took place here, in Chinatown, where we have control over the streets. Second, there's no way we would sell heroin to undercover police officers. We pay them substantial amounts of money to leave us and our business alone."

"But you do know what happened in the SOMA?"

"I know what was supposed to happen. Obviously, things didn't come off as smoothly as planned."

"Would you care to share what you know with me?"

"What do I get in return?"

She glared at him. He smiled and crossed one leg over the other. She bit back a colorful reply, which though gratifying wouldn't have served her purpose. Reminding herself that everything had a price, she replied, "Dinner."

"Deal." His smile widened. "Now, that wasn't so hard, was it?"

"I'm keeping my clothes on," she added for emphasis.

He smiled obligingly. "The restaurant staff will be disappointed but understanding."

"So tell me already. What happened?"

He leaned back in his chair. "Curiosity is both your weakness and your strength. Your nosiness leads you into situations you should be smart enough to avoid but instead drives you blindly forward with single-minded determination. I always find your exploits fascinating, like watching a train wreck in slow motion."

"I know all that," she said while windmilling her hand to move him along. "I'm a regular ferreting fool. Now, get on with the story."

He looked as if he wanted to wax on philosophically but abandoned the notion at her urging. "All right," he relented. "My understanding is that the narcotics task force hijacked product from a group of Mission District Norteños, then set up a meet in the SOMA, supposedly neutral ground, to sell them back their heroin."

"So the heroin wasn't China White. It was Mexican Brown."

"Correct."

"Aren't the Norteños distributing for the Sinoloa cartel?"

"Correct again."

"So what happened?"

He shrugged nonchalantly. "Put a bunch of armed idiots in a room, toss in a million in cash and a million in heroin, and what would you expect to happen? Maybe the Norteños took offense at being sold their own heroin. Maybe the task force thought they could keep the cash and the drugs."

"Did you hear anything about an Asian guy making off with the money or the drugs?"

His head came up. For the first time during their conversation, he looked genuinely interested. "Perhaps," he suggested, "you've something you'd care to share with me?"

She thought seriously about filling him in but decided against doing so for the time being. She still had too many unanswered questions in mind and didn't want him finding the answers to those questions before she did.

She slipped a smile onto her face. "We'll talk at dinner."

He cocked his head to study her. Brown eyes drilled into her before his face softened and a smile made its way to his lips. "I'll send a car for you."

"I'd rather meet you. Where are we dining?"

"I don't want to ruin the surprise. Be ready at five. I have something special in mind. And wear something elegant. I can't remember the last time I saw you in a dress."

"That means I'll have to shave my legs."

"We all make sacrifices," he deadpanned.

"Does that mean you're shaving your legs, too?"

"You're more than welcome to take my pants off and find out."

She smiled sweetly. "You don't expect me to fall for that trick . . . again, do you?"

"One can only hope."

chapter 3

Lee had called and left a message, asking Bai to meet him at a gym in the Mission District. The cab dropped her off on Bryant near an alley, the only entrance to the business.

As she stood on the street, a cold wind swept in off the ocean to nip at her cheeks and the tips of her ears. She tucked her hands into the pockets of her jacket and looked up. The fluffy white clouds had thinned and darkened to assume a more sinister appearance. Weather in the city, as usual, proved about as dependable as a politician's promises.

As she walked toward the entrance of the alley, the stench of stale beer and urine made the cold wind blowing down the street suddenly more appealing. She raised the sleeve of her jacket to cover her nose and paid careful attention to where she put her feet in the shaded, narrow lane. Broken glass, empty beer cans, and used condoms littered the cracked asphalt.

A soggy box with discarded clothes rested against the side of the alley. Crack addicts and the homeless still called the Mission District home. Despite efforts by the city to gentrify the area, life on the streets remained the same.

A green metal door at the end of the backstreet displayed the address in white paint. Above the door, a lifeless neon sign spelled out "BOO S" in darkened vacuum tubes. The missing letter left Bai to wonder.

She shouldered the door open to find herself in a cavernous space. Steel beams and brick walls supported a high ceiling. Boxing equipment filled the room. Heavy bags, light bags, and speed bags hung from the ceiling joists and jutted from the walls on metal frames. Sparring gear and weights lay scattered on the floor and racked along the walls. A large, heavy mat occupied the middle of the room. Over the mat floated a padded cage suspended by chains. The smell of musty socks and sweat permeated the atmosphere.

"You here to cage fight?" asked a scornful voice.

Bai turned to find a swarthy young man with black, close-cropped hair glaring at her. He appeared to be a couple of inches shorter than her, but what he lacked in height he more than made up for in girth. Below one of his brown eyes, a tattooed teardrop on his cheek informed her he belonged to a gang and had a kill to his credit. His cold gaze measured her while his lips curled back into a predatory grin.

She smiled. "You claim Norteño?"

"NORTENO," tattooed around his neck, made the question rhetorical. Norteño was a street gang affiliated with the *Nuestra Familia*, a violent prison gang reaching beyond the boundaries of Folsom's penitentiary walls.

He answered with a sneer in his voice. "Boobs don't ask no questions."

She dropped the smile. "That sounds like something a prick would say."

He scowled. "Boobs the name a the man what owns this place."

She had to think about that for a minute. "My bad. *Lo . . . siento*."

He leaned toward her to get into her face. "You my *chola*, I jack you up some."

Bai took offense at the implication a beating might make her more respectful. Moreover, she thought it highly unlikely. Smiling tightly and twitching her head, she replied, "I can see where beating a woman is the only way you'd get her respect."

"What you tryin' to say, *bruja*?"

"I'm not *tryin'* to say anything. I'm telling you the only thing hitting a woman proves is you're an asshole, which you've already admirably demonstrated. Thank you very much."

His face contorted into a mask of anger as his arm swung back. "You asked for it, bitch!"

She rolled forward onto the balls of her feet and brought her hands up to fend off a blow. A hand from behind locked onto the banger's arm to pull him off balance and spin him around, putting his back to Bai.

"I see you've made Rafael's acquaintance," Lee said, releasing the arm.

"The name is Rafe," the banger snarled.

Standing two inches apart, the men glared at one another.

Bai filled the silence. "Rafe was just charming me with his witty banter."

Rafe didn't take his eyes off Lee. "This ain't none a your business."

"Sadly, untrue," Lee said with a smile. "Think about it, Rafe. If you hit this woman, you're an asshole. If you fight her and lose, you're still an asshole. Come to think of it, no matter what you do, you're an asshole. And now, I've completely forgotten what it was I was trying to say."

Rafe took a swing at Lee. His arm muscles bulged as his fist came around like a sledge hammer. If the banger had chanced to come anywhere near landing a blow, Bai might have shown concern. He swiped at air while Lee easily slipped under his punch and moved to the side while landing a flurry of blows to Rafe's kidneys.

Rafe went down on one knee then stumbled up again. His eyes glistened with pain. He wasn't the brightest guy in the world, but he was smart enough to take a step back and reassess the situation. "She your *chola*?" he asked in a taut voice. "She looks butch to me. I can't see you doin' her."

"I like 'em butch," Lee replied with a sly grin. "What can I say?"

Rafe pondered Lee's words as he took another step back. His arms dropped and his shoulders hunched as if he might go another round. He stared menacingly at Lee then turned his attention back to Bai and raised an index finger to point the digit at her, like a gun. His thumb dropped the hammer as he backed away. "Some other time, bitch, when your boyfriend ain't around."

She turned to Lee as Rafe walked away. "I was right the first time. He is a prick."

Lee watched Rafe's back. "And a dangerous one. Be careful of him."

"What's his problem?"

Lee shrugged. "He's a psychopath, an enforcer for the Norteños. For the line of work he's in, being deranged doesn't seem to be a detriment."

"Lovely."

He changed the subject. "What did you find out at *Sun Yee On*?"

"I'm convinced Kelly wouldn't recognize the truth if it sat on his face," she said acidly. "I've learned the drug transaction wasn't a bust but an exchange. The Norteños were buying back a shipment of Mexican Brown, which the task force had hijacked. The swap went south—pun intended. Get it? Norteños—south?"

Lee ignored her attempt at humor. "So there was no China White?"

"No. That's why I tried, unsuccessfully, to strike up a conversation with Rafe. Since he's Norteño, I thought he might know something."

"He wouldn't give you the time of day, let alone divulge gang business. But it's interesting . . ." He paused in thought. "Kelly's lies contain a certain amount of logic. We wouldn't have any reason to help him recover stolen drugs or payola. So he feeds us a line about cops dying in the line of duty to motivate us. I'm still left wondering why Kelly came to us."

"I think Kelly's playing us."

"You may be right. Anyway, let's go upstairs. There's someone I want you to meet."

At the rear of the gym, stairs made from round pipe rails and diamond-pressed steel led to a second-story landing.

Preceding Bai, Lee turned his head to say, "This used to be a warehouse. About thirty years ago, Boobs converted the place to a gym. It's been dying a slow death the last few years. Health clubs have taken over most of the fitness trade. The people who work out here are a different breed—modern-day gladiators."

"With Rafe as the welcoming committee, I can understand why business might be slow."

"Your encounter with Rafe was probably his idea of romance. He's still at that awkward age where he slaps a girl to get her attention."

"Gives 'hitting on a woman' a whole new meaning."

At the top of the stairs, Lee pushed open a steel door to usher her into an enclosed loft space. She stepped into an office appearing to double as an apartment. A folding Murphy bed stood up against the opposite wall. A couch and coffee table occupied the center of the room facing a flat screen attached to the wall adjacent to the door. Overlooking the gym below, a three-foot square of plate glass filled the space next to the door where she stood.

A very big man with black verging on blue skin sat behind a desk at the far end of the room. From the graying at his temples and the fine lines around his eyes, he looked to be in his late fifties or early sixties. He had arms like bands of steel and shoulders like piled river rock. As he openly studied her with intelligent brown eyes, his lips pulled up into a smile revealing brilliant white teeth.

"The name's Jefferson Boob, but everybody just calls me Boobs," he said, extending his hand over his desk as he got up from his chair.

She stepped across the room to take his hand and felt the strength in his gentle grip. "Very nice to meet you . . . Boobs."

"The pleasure's all mine," he said, ushering them to sit in a pair of wooden chairs facing his desk. As he reclaimed his seat, he added, "Lee tells me you're looking for Daniel."

"Did he tell you why we're looking for him?"

"Yes. I'm sorry to say I don't have an address for him. I haven't seen him for a while."

She nodded in understanding. "How well do you know him?"

He glanced at Lee before answering. "I'm not sure how much Lee has told you about me or about this gym. As a matter of practicality, anybody walking through the door to my establishment leaves his business behind on the street. That's the only way I can operate. I have fighters coming in here who are Crips and Bloods from Hunter's Point, Norteños and Sureños from the neighborhood, and Santa Maria's and Joe Boys from Oakland. This place would be a war zone if I let that gang crap come in here. The only thing I need to know about a fighter is whether or not he can fight. That's the only thing I ask about."

"Could Daniel Chen fight?" Lee asked.

Boobs shook his head and looked at the ceiling with a thoughtful expression. When he dropped his gaze, he said, "He reminded me of you, Lee. Elegant. I get a lot of brawlers in here, fellas who like to take out their frustration in the ring, but that wasn't Daniel. When he fights, he's like poetry in motion—smooth, precise, and fierce. I don't know where he learned to fight, but he's had training. A lotta training."

"It sounds as if you like him," Bai said.

"I do like him. He's a good man, polite and well-read. Smart. Smarter than me by a long shot."

"We were led to believe he's an immigrant. What you're saying doesn't jibe with what we've been told," she explained.

He chuckled and leaned back in his chair. "You've been talking to that fat cop, haven't you?"

She nodded. "As a matter of fact, we have."

"He came in here demanding to know everything I knew about Daniel. So I did what I always do when a cop demands answers. I made up a bunch of crap and fed it to him."

"Is there anything you can tell me about Daniel Chen that isn't a load of crap?" she asked.

As he looked at her, his smile slowly drifted away. His gaze met hers in steady evaluation, as if he might be thinking about what, if anything, to tell her. She waited patiently.

"I like to think I'm a pretty good judge of character," he said, "but I've been known to be wrong."

"Haven't we all?" she said sympathetically. "I've got a teenager at home to prove it."

He smiled and took a deep breath as he leaned back in his chair. "Have a look in Berkeley."

"The town?" Lee asked.

"The school."

His response surprised her. "He's a student?"

Boobs laughed and shook his head. "Try teacher."

chapter 4

Lee hailed a yellow cab on Bryant Street to take them home. The asphalt streets glistened with a shiny, black wetness as street lamps equipped with modern light sensors blinked on to glow like haloed beacons. A heavy mist hovered overhead in a gray drizzle as dusk settled over the city.

By the time the cab dropped them in the heart of Chinatown, fog had enveloped the streets. Lee held the glass entry door open as Bai walked into her small lobby. The vestibule showed a mix of old and new. Shiny brass doors on the new elevator stood on the right. A white steel door on the left led to Lee's apartment, and a row of older brass mailboxes lined the far wall. White marble on the floor showed a gray patina of age.

She'd renovated the old manse, turning the top floor into a luxury apartment and the second into a private gymnasium. The ground floor housed the old lobby, a four-car garage accessible from the rear alley, and the smaller apartment where Lee resided. The only features of the building she'd left in place were the plain brick facade and the modest lobby, giving no indication of the luxurious accommodations within.

Lee put his finger to the biometric lock on his door while Bai pressed her thumb against a similar sensor on the elevator call panel. She turned to glance at his back while waiting for the elevator to descend. "Are you busy tonight?"

He turned to look at her. "Not really. Do you want to go out?"

"I already have a dinner date. I was wondering if you could cover for me and spend some time with Elizabeth and the girls."

His eyebrows lifted in question. "Why would I need to cover for you?"

"I'm having dinner with Jason."

The admission gave him pause. "I'll cover for you on one condition."

"What is it with men and conditions? Does every little thing have to be bartered? What happened to doing a friend a favor?"

"Never mind, then," he replied dismissively as he turned his back on her.

"Wait!" she said hurriedly. "Let's hear the condition."

He turned around slowly and leaned his back against his apartment door to fix her with his gaze. "You tell Jason what we're working on."

"Why?"

"Because nothing's adding up and this business with Chen has me worried. What's a Berkeley professor doing at a drug buy? Why does Kelly want our help? I have this tingling sensation," he said, rubbing the back of his neck, "like someone has us in their crosshairs."

"It could be a false alarm. The last time you tingled it was over an Olympic swimmer from Spain."

"This isn't the same thing."

She looked at him with a frown and let out a long, despairing sigh.

"What now?" he asked.

"I just had one of those enlightening moments: both of my best friends are men, and they're both prettier than I am."

"Don't be so hard on yourself. If you'd take the time to dress up and wear a little makeup you'd be stunning. Tonight, wear the red dress I picked out for you. You look amazing in red."

She produced a noncommittal shrug. "I'll think about it."

"Are you going to tell Jason about Chen?"

"I'll think about it."

He waited with his arms crossed.

She remained ambivalent about telling Jason anything he didn't absolutely need to know. If Jason meddled in her affairs, chances were good someone would die. Death heeled the man like a faithful hound.

She replied reticently. "All right, I'll tell him. But I'm leaving out the part about the tingling. I have enough trouble sorting out my own feelings without having to explain yours."

"Deal!" He smiled. "And, you don't have to worry about Elizabeth and the girls. We'll do a movie night. What do you want me to tell them if they ask?"

"I'm going to tell them I'm having dinner with a client."

"Do you think you can lie to Elizabeth and get away with it?"

She seriously considered the question. Elizabeth had been employed as her governess after Bai's parents had been vaporized in a car bomb. She'd been with Bai since childhood. What complicated matters was that Elizabeth was also Jason's mother and, for all intents and purposes, Bai's mother-in-law, even though she and Jason never actually got around to getting married—a little fact that hadn't escaped anyone's notice.

"Truthfully, I'm not really all that confident I can pull it off. Sooner or later she always finds me out. Look at me: I'm over thirty and still afraid to tell my mother I'm seeing a boy she doesn't approve of, even though that boy happens to be her own son. How messed up is that?"

"She worries about you. We all do."

She leaned forward and kissed him on the cheek. "I'll tell Jason what's going on. You do your best to distract the girls. I'll try to get home early."

He smiled again. "I love your optimism, even if it is delusional."

"I swear," she said, walking backward toward the open elevator, "this time I'm not going to end up in bed with him. This is just dinner," she vowed as the doors closed.

She pushed the button for the second-floor gym to check on her girls and waited while the elevator smoothly rose. The doors opened to the sound of blaring music. The girls, who were supposed to be practicing their martial arts, remained oblivious to her presence. They danced in front of a mirrored wall, shaking their booties to Beyoncé's demand to "put a ring on it."

Jia, the oldest at fifteen, didn't show any visible scars from the severe beating she'd received after being sold into the sex trade. She'd made a miraculous physical recovery. The emotional scars were proving more difficult to heal. Bai hoped that time and ongoing therapy would eventually mend the psychological damage. Jia remained more fragile than she appeared.

Bai's daughter Dan, thirteen, had other issues. A brilliant loner, she verged on being a recluse. She took after her mother, demonstrating a tendency to be moody. Studying college course material and attending special classes for the gifted further alienated her from children her own age. The child's brilliance and preternatural maturity worried Bai. She feared her daughter might someday withdraw into her shell like a turtle and never come out.

Dan had bonded with Jia while helping to nurse her back to health, the two becoming as close as sisters. Dan taught Jia how to fight to make her strong enough to beat off any attacker. Jia, on the other hand, seemed determined to teach Dan how to dance and talk to boys. Their bond made them each stronger.

Unwilling to barge in on the dance session, Bai pushed the button for 3. When the elevator doors opened on the top floor, she stepped onto a blue granite floor to be greeted by a coat of red-lacquer Chinese armor dating from the eighteenth century. A remnant of her grandfather's collection, the armor stood guard in her foyer just as it had in his home. She'd donated most of his collection to the Asian Art Museum shortly after his death, retaining only a few pieces for sentimental reasons.

Familiar sounds and smells wafted from the kitchen. Pans rattled as Elizabeth prepared dinner. The aroma of garlic and roasting meat enticed Bai. She followed the scent like a fish following a shiny lure. Standing in the doorway of the kitchen, she watched as Elizabeth bustled.

Elizabeth stood five-foot-nothing with delicate features, graceful limbs, and a tiny waist. Straight black hair, cut in a bob, framed a heart-shaped face. Her eyes were large and brown; her nose straight and petite. Full lips formed a perfect smile. She turned to see Bai. "You're home."

"Yes. But I have a dinner engagement at five with a client, so I won't be here for dinner."

"Anybody I know?"

Bai avoided the question. "Is that duck you're roasting?"

"Yes. It's a shame you won't be here." The tone of Elizabeth's voice carried a hint of reprimand. "Someone from *Sun Yee On* called to say the car would be a few minutes late in arriving."

"Thanks," Bai replied meekly.

"Are you having dinner with Jason?"

"It's business."

"I believe you mentioned that."

Bai checked to see if Elizabeth's breath frosted in the suddenly chill atmosphere. She thought it best to change the subject. "Lee wants to have a movie night with the girls."

"How convenient."

Bai knew that nothing she might say would mitigate Elizabeth's fears. Elizabeth had married a triad soldier and been widowed at an early age. They both knew of the danger associated with being any-where near Jason. A lot of people wanted him dead.

Bai took a deep breath and plunged in. "I'll be careful."

"If you're going to be with Jason, take protection."

"You don't have to worry about that. I'm not sleeping with him."

"I was referring to your gun."

Bai couldn't think of anything to say. She nodded while trying to make herself very small.

Elizabeth spoke softly as she turned back to the stove. "Do you want to know what I fear the most?"

Bai hesitated to answer. Their conversation had turned into a mine-field, and Bai felt as though she had tennis rackets strapped to her feet.

When she didn't reply, Elizabeth told her anyway. "My greatest fear is that you and Jason will die together, victims of some gang-related vendetta. No mother wants to outlive her children. No parent wants to feel that kind of torment."

As a mother, Bai understood. She walked over and wrapped her arms around Elizabeth from behind. "I get it," she said, holding her tightly. "I won't do anything stupid. I won't take any unnecessary risks. But life is uncertain, and I can't let fear dictate how I live. I'm pretty good at taking care of myself, if you haven't noticed."

Elizabeth sniffed and disentangled herself. "You mean, like the way you took care of yourself in Vancouver? I heard all about your escapade with Jason and how he almost got you killed. I thought you'd learned your lesson."

She accepted the rebuke. She'd barely managed to avoid an unpleasant death at the hands of a sadist. She just felt grateful Elizabeth wasn't aware of the assassin who'd try to kill her at the airport. One deadly encounter on her scorecard seemed sufficient.

"I'll admit circumstances got a little out of hand in Vancouver. And, I'll admit Jason was partially to blame for the situation. But if I hadn't gone to Vancouver, Jia would have died. I have regrets, but saving that child isn't one of them. If I had to do it all over again, I'd risk my life a hundred times over."

Elizabeth didn't look happy but nodded her head in understanding. "I can't fault you for saving a child's life. I just want my family safe."

"That's what I want, too."

"Good. Then there's someone I want you to meet. You have a date at the Grand Hotel tomorrow at seven for drinks under the name of Kwan. Don't be late."

"Not again," Bai lamented.

"There's nothing wrong with meeting someone new. Howard Kwan is a third son, but you can't be choosy. The family is in textiles and quite wealthy. They have factories in China and wholesale outlets here in the States."

Arranged dates remained the bane of all thirty-plus Chinese. If you hadn't found a mate by the age of thirty, relatives got involved to find one for you, even if they had to troll for one. This wasn't Bai's first blind date, and it probably wouldn't be her last. There were only two ways to avoid the arranged date—death or marriage.

"Is there anything else I should know?" she asked.

Elizabeth looked as if there were more she wanted to say but seemed reluctant to speak. Finally, she shook her head as if to discount her own concerns. "Try not to scare him."

chapter 5

The limousine arrived as promised. Jason wasn't inside. The driver, Martin, whom Bai knew well as a friend and trusted triad soldier, opened the rear door for her.

"You look nice, Bai," he remarked as he gestured toward the open door.

Having taken Lee's advice, she'd worn the red silk. The short cocktail dress barely covered the knife sheathed on the inside of her thigh. The length showed off her long legs. A draped bodice left one shoulder bare and deflected attention from her broad shoulders. A long black silk scarf wrapped her neck, while red and black Ferragamo stilettos flawlessly completed her look.

She turned to Martin. "Where are you taking me?"

A large, blocky man with a talent for taking orders, Martin wore suits too large in a wasted effort to disguise the weapons he carried. When he shook his head, his bulk made him look like an agitated elephant. His shoulders rocked back and forth in denial. "I can't say, Bai."

She took a step toward him. He took a hesitant step back with a startled look.

"You can't say, or you won't say?" she asked tersely.

"Yes," he replied while gesturing at the open door of the limousine. She balked with a scowl on her face, her arms crossed.

He grimaced and pleaded with her. "Please. I've got orders. I just do what I'm told."

She couldn't fault him for following orders. Jason could be a demanding and unforgiving man. He could also be amazingly kind and generous. Like most people, Martin had learned how to stay in his good graces: he did exactly what Jason told him to do.

"I hate surprises," she muttered as she slipped into the limo.

"Not nearly as much as I do," he mumbled as he closed the door.

She settled into the back of the limo where she found another surprise, a bottle of sixty-year-old Macallan's in a Lalique decanter. An ice bucket filled with frozen spring water the size and shape of golf balls sat next to the bottle. The scotch balls would melt more slowly than ice cubes while chilling the alcohol more efficiently.

She eyed the bottle suspiciously. The obvious ploy had all the earmarks of a trap. Jason knew she loved great scotch. He also knew she had a low tolerance for alcohol. Putting her in a comfortable car with deep leather cushions, gentle music, a fine scotch, and nothing else to do was his way of softening her up, a childishly transparent strategy.

Silently rebuking herself for giving in to temptation, she broke the seal on the decanter and made herself a drink. Knowing she was being manipulated didn't alter her appreciation for the fine whiskey. The amber liquid tasted like a combination of vanilla and licorice with heavy peat and a touch of smoke. Smooth and cold, it gently warmed her throat, the heat slowly spreading to her chest and belly.

She sighed and realized that for the first time in weeks she felt truly relaxed. Wrapped in the cocoon of a bulletproof limousine with the most amazing beverage, she luxuriated and raised her glass.

"*Xie Xie!*"

Two drinks and an hour later she vaguely remembered crossing the Golden Gate Bridge and traveling east off of the freeway into wine country. Eventually, Martin drove up a long lane between rows of grapevines. The limousine came to a stop in a circular motor court paved with brick.

The door opened, and Jason looked in to offer her his hand. She found herself genuinely happy to see him and smiled broadly as she stepped out of the car. After the noise and bustle of San Francisco, the absolute peace of their surroundings felt like a soothing balm.

"Did you enjoy the ride?" he asked.

"Very much, thank you. The scotch was a real treat. Where are we?"

"We're a little south of Healdsburg."

The sun settled over the coastal range as the sky turned a burnished gold. The warm air smelled of soil, freshly mowed grass, and honey-suckle. She reminded herself that late spring bloomed outside of the city. Most of California prepared for summer heat; San Francisco pre-pared for summer fog. The inclement weather in the city had some-thing to do with an inversion layer, a term she'd never really understood but which local weathermen never failed to blame.

"You look beautiful tonight," Jason said as he gave her a slow, appreciative glance.

Bai turned in place to show off her outfit and nearly fell as the heels on her stilettos caught on the pavers.

"Whoa," he exclaimed, catching her as she tumbled into his arms.

She looked up at him in surprise.

He smiled. "I didn't think it was going to be this easy."

She righted herself and stood to face him with a frown. "I still haven't learned how to walk in girl shoes."

"I have a solution for that," he said, and dropped down on one knee to slip the shoes off her feet. "We're dining al fresco tonight. You might as well be comfortable."

Standing, he took her arm to lead her around a modern brick and clapboard house with large picture windows. The walls of the building seemed to be mostly glass, a feature that would showcase the spectacular views. The expansive home rested on a hill surrounded by vineyards.

"It's beautiful here," she noted as she walked barefoot across a grassy lawn that looked out over the rolling landscape.

"I'm glad you like it. I put it in Dan's name."

She turned to him. "You put *what* in Dan's name?"

"This estate," he explained. "Eighty acres, forty of them in vines, ten in fruit trees, and thirty fallow. This is the main house. There's a caretaker's cottage the other side of the vineyard. The place is self-suf-ficient; the fruit pays for maintenance and taxes, with a little left over."

"Wait a minute. You bought our daughter a vineyard? Why?"

"I thought it might be nice to have a place outside the city where the girls could come to play. There's a pool on the far side of the house and room for horses, if she wants them. Also," he hesitated, "if anything happens to me, I wanted her to have something, a gift from her father. I haven't been able to give her anything before now."

She looked out over the vineyard then turned around to look at the house. "You're not planning on going anywhere, are you?"

He smiled. "Not intentionally."

She considered his offhand remark as well as the gift. On one hand, the gift seemed ridiculously extravagant. On the other, she wasn't sure she could deny him the right to gift his daughter. She had little choice, it seemed, but to accede graciously. "It really is beautiful. I'm sure the girls will love it."

"That's settled, then," he stated. "Let's have dinner."

He took her arm to lead her around the house to a flagstone patio where a table waited under an arbor covered in grapevines. Twinkling lights sparkled discreetly around the arbor and surrounding terrace. White linen covered a small circular table set for two with a lush, low centerpiece arrangement of tropical flowers. Blue plate chargers edged in gold rested on the table.

"Are you hungry?" he asked.

"Famished. And a little drunk."

He grinned at her with a predatory smile. "Good. There's hope, then."

She returned his smile while he pulled out a high-backed uphol-stered chair for her. As if on cue, crickets and frogs started their nightly concert while the fading light turned the sky dusky. As she settled in, he pulled a bottle of white wine from an ice bucket and poured each of them a glass.

No sooner had he filled their glasses when a woman, perhaps in her fifties, in a white chef's apron stepped out of the house to place chilled forks and delicate china plates with salad on the table before them.

Jason spoke to the woman. "Thank you, Coleta. The table looks lovely."

She smiled and nodded while Jason continued. "This is Bai Jiang. I've told you about her. I'm sure you'll be seeing more of each other as time goes on." He gestured at Coleta. "Bai, this is Coleta Corazon. She and her husband, Fausto, have been managing this vineyard for some time."

Bai greeted Coleta, who exchanged pleasantries with her before excusing herself to return to the kitchen. When she'd left, Bai turned to Jason with a questioning look.

"Coleta and Fausto are honest, hardworking people who've managed this property for the last fifteen years. It's up to you whether or not you want to retain them, but I'd suggest you do. Coleta, as you're about to find out, is an amazing cook."

Bai nodded and tried the salad. The dressing tasted delicious with the perfect balance of anchovy and garlic. An added textural interest of homemade croutons made the salad even better. The flinty, dry fruit of the white wine, a Pine Ridge Petit Clos, proved the perfect accompaniment.

"Have you spent much time here?" she asked.

"Not as much as I'd like," he replied. "The tranquility here is soothing."

"You'll always be welcome here," she stated in a magnanimous moment.

He smiled. "I would hope so, but I won't hold you to that. People change . . . the world changes. I'm happy just taking life one day at a time."

She'd finished her salad when Coleta came back wheeling a cart carrying covered plates. The first plates she presented to each of them held a grill-marked filet mignon. Completing the presentation on the plate were a rosette of foie gras and a fanning of sautéed mushrooms.

Jason reached over to fill another long-stemmed glass with red wine.

"What are we drinking?" she asked.

"In celebration of your wearing a dress, I decanted a 1980 Jordan Cabernet. You'll have to take a look at the wine cellar in the basement. I purchased the house in turnkey condition as part of an estate sale. The former owner had excellent taste in wine. He'd been collecting vintages from the Napa and Alexander valleys for the last forty years."

Coleta uncovered plates with squares of multilayered au gratin potatoes and lightly steamed green beans. She gestured to the two of them to try their steaks. Bai bit into hers and fell in love. She took a sip of the Cabernet with its subtle tannins and tasted overripe cherries with a slightly tarry finish and butt-danced with joy.

Bai asked, "This steak is amazing. What's your secret?"

Coleta smiled at the appreciative comment. "I put a dollop of Gorgonzola butter on the steaks right after pulling them off the grill."

Bai smiled and wondered, distractedly, if the former owner had died of heart disease. She took another bite of steak and couldn't bring herself to care. Some things were worth dying for. The meal ended with chocolate raspberry torte and port. She found herself pleasantly inebriated.

Jason leaned across the table to get her attention. "Would you like me to call Martin?"

"Why? Do you want to spend the night with Martin?"

"He's not my first choice," he confessed. "I thought you might want to take the limo home."

Confused, she looked around. "I thought this was home."

He smiled. "And so it is. Can I show you to your room?"

"I'm afraid you'll have to carry me. There's no way I could possibly stand on my own. You've managed to get me wonderfully drunk. As a reward, you can have your way with me, farm boy," she said, throwing her arms wide in surrender.

"'Farm boy'?"

"That's your new name. We'll live like farmers, up at the crack of dawn to feed the grapes. And, there must be something that needs plowing," she said, grinning. "Oh yes . . . that would be me."

"I can see this will be a night to remember," he said as he stood to scoop her into his arms. He carried her effortlessly as he walked toward the house. Coleta must have been keeping an eye on them because she opened the French doors at their approach.

"Thank you for the wonderful meal," Jason said.

He turned so that Bai could wave good night. She couldn't seem to form words. The world had acquired fuzzy edges.

Coleta nodded and covered her mouth to hide her giggles. "I'll come by tomorrow to finish cleaning up, Mr. Lum."

"Thank you. I'll be leaving early, but Bai will probably still be here."

Bai waved again at the sound of her name. He turned to carry her across an open living room and down a hallway to a large bedroom where he leaned down to gently lay her on cream-colored satin sheets. Fanning her arms on the slippery fabric, she reveled in the sensation as she wrapped herself in the linens like a caterpillar in a cocoon. And promptly passed out.

chapter 6

Bai awakened with a throbbing head and a tongue like a wool sock. She raised a hand to pull the sheet away from her face. Bright sunlight made her gasp.

"You're awake."

She turned her head slowly to find the source of the comment. Lee sat in an upholstered armchair across the room reading a book.

"What are you doing here? Where's Jason?"

"I'm here because Jason can't be. He had an early flight and didn't want to leave you stranded. He offered the limo, but I drove instead. How do you feel?"

"While I was asleep, someone knitted little wool sweaters for my teeth, and there's a monkey banging a drum in my head. Can you make him stop?"

He ignored her obvious discomfort. "Did you know you talk in your sleep? Who is 'farm boy'?"

"Get me coffee and aspirin, and I'll tell you."

"There's a nice woman in the kitchen who wants to feed you. She's making biscuits and gravy, and who knows what else. I didn't have the heart to tell her you don't eat breakfast, unless, of course, a doughnut could be considered breakfast."

"I'm begging you. Don't talk about food. Aspirin and coffee. Please!"

"All right. But after you've had your coffee, I want the whole sordid story."

She pulled the sheet back over her head and realized she was naked beneath the linens. Jason must have disrobed her. She wondered where he'd put her dress and her knife. It bothered her that she couldn't remember anything beyond landing on the bed. If he'd joined her between the sheets, she had no memory of the tryst.

Lee returned with coffee and aspirin on a tray. He placed the serving dish on a nightstand next to the bed before sitting again in the chair across the room. Slowly, she sat up to acclimate to a higher elevation while her stomach flopped like a fish out of water. Holding the coffee cup in both hands, she sipped carefully and waited to see if her stomach would rebel. When she felt reasonably certain the coffee would stay down, she swallowed the aspirin and leaned back against the upholstered headboard to drink with her eyes closed.

"I brought a change of clothes for you."

She opened her eyes reluctantly. "Thanks. Have you seen my dress or my knife?"

"Your dress is hanging in the closet. The knife is in the top drawer of the nightstand. So, what happened?"

She eyed him over the rim of the cup as she drank. "I got drunk. I passed out. If there was any whoopee, sadly, I missed it."

"Who's 'farm boy'?"

"'Farm boy' is Jason's new nickname. He bought this vineyard for Dan. I'm not entirely sure what he was thinking. Anyway, Dan now has a summer home, which seems a bit much for a girl just entering puberty."

Lee seemed to weigh the news. "Putting this property in her name was smart. The land is valuable now. It will only get more valuable with time. If she ever needs money, she can sell the property whole or piecemeal. You can't fault the investment strategy."

"I suppose not. And Jason was right in thinking the girls would enjoy summers here. I have the feeling we'll be shopping for horses in the near future. Do you know anything about horses?"

"They're large, hairy, and a bit brutish, like professional wrestlers. I like betting on them, but I've never felt the need to actually touch one—horses, that is. I can't say the same about professional wrestlers."

"A simple 'no' would have sufficed."

"Have more coffee and let me know when you're civil."

She looked at him, stifled a response, and took another drink of coffee. The restorative properties of caffeine helped. Her headache started to subside.

"I can't seem to get out of my own way," she moaned. "I completely ruined Jason's big seduction scene." She smiled at the memory of his carrying her into the bedroom. "There were candles and flowers and dinner with wine. Everything was wonderful. And then I got drunk and slipped into a self-induced coma."

"It happens to the best of us."

"So this has happened to you?"

He smiled. "Not really. I was just trying to be supportive."

She closed her eyes and sighed. "My behavior was pretty adolescent, but I felt really good at the time. I just forgot to put on the brakes."

"Lesson learned." He seemed way too chipper. "Are you ready to hit the shower? We're supposed to be in Berkeley today looking for Daniel Chen. Remember?"

She nodded her head and felt a wave of dizziness. "Sure, give me about thirty minutes. I'll be with you."

"I'll wait for you in the kitchen."

She staggered out of bed to slowly make her way toward the bathroom. Adjusting the spigot to the proper temperature, she put her head under the hot spray to let the water wash over her. Steamy air and deep breaths helped to clear her head. The residual pain and nausea slowly slipped away.

As she carefully stepped out of the shower, she discovered her equilibrium had returned. She dried herself and ran her fingers through her short, coarse hair. Her clothes—a black tee, black jeans, and black trainers, along with a change of underwear—were rolled up in a small satchel next to the bed. She dressed hurriedly before making her way to the kitchen.

Coleta stood at the stove and smiled knowingly at Bai while welcoming her in a cheerful voice. "Good morning. I hope you're hungry. I wasn't sure what you liked, so I made a little of everything."

A warming plate filled with bacon and sausage, biscuits, gravy, and potatoes rested on the counter. The expectant look on the housekeeper's face compelled Bai to take a seat at the table while hiding her embarrassment. In a soft and reticent voice, she said, "Perhaps just toast and coffee this morning."

"I can prepare eggs any way you like them. The pancake batter is already made."

"Thank you, but no. This is fine," she said, pouring herself a cup of coffee as Lee watched her from across the table. "You're not eating?"

"I had pancakes earlier." He turned to Coleta. "They were delicious."

Obviously taken with him, Coleta beamed. "I'm so glad you enjoyed them."

"Would you care to join us?" Bai asked.

Coleta hesitated a moment before pulling at the ties on her apron and removing the garment as she walked around the stove to join them. She sat across from Bai and filled a cup with coffee. After she'd taken a sip, Bai addressed her. "I'd like it very much if you and your husband would stay on as caretakers for this property."

Coleta visibly relaxed and seemed to brighten at the news. "Fausto and I were hoping that would be the case. We've lived here for fifteen years and have come to think of this as home."

"I'm a little pressed for time today. Perhaps later in the week we might get together to go over the details."

"That would be fine."

"I'd like to thank you again for the wonderful food," Bai said as she stood.

"You're leaving so soon? You've barely touched your breakfast."

Lee stood as well. "It's been a pleasure, Coleta. Thank you again for the lovely pancakes."

"I do so hope you'll come again soon."

He nodded and led Bai out of the kitchen through a side entrance. The sun nearly blinded her as she stumbled out the door. He took her elbow and walked her around the side of the house where the limousine had deposited her the night before. In its place sat Lee's 1965 Cadillac Coupe de Ville convertible, red with white upholstery.

"You drove the land boat?" she asked.

"The sun was out. It seemed like a nice day to get some air."

She noticed her leather jacket lying on the backseat as she walked around the car to get in the passenger-side door. As usual, he'd thought of everything. She got in and turned to him as he put the keys in the ignition and started the car. "Did I thank you for coming to get me?"

"My pleasure. Like I said, it's a beautiful day for a drive."

They backtracked to Highway 101 heading south until they reached San Rafael. The sun shone brightly on the crisp spring day as they crossed the Richmond-San Rafael Bridge, which took them to Highway 80. From there, they had only a short hop to Berkeley. In less than an hour, they pulled off the freeway under leafy trees and into a visitor parking space adjacent to the University of California at Berkeley's administrative offices.

A light mist covered the campus. The temperature had dropped twenty degrees. Bai pulled her jacket off the backseat and put the garment on as she walked around the car to join Lee.

"What was it Boobs said Daniel Chen taught?"

"Asian Studies."

"I wonder what a professor of Asian Studies was doing in a fight club."

"When you think about it, many of history's greatest warriors were also scholars."

"Like Genghis Khan?"

"Maybe not the best example," Lee replied as they made their way across the parking lot.

UC Berkeley's administration offices were located in Sproul Hall, a white-columned building the size of a football field. They found an information kiosk that directed them to directory services on the second floor. A counter with a ticket dispenser dictated the order of service. Lee pulled a ticket with the number forty-two.

The room was crowded even though the university was on summer break. Students carrying paperwork and registration packets waited patiently for their number to be called. Bai and Lee took seats in a row of chairs along the back wall to wait.

"Number forty-two," a short elderly woman finally called. She stood at the far end of the room behind the counter and wore a pastel-pink suit that matched her hair.

Handing the ticket across the counter, Bai asked, "We're looking for Daniel Chen. I understand he teaches here. Where might we find him?"

The clerk smiled and replied in a voice that reminded Bai of Mrs. Blight, her third-grade teacher. "The university is on break. Summer session doesn't start for another week."

"Do you have a home address for him?" Lee asked.

"Certainly," said the clerk in a matter-of-fact manner.

"May we have his address?" he asked.

"Certainly not," she replied briskly.

"We need to speak with him about an important matter," Bai explained.

"I'm sorry, but school policy prohibits me from giving out personal contact information on faculty members. There's nothing I can do."

Bai turned to look at Lee. He shrugged to let her know he was also stymied. She decided to change tactics. "Does Professor Chen have an office on campus?"

The clerk smiled in encouragement. "He does."

Bai returned the smile. She felt like they were making progress. "Does he have office hours?"

"Not during break."

The smile melted from Bai's face. "Isn't there some way to get in touch with him?"

"You might try his office."

"You just said he doesn't keep office hours during break."

"That doesn't mean he isn't there," the clerk replied sweetly. "It just means he doesn't keep regular hours. If he isn't there you can always leave a note on his door. Sometimes professors stop by to collect mail and pick up notes from their students. That's probably your best bet for getting in touch with him before classes start next week."

The woman pulled a pink Post-it from a tablet sitting on the counter and scribbled on it. "This is his office number. He's in Barrows Hall, right next door. Have a nice day."

Bai smiled back half-heartedly. The clerk's demeanor seemed a little too cheery. She couldn't be sure, but she suspected she'd just been schooled.

chapter 7

Lee and Bai took an elevator up to the sixth floor of Barrows Hall. They stepped out into an empty corridor and walked down the hall to Room 623. A nameplate read, "Daniel Chen Ph.D." She rapped on the hard metal of the door with bare knuckles. No one answered. She pounded a couple of times with the flat of her hand, but there was still no response.

Lee grabbed the door handle and twisted. Surprisingly, the knob turned. He queried Bai with raised eyebrows. She nodded, and he pushed the door open.

A desk rested on its side. Papers covered the floor. Upended chairs littered the room. Two bodies lay sprawled, face up, amid the jumbled mess. The smell of feces and urine choked the air.

"This couldn't be good," she observed.

In a tentative manner, Lee asked, "Do we run, or do we report?"

She turned her head to gaze down the empty hallway then looked up at blinking red lights encased in black plastic domes. "There are closed-circuit cameras on the ceiling. Plus, there's no way that clerk in administration is going to conveniently forget us. Why don't you check these guys for a pulse while I call the police?"

"I make it a rule not to touch dead people," he informed her. "Dead people fit into the same category as horses. But you needn't worry. See the way that guy's neck is bent the wrong way? He's definitely dead."

She looked at him soberly and shook her head. "Fine. Be that way. You call it in, and I'll check for signs of life."

Stepping into the office, she walked around the papers and books strewn across the floor, trying not to disturb anything. She dropped to one knee next to the first victim, the one with the crooked neck, and pressed two fingers against the hollow of his throat. "He's cold. This one's been dead for a while. No blood I can see. I'm not a medical examiner, but from the looks of him, I'd guess he died from a broken neck." She leaned over to look at his hands. "His knuckles are scraped."

"He's a big man," Lee observed. "I don't suppose he went down without a fight."

Lee's assessment matched hers. The stiff appeared to be Latino, over six feet tall, and probably weighing more than 250 pounds. Muscle wrapped his arms as if he'd been a weight lifter. His clothes didn't tell them anything. He wore jeans and a black sweatshirt with the sleeves torn off.

She stood to walk over and check the second body. Not as large as the first victim, he too looked to be Latino—skinny, wearing a wife-beater T-shirt and a red bandana wrapped around his head like a sweat-band. His arms were also ropy with muscle. The stiff rested on his back with his hands around his neck where his nails had raked the flesh raw. She reached down and checked for a pulse. Cold skin met her finger-tips. She could tell he'd died long before they'd arrived.

"This guy's blue underneath his tan," she said. "His eyes are red. It looks like the little blood vessels burst from lack of oxygen. From the way he's scratched his throat, I'm guessing he suffered a crushed windpipe."

"Both of them are tatted up pretty heavily," Lee said, referring to the numerous tattoos on their exposed arms.

"I noticed the tattoos, but I can only guess what most of them mean. You can see they're both flying the number fourteen on their shoulders."

"The fourteenth letter . . . 'N,'" Lee stated, "for Norteño."

She nodded and stood to carefully retrace her steps out of the room.

Lee spoke into his phone. "I'd like to report two bodies discovered in Barrows Hall on the UC Berkeley campus, Room 623. Yes, that's correct. They're definitely dead. Take your time. They're not going anywhere."

After closing his phone, Lee turned to Bai as she expressed a theory. "I'm guessing they came here looking for Professor Chen, just the way we did. Do you think they found him? If so, do you think he killed them?"

Lee shrugged. "If that's the case, maybe we're lucky we didn't find him."

"Something about this doesn't feel right. Whoever killed those two had to be a professional. A neck on a man that big doesn't snap easily. My gut's telling me something is all wrong about this."

Lee shook his head. "You're making too many assumptions."

"You're right. I'm getting ahead of myself."

They didn't hear the approaching sirens. The concrete walls in the interior corridor acted as sound barriers. It wasn't until officers skulked down the hall with weapons drawn that Bai and Lee realized the police had responded to their call in record time.

"Put your hands up and face the wall," the first officer ordered in a loud voice.

Startled, they both stared at the officers. They slowly raised their arms to put their hands against the wall, spreading their feet in anticipation of the requisite pat-down.

Lee spoke before the officers reached them. "I have a revolver in a holster under my left arm. The concealed carry permit is in my wallet inside my jacket pocket."

As one officer roughly jammed a gun barrel into the back of Lee's neck, a second reached around to yank the gun from his holster. Bai could smell their fear as the officers hurriedly frisked Lee then more gently patted her down. They failed to find her knife in the sleeve of her jacket.

The first officer spoke into a communication device clipped to his shoulder as he peered into Daniel Chen's office. "The scene is secure. Send up the paramedics." When he'd finished, he turned his attention back to them. "You can put your arms down and relax. I'm sorry if we scared you. We have to take precautions when we respond to a potential murder scene."

Neither Bai nor Lee replied.

The officer looked at them expectantly then frowned. "Why don't we step down the hallway, someplace out of the way, where we can talk?"

They followed the officer down the hall to a cross corridor. The second officer held a gun at his side and followed them. As they turned into the side corridor, two paramedics carrying field kits and accompanied by more officers raced past in the direction of Chen's office.

The leading officer turned to face them. "My name is Sergeant Meadows, Berkeley Campus Police. May I see your identification, please?"

Lee handed the officer his wallet. Bai produced a driver's license from the breast pocket of her jacket. The sergeant looked at her information then at Lee's license and gun permit before handing Lee back his wallet. The officer held their identification up for them to see. "You'll get these back before you leave. What can you tell me about the bodies you found?"

"They're dead," Bai offered.

"That's not very helpful," the sergeant replied with a deepening frown.

"They're cold," she added.

"So you entered the office and made contact with the victims?"

"How else could I determine they were dead?"

"You don't seem very upset. Most people would be visibly shaken at discovering a couple of cold stiffs," Sergeant Meadows observed.

"I didn't know them," she responded.

"Nor did I," Lee added.

The sergeant crossed his arms and stared at them. "Why do I get the feeling you're not being completely forthright with me?"

Bai looked to Lee, who shrugged.

"Fine," Meadows relented. "Can you tell me what you were doing here in Barrows Hall?"

"We're looking for Professor Chen," Lee said.

Bai nodded her assent.

"Why were you looking for Professor Chen?"

"Because he teaches Asian Studies," she replied.

Lee nodded.

"And you're looking for him because . . . ?" the sergeant urged.

"Isn't it obvious?" she asked.

The sergeant looked at her blankly.

"I'm Asian."

Lee nodded enthusiastically. "Me, too."

The sergeant looked at them as his lips drew into a thin line. "Officer Randle," he said, addressing the policeman still holding a gun at his side. "Take these witnesses down to a squad car and make them comfortable in the backseat until we can make inquiries and get statements."

Officer Randle motioned with his free hand for them to precede him. He didn't point his gun at them, but he didn't put it away, either.

The squad car proved to be reasonably hospitable, except for the locked doors and windows and the metal screen separating them from the front seat. They settled in to wait while remaining silent, aware the dash camera might have been left running to record their conversation.

More than an hour later, Sergeant Meadows approached the car and opened the rear door. He ushered them out with a sweep of his arm. "We've reviewed the digital evidence from the hall cameras and run your licenses. Your story checks out. We got a call from SFPD vouching for you." The officer paused to nod at them in acknowledgment, his demeanor more deferential. "I don't have any reason to hold you, but if there's anything you want to tell me about the two stiffs in Professor Chen's office, now would be a good time."

"Have you talked to Professor Chen?" she asked.

"We haven't been able to contact him. I don't suppose you know where we can find him?"

"We'd hoped to find him here," Lee answered. "Have you checked his home address?"

"Officers have done a safety check at his residence, but there was no response. We're pursuing a warrant, but that takes time." Giving them a meaningful look, he handed them back their identification and Lee's gun as he spoke. "Here's my contact information, in case you remember anything," he said as he handed Bai a business card. Before she could grasp the card, the sergeant flipped it. An address had been scrawled across the back. "Inspector Kelly at SFPD asked that I assist you in any way possible. I'm sure you'll keep me informed if you find anything."

She nodded as she tucked the card into the pocket of her jacket along with her driver's license. "Have you been able to identify the victims?"

"They were carrying identification. We have names and addresses, but we don't know why they were in Chen's office or why they were killed. When the medical examiner works up a time of death, we'll have a better idea of when they died. We're still looking at video from the cameras."

She patted her pocket holding the sergeant's card. "Thanks for the card."

Sergeant Meadows frowned before speaking. "When a brother asks for a solid, you do what you can. Kelly vouched for you. That address is the best I can do."

Lee exchanged a questioning look with Bai. She had her own misgivings. They were obviously being maneuvered into investigating Chen's whereabouts. The police had literally invited them to break into a private residence. Her gut instinct told her to walk away, but she couldn't do that. Giving up wasn't in her nature.

chapter 8

Daniel Chen lived in a cottage in the Berkeley Hills. The neighborhood behind the campus featured scenic walking trails and picturesque parks. Narrow streets wound through wooded hillsides. Houses blended into the natural landscape by using organic materials like shingles and stone. Many of the homes were architecturally stunning, if you could find them.

Lee pulled off the road at a widening of the street allocated for parking. The Coupe de Ville barely squeezed into the shallow set-aside. Bai followed him in exiting the car via the driver's door.

"Are you sure this is it?" she asked.

He looked around at the surrounding woods. "According to my GPS, this is the address Sergeant Meadows provided."

Trees and bushes screened the hillside to obscure whatever lay on the other side of the foliage. A path, paved with stones, wound through shrubbery to disappear into lush greenery.

Bai nodded at the trail, the only visible access through the verdant growth. "I think it's the yellow brick road for us, Dorothy."

Lee didn't look happy. "I don't like anything about this. I don't like the fact we're here at the behest of the police. I don't like that we're on our own in an isolated neighborhood. And, I don't like all these trees. They make me nervous."

"Wasn't there a poem about how wonderful trees are?"

"You're probably referring to the poem by Joyce Kilmer. *I think that I shall never see A poem lovely as a tree, A tree whose hungry mouth is prest Against the sweet earth's flowing breast*, et cetera, et cetera," Lee recited. "With all due respect, it's pretty obvious Joyce Kilmer wasn't worried about snipers. Do you realize the word 'ambush' contains the word 'bush'? Coincidence? I don't think so."

She nodded sympathetically. "If the trees scare you, you can always wait for me in the car. Of course, you might miss out on the chance to finally meet the mysterious Daniel Chen. I have to admit, I find myself more than a little curious."

He scowled. "I said I was nervous, not scared."

He turned to lead the way. As he stepped onto the path, he reached into his jacket and pulled out his gun, which he kept at his side pointed at the ground. Bai's eyes scanned the dense foliage as they walked in a generally upward direction. About thirty paces up the hillside, the path opened into a large clearing surrounded by evergreen trees. In the center of the clearing sat a very large stone cottage. An asphalt drive meandered down the hill from the other side of the residence.

"The road must loop around," Lee observed. "I think we've managed to come in the back way."

"That's the problem with GPS. It can't tell the back door from the front."

The house looked like a storybook dwelling made of gray stone and rough-hewn timber with a red slate roof. A second story boasted gabled, leaded windows looking out over a green expanse of lawn. A cloudless day allowed the sun to bathe the clearing in light. Serene and secluded, the house was set apart from the world, a secret hideaway in the forest.

"Being a professor at Cal must pay well," she said distractedly. "Let's take a look around before deciding whether or not to announce ourselves."

They walked to the side of the house where the black asphalt driveway ended. A late-model Lexus sedan sat in the drive next to the entrance of the home.

Bai looked from the car to the house. "The reasonable thing to do is knock on the front door and see if anyone's home."

"I agree," he replied.

Lee slipped his gun into the holster inside his jacket as they walked yet another stone path leading to the front entrance. They stepped up onto a porch covered in gray slate, where he pressed his finger against a doorbell set into the wood trim of an arched doorway. They waited, but no one answered. He pushed the bell again. When no one responded, he put his hand on the wrought iron handle of the door and pushed. A bolt clicked and the door opened.

He turned to her. "Haven't we been here before?"

"This does have a certain sense of déjà vu all over again."

He retrieved his gun from its holster, this time bringing the pistol up to his waist. He let the barrel of the gun lead the way as he stepped through the doorway. She slipped her knife out of the sheath in her sleeve and palmed the blade at her side as she followed.

They stepped into an entry hall of sculpted hardwood walls and granite flooring. To the right, a large formal living room touted over-stuffed furniture facing a fireplace massive enough to stand up in. Lamps, appearing to be real Tiffany, sat on end tables. The place smelled of money.

Lee gestured with his head toward the back of the house to let her know the direction he intended to go. She jerked her head up to indicate she'd take the top story. Separating wordlessly, they moved quickly and silently to search the home.

She stepped on the edges of the treads to avoid squeaking boards as she carefully worked her way up the stairs on the balls of her feet. When she reached the top of the stairwell, she opened the first closed door to discover a guest room with a bare closet and empty shelves.

Two more empty bedrooms and an unoccupied bath led her to the one remaining door at the end of the hall. She entered a large master suite that looked to be three or four times the size of the other chambers. A big four-poster bed with heavy red curtains anchored the center of the room. Curiosity drew her in as she pulled a curtain aside to reveal rumpled quilts and red satin sheets.

A click . . . the safety catch releasing on an automatic weapon froze Bai where she stood. A woman's voice from behind queried, "Can you think of a good reason why I shouldn't shoot you?"

Bai thought for a moment. "I can think of a lot of reasons you shouldn't shoot me. Where would you like me to start?"

"You can start by turning around," the voice ordered.

She turned to face a very pretty woman, probably in her early- to mid-twenties, Chinese, and naked. Being naked didn't seem to bother her.

"Who are you?" the woman demanded.

"Bai Jiang. I'm looking for Daniel Chen. The door was open."

The hammer ratcheted back on the small automatic pistol in her hand. "None of those is a good reason."

Bai hastily replied. "If you want a really good reason, how about a man standing behind you with a gun?"

The woman grinned. "Nice try."

The sound of Lee's cocking his pistol managed to get her attention. Bai smiled and shrugged. The naked woman frowned as the barrel of her gun dipped before coming up again indecisively.

She gestured with the gun in Bai's direction. "He shoots me. I shoot you."

"Works for me," Lee stated flatly.

Bai frowned. "I have a better idea. How about nobody shoots anybody? This is all just a big misunderstanding. We're here to make sure Daniel Chen is all right. Two men were found dead in his office this morning. People are concerned for his well-being."

The woman looked torn. She stepped away from Bai but kept the gun trained on her. "How do I know I can trust you? If I lower the gun, you could kill me, or worse."

The comment struck Bai as odd. "What could be worse than being killed?"

The woman hesitated. She chewed on her lower lip. "You might shame me."

It took Bai a moment to piece the words together. She looked at Lee. He chuckled.

"That would be a first," Bai blurted. She looked at the confused woman and shrugged. "It seems neither one of us has any desire to shame you. Sorry."

The woman turned to look at Lee with an appraising stare. He shrugged an apology. Her gun barrel dropped to point at the floor. His gun dropped in response.

"I don't believe we've been properly introduced," he said with a smile, "though I feel like we're on familiar terms. We can wait, if you'd like to put something on."

Dropping all pretense of fear, she shrugged and turned to casually walk toward the back of the room, where she disappeared into what Bai assumed to be the master bath or perhaps a dressing room. When she returned, she wore a white terry robe and no longer carried the gun. She took a seat on the bed facing them.

Lee put his pistol back into its holster. Bai kept her knife concealed in the palm of her hand.

"We're sorry for intruding like this," Bai said. "Like I said, my name is Bai, and this is my associate, Lee. We're looking for Daniel Chen."

"Are you the police?" The young woman pulled a cigarette from the pocket of her robe and held out a lighter to Lee as she put the smoke to her lips. He obliged and accepted the lighter. She cupped her hands suggestively around his when he lit her cigarette.

"No. I'm a *souxun*," Bai replied.

The woman seemed to consider the explanation a moment before discarding it. "If you're not the police, then you're trespassing. Leave before I have you arrested." She turned to Lee. "You can stay."

"I thought this was Daniel Chen's house," he replied.

"This is my house. Daniel sometimes stays here."

"Aren't you afraid of being shamed?" Bai asked.

The woman looked annoyed.

"Call the police," Bai insisted. "I'd like to hear what they have to say concerning the ownership of this house. Who knows? Maybe we'll all make the five o'clock news."

The woman's head turned to meet Bai's gaze with a frosty glare. Bai smiled. A proper upbringing didn't bar illicit affairs, but it did frown upon scandal.

"What do you want to know?" the woman asked bluntly.

"What's your name?" Bai asked.

"Wen Liu."

"This is a beautiful home, Wen. Yours?"

"It belongs to my parents."

"Where are your parents?"

"They live in Hong Kong."

"Is Daniel Chen your boyfriend?"

Wen looked thoughtful. She turned to look at Lee before answering. "We're not exclusive."

"When was the last time you saw him?"

"Several days ago."

"Has he called?"

She shook her head, her expression suggesting she'd lost interest and patience with Bai's questions.

"When do you expect him back?"

Wen smiled and shrugged while blowing smoke in Bai's direction, a symbolic gesture that wordlessly ended the interrogation. Bai pulled a business card out of her pocket and handed it to the recalcitrant woman. "If you see or hear from him, give him my number. Tell him I can help."

"Help with what?"

"He'll know. Just tell him."

Wen looked at the card with indifference but put it into the pocket of her robe anyway.

Bai started for the door then turned back on impulse. "Listen. I don't want to scare you, but it seems Chen crossed some very bad people. If we could find this house, so can they. If you have someplace else to go, this would be a good time to be there. We can wait while you pack a bag to make sure you leave here safely. I'd feel better knowing you weren't staying here by yourself."

Wen looked at Bai then at Lee, who nodded almost imperceptibly. The nod seemed to do the trick. She stood and walked into the back while they waited. When she came out a few minutes later she wore what was clearly very expensive designer clothing and carried two Louis Vuitton bags.

"I'm ready," she announced.

Lee carried her bags and led the way. They walked down the stairs and out to her car, where he tossed Wen's bags into the trunk and closed the lid.

Wen hesitated. She looked Lee up and down with a calculating stare.

"If you change your mind, give me a call," she said, pressing a card into his hand.

"How romantic," Lee replied, palming the card.

Frowning, Wen flopped herself into the driver's seat, backed out of the drive a short ways, and spun the car around to drive up the hill before turning onto the road without a backward glance.

"What do you make of that?" Bai asked.

"Spoiled, rich, sexually promiscuous, and potentially dangerous. She wasn't afraid when I held a gun on her. She seemed to be enjoying it. The only thing that frightened her was the thought of going public. She has something to hide."

"I was thinking the same thing. I got a couple of pictures of her with my phone while she was trying to seduce you. Did you manage to drop your phone into the trunk?"

He smiled. "I liked that phone. It's fully charged, so we can monitor her movements for the next week. Let me see the pictures. Did you get my good side?"

"Which side is your good side?"

He smiled. "All of them."

chapter 9

Bai monitored the GPS coordinates of Lee's phone by using an application on her cell. The app provided the location of Wen's car to within a few meters.

"You've got to love technology," she said.

They drove past the Emeryville exit on Highway 80 just north of the Bay Bridge. Moderately heavy traffic moved along at about forty miles an hour. A mist formed over the water of the bay. As they neared the bridge, blue sky turned gray.

"Where is she?" he asked.

"Almost over the bridge. Coming up on the city."

"Are we going to keep following her?"

"That depends on Miss Liu. Let's follow her until we get some indication how far she's going."

"Do you think she'll lead us to Chen?"

"Wen is a woman with secrets. Daniel Chen is a man who also has secrets. I suspect some of those secrets are shared, but that's just my gut feeling." She looked down and tapped the screen on her handheld. "The map has stopped moving. It looks like she's stopping at the Embarcadero."

"She's either shopping or decided to take up residence at the Grand."

A high-rise hotel known for its scenic bay views, the Grand at the Embarcadero coexisted with a multistory shopping complex rivaling Union Square for designer shops and restaurants. The Embarcadero provided lodging, fine dining, and entertainment in one location.

"If that's the case, let's go home and drop off the Caddie, pick up another car, and grab a surveillance kit. If she stops at the Grand, maybe we can secure an adjacent room and get a camera or microphone inside to keep tabs on her."

In less than thirty minutes, they'd crossed the bridge and arrived in Chinatown. They traded the Cadillac for Bai's MINI Cooper and picked up a suitcase filled with eavesdropping spyware. Lee drove them to the rear of the Grand Hotel and parked across the street, where they could watch employees entering and leaving the building through a service entrance. Bai made a call on her cell.

A woman's voice answered, "Grand Hotel Registration Desk. May I help you?"

"I have a friend staying at your hotel, a Miss Wen Liu. Could you tell me what room she's in, please?"

"I'm sorry. We can't disclose that information. I could connect you, if you'd like."

"No, that's all right. I wanted to surprise her. Thank you."

Bai disconnected. "That's pretty much what I expected. There's another way to get her room number, but we need a male, youngish and alone, to get me through the service entrance."

"You think you can talk your way inside?"

"Am I not a beautiful and alluring woman?"

Lee smiled. "You're asking the wrong man."

She pointed through the glass of the windshield. "That's exactly what I'm looking for."

A young Asian male, wearing black slacks, a white shirt, and a black leather motorcycle jacket, walked toward them on the sidewalk. He had a handsome face, verging on feminine—a child's face with soft edges and long eyelashes. His hair had been cut short on the sides with long bangs draped over one eye. Wires from earplugs dangled around a cleft chin.

"Almost too pretty," Lee replied.

Bai got out of the car to intercept the young man before he reached the back entrance. When she ran up to him, she asked for his help in Cantonese.

The young man stared at her blankly and said, "Wow! You're really beautiful!"

His statement took her by surprise. She forgot what she was about to say.

"I don't speak Chinese," he continued. "I was raised in the Sunset. Right now I'm really wishing I'd learned Chinese."

She laughed. "That's all right." She grabbed his arm with both hands. "I speak English. I stepped out for a smoke and forgot my key card. Can you let me in? Please? Please? Pretty please?"

Frowning, he looked at her, then at the service entrance of the hotel. "I'd definitely remember you if you worked at the hotel. If you're thinking about ripping this place off, I have to warn you there are cameras everywhere." He nodded up at a closed-circuit camera mounted over the door. "Security is really tight."

"I'm not here to steal."

Two Hispanic women walking past them cast curious glances their way before using badges to enter the building.

The young man smiled at her. "I'll get you into the building if you'll do something for me."

She looked at him warily. "Men are so predictable. What do you have in mind?"

"I want you to go out with me."

"Wouldn't you rather be with someone your own age?"

"No. My mother taught me to trust my instincts. Everything about you tells me you're special. You're smart: you're fluent in at least two languages. From the way you approached me, you're capable and confident. And from the knife in your sleeve, I can assume you know how to take care of yourself."

His analysis made her pause as she looked at him with interest. His steady gaze belied his age. She smiled at his coolness.

"Trust me," he said, and made the words sound sexy.

She almost batted her eyelashes. "Where have I heard those words before?"

"Aren't you asking me to trust you?"

"How old are you?" she asked.

"I'm twenty-five. My baby face is misleading. I know I look a lot younger."

"You seem to be full of surprises."

His tone offered a challenge. "I believe in fate. What about you?"

She relented, more than a little taken by his disarming charm. "All right, I'll go out with you. How do you want to play this?"

"Follow me and keep your head down. I'll badge in and kick the door wide. Just stay close and tailgate me through the entrance. I won't look back. Once you're in, you're on your own. I won't be able to help you if you're caught."

"What's your name?" she asked.

"Michael Chin." He smiled at her. "Let's trade numbers. I'll call you later. A deal's a deal."

She handed him her phone, and he transferred their cell numbers.

"My name is Bai Jiang." She held out her hand to shake. "A deal is a deal."

He held onto her hand as he spoke. "I wait tables in the lounge up top." He pointed with his free hand, a gesture that suggested he wasn't sure she knew which direction was up, and winked at her. "I'll call you later, Bai."

He turned and walked toward the service entrance. She did as instructed, staying close as he badged his way through the back door. Once inside, Michael went right, toward a service elevator, while she turned left to the stairwell leading into the bowels of the hotel. If Wen Liu had taken refuge in her room, she'd have to eat. And if she ate, the kitchen would have a record.

The room service kitchen was in the midst of lunch rush. Cooks yelled in English, Spanglish, Chinglish, and something that sounded a lot like Russian. The banter hummed like a giant engine amid clattering plates, sizzling food, and mechanical dishwashers that spouted steam in cloudy bursts. Garlic, curry, bacon, and a dozen other odors mingled. In the hub of the uproar stood a woman in kitchen whites with an electronic notepad in her hand and a blue scarf around her neck. She yelled instructions and fielded questions, like a ringmaster at a circus.

Bai stood in the hall and yelled, "Room number for Liu, L, I, U, first name Wen."

"Room 626," the woman in kitchen whites replied. "What the

hell? That order should have gone out thirty minutes ago. Who has the order for 626?"

Bai had what she wanted and turned to leave.

Standing behind her stood a large man in a blue blazer with a frown on his face. He was Caucasian with a square jaw and short hair, cut military style; his voice oozed contemptuous authority. "May I ask what business you have at this hotel?"

"I'm certainly glad to see you," she said enthusiastically. "I seem to be lost. Could you direct me to the mezzanine level?"

He reached out and held her arm. She wrapped his arm with hers and brought her hand up under his armpit, applying pressure to his elbow. Smart enough to let go, he stepped back warily.

She scolded him. "You can look, but you can't touch. Didn't your mother teach you manners?"

She thought he'd make another attempt to physically detain her, but he surprised her and took a quick step back. "Our security manager is on his way. He's asked that you wait for him, Ms. Jiang."

The use of her name halted any thoughts of her running. "Oh crap, that doesn't sound good. Who, exactly, is your head of security?"

"Gary Yan."

She nodded in understanding and looked up at the blinking camera mounted on the ceiling, one of several she'd passed on her way to the kitchen.

Yan had a younger sister she'd gone to high school with. She couldn't recall what he looked like, but he'd obviously not forgotten her. Five minutes later, Gary Yan rounded a corner to stride down the hall toward her. He stood around five foot eight with a beefy physique that strained the seams of his blue jacket. A round face smiled at her as he put out his hand in greeting. "Bai Jiang, it's been a long time."

Although he spoke with a smile, his eyes, tight at the corners, informed her he wasn't really happy. She took his hand and returned his smile. Getting caught left her feeling chastened.

"How is Anna?" she asked, referring to his sister.

"Married to a dentist," he replied perfunctorily as he released the grip on her hand then turned to his subordinate. "I'll take it from here, James. Thank you."

James didn't look pleased, but he nodded then turned to walk away. Yan watched him leave before returning his gaze to her. "Would you allow me to escort you to the nearest exit?"

"Certainly. I'm sorry to have troubled you, Gary."

His smile disappeared as he walked with her toward the stairwell. "I'm hoping there isn't going to be any trouble, Bai." He glanced aside at her briefly. "Is this *Sun Yee On* business?"

"I'm not part of *Sun Yee On*, Gary. If you have concerns, you can call Inspector Kelly with SFPD. I'm doing some police work for a change."

"That won't be necessary, Bai. If you tell me there's no need to worry, your word is good enough for me. Should I worry?"

"No."

He opened the back door for her and ushered her out.

She walked out the door and turned back to face him. "Thanks for the free pass, Gary."

He nodded. "Next time, use the front door, Bai. It'll be better for both of us."

As the door swung closed, she turned away. Getting caught red-handed had ruined her mood. When she reached the car, she settled into the seat next to Lee and turned to him with a weary smile. "Gary Yan is head of security at this hotel."

"I didn't know that."

"Surprised me, too." She handed him her phone. "See if you can get a reservation for Room 624 or 628. Wen is in Room 626."

He made the call and reserved the room. They decided he would check into the hotel and use their surveillance equipment in an effort to get "eyes and ears" inside Room 626. She would monitor Wen's car on her phone app remotely. If Wen decided to use a taxi, they were screwed. Bai had neither the time nor the inclination to sit outside the hotel lurking like paparazzi. She had a blind date to get ready for.

chapter 10

Bai planned to simply have a drink at the Grand Hotel and fulfill her obligation to Elizabeth. She didn't feel the need to dress up for her date. An outfit of black slacks and her black leather jacket over a white, pleated tuxedo-style shirt worked as a compromise between dressy and casual. She wore black pumps as a concession to femininity, while minimal lip gloss and a brush of mascara emphasized her lips and eyes.

As she stepped out of the elevator on the twentieth floor and into the lounge foyer, she noticed four Asian men in black suits wearing earbuds. Everything about the men suggested they were private security. She nodded to them as they made eye contact with her. They bowed slightly before she turned to walk into the lounge.

Howard Kwan sat on the far side of the room at a window table with a view of the brightly lit Bay Bridge. She recognized him from photos she'd researched online. Except for Howard and the staff, who stood idly by, the lounge appeared unoccupied. Music played softly in the background.

She walked up to stand before the table. "Howard Kwan?"

Looking up, he turned to study her. He subtly nodded his head to acknowledge her without offering her the courtesy of standing.

She forced a smile. "I'm Bai Jiang."

He waved his hand wordlessly for her to be seated. Handsome in a soft way, he had a straight nose, calculating eyes, and sculpted cheekbones that framed pouty lips formed into a disapproving frown. Long hair with bangs trimmed asymmetrically finished a look popular among chic Asian males.

He studied her from across the table as she settled into a seat facing him.

When he spoke his voice sounded flat. "You're old. Since I believe in being honest, I'm only stating a fact. I'm rich. That is also a fact."

Her smile fought to stay in place. She assumed his words were
intended to aggravate her. "Don't forget 'rude,' as long as we're being
honest. You're rude. And my age is something you'd best not mention
again. If you do, I'll hurt you. That is also a fact."

She waved the cocktail waitress over and ordered a Macallan's,
neat. When the waitress left to fill her order, Bai turned back to face
him. "How old, may I ask, are you?"

"Thirty."

"That makes us the same age."

"Thirty is young for a man."

"Younger for some than others," she observed. "From your
behavior, I can only assume you're even less enthusiastic about being
here than I am. Since that's the case, why don't we have a quiet drink, let
our respective elders know we're not a match, and part amicably. If you
keep talking, I fear you'll succeed in making me angry."

Her drink arrived. She sipped while guardedly ignoring the man
across the table. Mercifully, he didn't feel the need to entertain her. The
knots in her shoulders and back slowly relaxed as the scotch mellowed
her.

"Are you gay?" he asked. "I'm only asking because of the way you
dress. And your hair. It's perfectly all right if you are gay. My masculinity doesn't feel threatened or anything."

She no longer felt the need to smile. "It's been my experience when
a man confides his masculinity is *not* threatened, it generally is. As to
whether or not I'm gay, I hadn't been up until this moment. Meeting
you has given me a reason to reconsider."

He smiled. "You're very direct. I'm not accustomed to that. Most
women tell me what I want to hear. My family has lots of money, an
economic fact with a tendency to make the women I encounter meek.
But you're different. I'm trying to decide if I like that."

"Don't bother deciding. You're not my type. I'm not interested."

"What is your type?"

"Men who aren't afraid of their mothers."

"What makes you think I'm afraid of my mother?"

"You're here, and you don't want to be."

"Don't jump to conclusions. I made a special effort to be here."

She waved his comment aside. "I'm still not interested."

"Older women can't be choosy."

"I thought we agreed not to mention my age."

"Thirty isn't young."

"For a woman, you mean."

Distracted, he looked up. She turned aside to find Michael Chin in a waiter's uniform standing next to her. A short-waisted, black coat showed off his broad shoulders and narrow hips.

He smiled down at her. "Hello, Bai. Can I get you anything? A cab, perhaps?" He eyed her date speculatively and smiled. "I hope I'm not intruding."

She had difficulty hiding her amusement. "I'm fine, Michael. Thanks for your concern. You look good in a uniform."

"Thanks. You look terrific too. I'll be sure to call. I really can't wait," he said, and turned away, his smile vanishing as he nodded curtly at Howard before walking away.

Howard pursed his lips and stared at her. "What is it he can't wait for?"

"I promised him a date."

He seemed to ponder the prospect. "Is it too late for me to apologize?"

"Yes."

"I feared as much. As long as we're here, would you like to hear about me?"

She folded her hands under her chin and blinked at him. "What better way is there to pass the time than to sit and listen to *you* talk about *you*?"

"See . . . that's what I mean. That's not at all what I expect from a woman. But coming from you, it's attractive."

"I'm trying to determine whether you're remarkably dense or just droll. I'm leaning toward dense, but the biographical material I found on the Internet tells me you're not."

"What did you find? I'm curious."

"You're the third son of Kwan Industries. Most of your family's operations are in textiles, but you also have a finger in the emerging pharmaceutical industry in China as well as high-tech startups. At a *very young* thirty, you have a bachelor's in computer engineering from Harvard and a doctorate in applied medicine from USC. Rumors say you're the likely successor to the family business, even though you're neither the heir nor the spare, which indicates that your older brothers, for one reason or another, aren't suitable. Hence the reason your mother wants you married. The only question I have is why me? I'm an unmarried mother with a history."

He sat back in his seat to look at her. The pretense dropped from his face, and he took a deep breath. "You know almost as much about me as I do. The reason you're here is I asked to meet you."

"Why?"

"Curiosity, I suppose. I saw your picture and bio. The picture was flattering but accurate. You're a beautiful woman. The bio wasn't nearly as flattering."

She nodded in acknowledgment. "I have a history."

"To be honest, I wasn't sure how to approach you. You're somewhat intimidating. Your 'history,' as you call it, reads like a crime novel."

"Give me a minute. I'm trying to figure out whether I'm being flattered or insulted."

"I'm attracted to you," he stated bluntly.

"You have an odd way of showing it."

"I'm not good with people. I'm good at making money, but people, especially women, are a mystery to me."

"I'm sorry, Howard, but I'm not attracted to you."

"You don't know me."

"I don't believe I want to know you."

He leaned back in his chair to study her. They gazed at each other while they sipped on their respective drinks in a state of fragile détente.

When he spoke, he sounded as if he were reciting. "You have one daughter, age thirteen, father unnamed but generally assumed to be a high-ranking triad member. You have another child living with you, age fifteen, relationship unknown. Your mother is actually your childhood governess and not a blood relation. Various real estate holdings in your name as well as corporations under your control place your wealth in the range of a hundred million American dollars. You work sporadically as a *souxun* finding lost people, an activity that seems to take up most of your time. Did I miss anything?"

She shrugged. "That pretty much says it all: unmarried mother, crime family affiliate."

He dismissed her words with a wave of his hand. "The details don't really matter. The salient point is, although you're wealthy in your own right, your fortune pales compared to my family's assets. Don't you find all that money attractive?"

She paused to reflect on his question. "I have difficulty keeping track of the money I have, which is far more than I'll spend in a lifetime. At some point, money becomes a burden."

"You surprise me," he said with a frown. "The more we talk, the more I like you. This date was just a lark, a way to ingratiate myself to my mother and entertain myself. Getting to know you has complicated matters."

"I'm unsuitable. Your family would never accept a woman with my background."

"You've been direct with me, so I'll be direct with you. My oldest brother is a gambling addict. My father bought him a casino in Macau thinking my brother would get his fill. Instead, he managed to gamble away the casino. My second brother is a drug addict. He's in rehab in Sweden. If history repeats itself, as soon as he gets out, he'll get high until he gets thrown back into rehab. My family isn't in any position to make judgments."

"So what are you suggesting?"

"I'm suggesting we date and get to know each other. There's something about you I find very appealing."

"Are you sure you just don't like women who dress like boys?"

He laughed. "Touché. I deserved that. And the answer is no. I assure you. I'm very fond of women. Some might suggest, too fond."

"The problem I have with dating you, Howard," she confided, "is I find you to be a bit of an ass."

"I can be a complete ass," he assured her. "That's just one more reason to have someone like you around to put me in my place."

She finished her drink and tipped the empty glass at him. "Sorry. Time's up. I still don't want to date you. I hope you find what you're looking for."

As she stood to leave, he got to his feet. "Then I want to hire you."

"I'm not that kind of girl," she asserted dryly.

"I'll pay you a thousand a day and expenses."

"No thanks."

"Ten thousand a day and expenses," he said loudly enough for the wait staff to turn and stare.

She gave him a withering look, which he ignored. "Are you done throwing money around?"

The remark seemed to set him back. "At least let me give you a ride home. I have a car and driver downstairs. It's the least I can do."

"No, thanks," she said, and turned to walk out of the bar.

He followed her. She ignored him and stepped into the elevator. He stepped in with her, and the security team formed around him to fill the lift. At ground level, he continued to follow her alone through the hotel lobby to the taxi stand next to valet parking. She stood in line with two couples on holiday while a parking attendant with overdeveloped cheek muscles puffed on a pipe whistle in an attempt to attract the attention of a passing cab.

As she waited, a black van with dark tinted windows pulled to the far curb. Three men jumped from the side door of the van. Dressed in black and wearing balaclavas to hide their faces, the men seemed to have their sights set on Howard.

Howard spotted them and turned to run toward the hotel lobby where his security team waited. As the men ran to intercept him, Bai ran toward them. She blindsided them and knocked the first assailant sideways into the path of the second, who managed to get tangled in the legs of the third. All four of them tumbled to the pavement. She rolled on her shoulder to spring back to her feet. By the time the three men got themselves sorted, she stood between them and Howard with her knife in her hand while his security team hustled him through the glass door of the lobby to safety.

Seeing the opportunity to grab their intended victim spoiled, the men turned and ran back toward the waiting van. Tires screeched, and the smell of burning rubber permeated the air as the black-clad assailants dove into the moving van. Unwilling to give chase in pumps, Bai stood watching, with the knife in her hand. Only then did she realize onlookers had congregated to stare at her.

She quickly slipped the knife back into the sleeve of her jacket and turned to walk back into the hotel lobby. Meanwhile, Howard issued orders to his security. "Get the CCTV discs as well. I don't want this getting out."

When he'd finished, he turned to her. "Sorry. This is probably my fault. I asked my security to stay back so I could talk to you. I wanted some privacy. Apparently, someone saw my lapse as an opportunity."

"Seems like more than happenstance a van would be waiting for a lapse in your security. Does this happen often?"

"This isn't the first attempt. I suspect this is the work of my oldest brother. I also suspect he's subverted some of the people closest to me." He turned to look at his security detail with a wary expression before turning back to Bai. "He doesn't want me dead, just out of the way until after the board meeting next month."

"Your family plays rough."

He smirked. "You don't know the half of it."

A black limousine pulled to the curb outside the door.

"Are you sure I can't give you a ride home?" he asked.

Her cell phone rang. Lee's voice sounded anxious. "I think you should come up to the room. We have a problem."

"I'll be right there."

She turned back to Howard. "Thanks anyway. It seems I still have business here."

As she walked away he called after her. "I'll be in touch, Bai. I don't give up easily."

chapter 11

Bai rode the elevator to the sixth floor then walked down the hall to Lee's room. A blue-jacketed member of hotel security opened the door for her and wordlessly ushered her into the suite. She stepped cautiously through the entry to see Gary Yan standing at the doorway adjoining Wen Liu's room. Lee stood next to him with a grim expression on his face.

She walked toward them and saw that the double doors between Lee's and Wen's rooms stood open. The men shifted their stances, so she might see past them. Wen lay on the beige carpet next to her bed. She wore a white terry robe with a hotel logo. With her legs and arms splayed, she looked as if she'd been making snow angels. Her head was turned to the side. Her eyes stared sightlessly. Two holes the size of dimes marred her unlined forehead, trailing blood that streaked across the bridge of her nose to form a small pool on the carpet beneath her cheek.

Bai turned to Lee with a stunned expression. "What happened?"

"I had a pencil mic under the door," he explained as he gestured at the long, slim microphone still lying across the doorsill. "I was monitoring her with earphones when I heard a knock on her door. She answered. I heard two gunshots and the sound of something hitting the floor. By the time I got my corridor door open, the hallway was empty. I called security."

Yan affirmed Lee's story with a terse nod. "Camera footage corroborates his story. We have a man in a black windbreaker wearing a black baseball cap and sunglasses standing in front of Miss Liu's room at the time indicated. The gun is visible in the video. The perp then exited the building by way of the stairwell located directly across the hall. He was in and out of the room in seconds. Out of the building in a matter of minutes."

"There were gunshots," she said, "so the shooter didn't use a silencer. He obviously wasn't worried about making noise."

"It's like the killer wanted it known she'd been executed," Lee said. "I think someone is sending a message."

"Murder isn't a message," she replied. "It's a declaration of war."

Yan voiced his opinion angrily. "You must have some idea of what this is all about!"

She looked at him and frowned. "I wish I did. Have you called the police?"

He nodded. "I asked for your Inspector Kelly. He wasn't available. I explained the situation but left out the part about the microphone. The hotel would like to avoid publicity. I asked the police to respond discreetly. No uniforms. I'd suggest you put your surveillance equipment away before they arrive."

He obviously didn't want any more complications than necessary. Considering his perspective, Bai could understand how having hotel guests spied upon would definitely be a complication.

Lee didn't waste any time in scooping up the microphone off the floor. He packed the listening device along with the rest of his equipment into the surveillance kit and placed the suitcase on a stand next to the dresser. He'd barely finished stashing the suitcase when the police arrived.

Homicide detectives nonchalantly strolled into the room to introduce themselves. "My name is Meyers, and this is my partner, Detective Gomez," said one of the men, a Caucasian with a paunch and pitted skin. He wore coffee stains on a white shirt with an open collar under an off-the-rack gray suit.

After walking over to look at the victim through the open doorway, he tilted his head and frowned. "What a waste! Who would shoot a beautiful woman like that? That's just criminal."

He turned around and walked back to observe Bai and Lee. His cavalier behavior suggested he wasn't in a hurry.

Gomez, Meyers's partner, a middle-aged Latino in a tailor-made blue suit, broke the silence by directing a question at them. "Did either of you witness the killing?"

"No," Lee replied. "I was in the room alone when I heard the shots

fired. Bai was upstairs in the lounge having a drink. I called hotel security as soon as I heard the shots."

"You didn't see anyone or hear anything else unusual?"

"Just the shots."

The detectives looked them over then seemed to dismiss them.

Gomez turned his attention to Yan. "We understand you have the
perp on video."

"Yes. If you'd like to follow me downstairs to our security offices,
I'll provide you with the disc."

Gomez nodded to Meyers, who followed Gary Yan out of the
room. Once they were gone, the medical examiner and crime scene
investigators showed up.

Gomez spoke with the CSI technicians then turned to Bai and
Lee. "We'd like to use your room as a staging area for our investigation.
Doing so will leave the door the killer used free from contamination
until CSI can collect any possible evidence. I'm sure after we've collected your statements, the hotel will find other accommodations for
you."

Gomez didn't voice the statement in the form of a request; neither
did he wait for their reply. The medical examiner walked through the
adjoining door to anticlimactically pronounce Wen dead. Technicians
then took photographs of everything in her room before wrapping her
hands in plastic bags to preserve any potential evidence, though the
likelihood she'd come in contact with her killer seemed remote. They
then placed her into a black plastic body bag for the trip to the morgue.

Meanwhile, Lee provided Detective Gomez with a recorded statement, neglecting to mention the microphone under the door. As Lee
spoke into the recorder, the techs wheeled the body out on a gurney
through his room for a ride down the service elevator. Bai watched
silently as homicide detectives gathered Wen's personal possessions.
They took her clothes hanging in the closet and her cosmetic case out
of the bathroom, stripping the room of all her possessions. The police
hastily inventoried the contents of her handbag before sealing everything in plastic. Curiously, they didn't find a cell phone.

Meyers returned, and the detectives thanked them for their assistance then nonchalantly left the room with the same lack of urgency they'd shown upon arrival. Gary Yan returned as the last crime scene technician closed the doors between the two rooms before departing.

"I've arranged another room for you on the eighth floor," Yan said, holding out a key card for Lee.

"That won't be necessary," Bai said.

Yan smiled tightly. "I insist."

She looked at Lee, who shrugged and took the proffered card. "I'll just need a few minutes to collect my things."

"I'll wait for you," Yan said as his earbud squawked. He frowned as he listened then refocused on Lee and Bai. "I'll be back to make sure you've vacated the room."

As soon as the door closed behind Yan, Lee retrieved leather gloves and a set of locksmith's tools from the surveillance case. In only moments, he had the double doors between the rooms open again.

"Wen's phone is still in here somewhere," she said to Lee. "I'm sure of it."

A quick search between the mattresses and under the bed proved futile. Crawling around on all fours, she looked under the dresser while Lee hurriedly searched the bathroom, including the toilet tank. The room safe sat open and empty. She checked the safe and felt along the back of the metal box for a false wall; there wasn't one. Lee pulled out the drawers from the bureau and the desk; they were clean. They'd run out of places to look and were about to give up when a thought occurred to her.

"Lee, do you still have the card Wen gave you?"

He fished the card out of his pocket and handed it to her. She tapped the number into her cell and hit the call button. A current Chinese pop song played through a tinny speaker. Following the sound, they walked across the room to a flat-screen television attached to the wall. Lee played his hand over the top edge of the screen until his fingers came to rest on something that shouldn't have been there—a cell phone. He retrieved the phone from its hiding place and pulled the battery out of the back of the device before putting the pieces into the pocket of his jacket.

"If someone is tracking this phone, I don't want them to follow us," he explained.

They put everything back the way they'd found it, then exited the room the way they'd entered by relocking the doors. Lee picked up the surveillance case and accompanied Bai out of their room.

They talked as they waited for the elevator.

"I've had worse days," she confided. "Not a lot of them, but some."

He sighed. "I feel bad. Maybe if I'd done something differently, Wen would still be alive."

"And maybe she'd have died a lot sooner if we hadn't gotten her out of the house in Berkeley. Someone, other than us, tracked her here. She'd only been here a few hours. That's pretty short notice to put together a hit. I'm guessing she was targeted long before we met her. Black karma."

"There's no such thing as black karma," Lee said derisively.

"Tell that to Wen Liu."

Lee turned his head to look at her and shook his head. "Whatever the case may be, I feel sorry for her. I was right there and still couldn't do anything to prevent her death."

"Don't dwell on what can't be changed. You had no way of knowing Wen was in danger. Instead of feeling guilty, think about what we can do to help bring her killer to justice."

He looked at her and nodded. "She must have had a good reason to hide her phone. I'll want to clone the cell's memory before I attempt to hack through the security on her device. I'll need my lab machine to do that."

"How long will that take?"

"That will depend on the level of security and the type of encryption she used. If the key to the encryption is stored on the phone, I'll have the memory card cracked in a couple of hours. If she was sophisticated enough to keep her encryption key elsewhere, we could have a problem. I'll probably have her call log and address book within an hour or two. They're rarely encrypted."

"I'm curious to find out who she's been talking to. While you're working on the phone, I'm going to do another Internet search on Daniel Chen. His profile doesn't add up. The background I've found on him so far only dates back a few years. Before that, Chen didn't exist."

"Looking for Chen is turning out to be a risky business. Are we really sure we want to find him?"

"Wen Liu is dead. So are the Norteños we found in Chen's office. He may be the only one who can tell me why they died. Now I absolutely have to find him."

Lee turned to give her an appraising stare.

"What?"

"Your logic just reminded me you're a girl."

She shrugged off his comment. "Do you think thirty is old?"

He looked at her blankly. "Not since I turned thirty."

"Funny how that works, don't you think?"

chapter 12

Bai went to Lee's apartment to watch him clone Wen's phone. He settled in at his desk and turned on his lab machine, a basic desktop computer without Internet or network capability. The barebones machine had a simple operating system and a myriad of ports for accessing and copying data. He took the secure digital memory card with built-in encryption out of Wen's phone and put it into an SD port on the lab machine to copy the contents onto a hard disk for backup.

"If there's a fail-safe program on the phone to protect the contents against unauthorized access, the backup will give us a second chance to decrypt the data," he explained.

"Great! Whatever that means," Bai replied, mystified by Lee's jargon.

"I'm just copying the data in case I screw up."

When the backup finished, he removed the original SD card and put it into a desk drawer. "While I'm doing this, why don't you go upstairs and rest? I'll call you when I have something."

"Are you sure you don't mind? I can stay and help."

"That's what I'm afraid of."

He smiled but didn't look up from his task.

"I'm a distraction. I get it. All right, call me if you find anything of interest. I don't care how late it is."

He nodded to let her know he'd heard, too immersed in his task to verbally respond. She let herself out of his apartment and took the elevator up to the third floor. Since it was past eleven, the girls would be in bed. When she stepped out of the lift, she found Elizabeth waiting for her. A worried expression on the older woman's face informed Bai her long and crappy day wasn't over.

"The pictures didn't do you justice, but I could still tell it was you."

"What are we talking about?"

"You made the ten o'clock news."

Someone at the Grand Hotel had photographed the altercation in front of valet parking and sold the pictures to a local television station. The shots led the 10 o'clock news report. Bai had been hailed as an unassuming, and presently unknown, hero.

"I've made tea," Elizabeth said. "I was just about to have a cup in the living room, if you'd care to join me?"

Bai recognized the subtle tone that turned what might have been considered an invitation into an edict. They adjourned to the living room, where polished natural bamboo floors and contemporary leather furniture lightened the atmosphere. Large ceramic cups glazed a dark blue rested on the brass and glass coffee table between them.

"I was protecting my date," Bai declared in her own defense. "Dates are few and far between. I couldn't let someone just steal him."

Elizabeth didn't appear to be amused. "You could have been hurt."

"But I wasn't. As a matter of fact, there are a couple of men running around with bruises wishing they'd tried to steal somebody else's date."

"How do you feel about Howard?"

Elizabeth's mercurial change in subject surprised Bai and made her wary. She decided to nip the older woman's matchmaking attempt in the bud. "If I had to sum up Howard in one word, I'd say he's an ass. He might even be a complete ass."

"I believe he's a nice man," Elizabeth replied, pointedly ignoring her opinion. "He can be kind, I'm told. That's not to say he doesn't have his flaws. We all do."

"Did I mention he's an ass?"

"I'm just asking you to keep an open mind."

Bai held her cup in both hands and leaned back into the soft leather cushions to study Elizabeth. A subcurrent of conversation had taken place that left her puzzled. "Is there something you're trying to tell me?"

"I think it would be a good idea to give him a second chance. I know his mother quite well, and I feel there's more to him than what you've seen. I'm told he hides his true nature . . . that he's sensitive."

"He told me I was old."

Elizabeth spoke over the rim of her cup. "Most women are married by thirty."

"So now you're defending him?"

She smiled. "Facts are facts."

Bai let out a deep sigh and took a sip of bitter green tea. "Is it the money you find so attractive?"

"There's nothing wrong with having money, but that isn't my main concern."

"I have plenty of money. I don't need billions of dollars to be happy."

"You're wasting your life finding people who don't want to be found. The Kwan holdings are extensive, and you have an aptitude for management. Wouldn't you like to challenge yourself?"

"I challenged myself yesterday. I only ate two donuts when I could have eaten the entire bag. Doesn't that count for something?"

Elizabeth tilted her chin, which packed the emotional impact of Bai's slamming her forehead on the table. "If you're not willing to have an adult conversation, there's no point in continuing."

With a sullen expression and a stiff posture, she stood to leave the room. Bai considered replacing her tea with scotch when her phone interrupted the thought. The caller was Jason.

She answered in a rapid-fire manner. "I'm tired. I've had a crappy day. You're not going to make it worse, are you?"

"There's a strong possibility I will."

"Where are you?"

"Macau."

"What are you doing in Macau?"

"Running a casino, but that's not why I called."

There was silence on the line.

She wondered if Jason wanted her to guess why he'd called. Too tired to play games, she replied, "I'm hanging up now and going to bed."

"I'm told you made the ten o'clock news."

"Word travels fast."

"I understand you were with Howard Kwan."

"I had a date."

"That's not a good idea," he said in an ominously flat voice.

She found her temper rising. "Since when do I need your permission to date?"

He hesitated before answering. "Stay away from Howard Kwan. His family is poison."

"I'll take your advice under consideration," she replied, unwilling to cave in to his demands without at least token resistance.

"I'll be back in a day or two. Don't do anything foolish while I'm gone."

"How do you define 'foolish'?"

"'Foolish' would be taking on three thugs with a dozen witnesses around to take pictures."

He might have had a point, but she couldn't see any advantage in ceding it to him. "It was a spur-of-the-moment reaction. A girl has to do what a girl has to do."

"There you are. You just defined 'foolish' and saved me the trouble. I'm serious, Bai. His family is bad news."

"Then we have something in common. Don't we?"

"More than you know." His flat tone made the hair on the back of neck rise. "Give my love to the girls. I'll see you in a day or two."

He hung up before she could reply.

She huffed into the phone and tossed the device to the other side of the couch. The phone hadn't finished bouncing on the leather cushion when it rang again. She belly-flopped onto the cushions and stretched to retrieve the device. It was Lee.

"Did you find something?" she asked.

"Yes. You need to see this."

"I'm on my way."

She ended the call and walked across the living room to the foyer where the open elevator waited. The lift took her to the ground floor where she took three steps across the lobby and through the door Lee held open.

He smiled and put an arm around her shoulders to direct her

into his study. "Let me show you what Wen was trying to protect." He pointed at the monitor on his desk. "Come and look at this."

She walked around the desk in order to see the screen. "What am I looking at?"

"These are the encrypted files on the flash drive," he explained, pointing at small icons on the screen's monitor. "I've just started to look at what's inside the files, but I've already come across a half dozen confidential documents. What I've seen indicates she had a wide range of interests, everything from pharmaceutical research to engineering diagrams."

"What do you think the files mean?"

"I think she was an information broker, someone who buys and sells confidential information, like a fence for stolen secrets. From the correspondence I've seen, she appears to have had a number of aliases. That's assuming 'Wen Liu' is her real name and not an alias. Look at this."

He clicked on another folder, and a list of names with contact information appeared on the screen. "This is her address book. She has hundreds of contacts listed."

He scrolled down the list. "Here's someone we know who might be able to shed some light on her activities."

Jason's name was listed under "L" for Lum, along with his private cell number.

"It seems I'm not the only woman to have his private number," Bai said. "How about a Daniel Chen?"

"I looked," Lee stated. "There's nothing under Chen, and I wasn't able to access her call log to see whom she called and when. I may have to activate the phone to do that, and I want to get as much data as possible first in case I trigger a defensive program that will shut down or wipe the phone."

She nodded without really understanding. "I can see why she'd want to hide her identity. Selling confidential information is a dangerous business. Do me a favor: see if Howard Kwan is on her list."

He did as requested and scrolled the screen up. There were about a dozen Kwans on the list, Kwan being a common name. Howard was among them. Whether or not the Howard Kwan listed happened to be the one she'd just met, Bai had no way of knowing.

She tapped the number listed for Howard Kwan into her phone, which had a blocked caller ID.

"Who is calling?" asked a voice she recognized as Howard's.

She ended the call without responding. "Wen, it appears, led an interesting life."

"Yes," Lee replied with a thoughtful expression, "the kind of interesting life that can get you killed. I have the sneaking suspicion the more files we decrypt, the more suspects we'll find who might have wanted her dead."

chapter 13

The day started out humid and warm with the scent of rain in the air. Bai decided to take advantage of the balmy weather and walk the three blocks to her office. While she stood at the crosswalk waiting for the light to change, a limousine pulled to the curb in front of her. A man in a black suit wearing an earbud stepped out of the front passenger door to walk back and hold the rear door open. She regarded him as she crossed her arms, her hand on the sleeve of her jacket.

"Who?" she asked.

"Chairman Kwan," he replied and bowed deeply.

Frowning, she hesitated before stepping into the car, curiosity overruling common sense. The car pulled back into traffic and headed west. The limo rolled up California Street and into the Nob Hill District to stop in front of the venerable Mark Hopkins.

An opulent hotel, the Hopkins once served as a destination for celebrities and royalty. During the thirties and forties, music greats such as Tommy Dorsey and Benny Goodman provided a swinging nightlife. John Barrymore had been a regular. Located at the top of Nob Hill, the hotel still retained its charm and a fabulous view.

Bai's escort led her through the lobby and into the elevator that took them to the eighteenth-floor penthouse. When she stepped out of the lift, six Asian men in similar dark garb stood guard. A couple of them frowned at the sight of her. She returned their measured gazes without smiling.

Her guide ushered her through a set of dark-paneled double doors. She inhaled deeply and braced herself before walking into a lavish apartment decorated with neoclassical furniture. Fresh long-stem roses in large vases sat on leather-topped tables embossed with gold filigree. At the far side of the room sat a diminutive woman in a high-backed upholstered chair with her hands folded and her legs tucked to the side, the embodiment of appropriate comportment.

She wore a perfectly tailored black suit that showed off a fortune in diamonds. Rings stacked her fingers, and a necklace wrapped around her throat in a glistening display of wealth. Her bob was perfectly cut and framed a lovely face with a welcoming smile. Bai stood transfixed for a brief moment. Somehow, the woman seemed familiar.

"I can't help feeling we've met before," Bai said.

The woman smiled and gestured to the matching chair facing her. "My name is Jade Kwan. I'm Howard's mother. Won't you be seated and have tea with me? I believe we have a great deal to discuss."

Bai balked. "I've already told Howard I'm not interested. You have nothing to worry about."

Jade's smile widened as she nodded. "Please, have a seat and let me explain."

Bai sat down cautiously. Her eyes remained fixed on Howard's mother, who continued to smile as she poured tea from a porcelain pot into matching delicate cups of fine bone china.

With a gesture of her hand, the woman indicated the steaming cup of tea. "Please."

Bai lifted the cup to her lips and sipped. The fragrant green tea tasted delicately bitter.

Jade sipped her tea before speaking. "You needn't be afraid. You're among family."

The statement surprised Bai. "What do you mean?"

"I'm Elizabeth's sister. Please, call me Jade."

Jade's smile remained fixed in place as she studied Bai in obvious amusement.

Bai wasn't sure what to make of her assertion. "Elizabeth never mentioned a sister."

"We've been estranged since she decided to marry a gangster and waste her life. I was surprised to hear from her. It seems we have a common interest."

"And what would that be?"

"You. My sister and I agree your talents are being wasted. You should be flattered. My sister and I don't agree upon a great many things."

Bai leaned back into the chair to quietly decipher Jade's words. Obviously, forces were at work she hadn't foreseen. She found the thought disturbing. And, as she observed the determination on Jade's face, a bit frightening.

Jade seemed to read her. "Have I scared you?"

"Maybe, a little."

One side of the older woman's mouth drew up in a lopsided grin. "I don't mean to alarm you. I brought you here to offer you a challenge— one, I feel, you're well-equipped to meet."

"I don't understand."

"Marry my son and help him build Kwan Industries into the largest consortium in the world."

Bai's mouth flopped open as command of her jaw, along with her ability to speak, abandoned her. Jade laughed and sat back to sip tea.

When Bai finally got herself sorted, she had questions. "Why me?" she asked tentatively. "I'm an unmarried mother—old, as Howard likes to remind me. I'm not exactly virgin bride material."

"I'm not looking for a virgin or a naive young woman for my son. He's like his father in many ways—brilliant, talented, and timid."

She reached for a remote sitting on the tea table between them and pointed the device at the wall behind her. A flat screen came to life showing a video of Bai tackling the three assailants from the black van. "You attack," she stated, "while Howard retreats. One doesn't win wars by retreating."

She turned off the monitor before continuing. "For thirty years I've been the strength behind my husband's genius. Together, we've managed to build an industrial empire from one tired, outdated textile mill. Kwan Industries employs more than thirty thousand people. I want to ensure expansion continues. I believe you're the woman capable of bringing my dreams to fruition."

The dour expressions on the faces of Jade's bodyguards suddenly made sense to Bai. They'd been the men she'd tumbled to the tarmac in front of the Grand. Everything fell into place. The attempt to kidnap Howard had been a ruse to test her. She didn't know whether to be flattered or outraged.

She settled for blunt. "I have a life here and children who need me. I'm not naive, as you pointed out. Marrying into your family would require that I produce children to inherit the empire you envision. I won't set aside my own children for the sake of your family."

"You don't have to. Your daughter, my sister's granddaughter, has my bloodline. She's also brilliant and, from everything I've heard, fierce. Then, too, there's something about which you're not aware. Howard's been a prolific womanizer for more than a decade, yet not one illegitimate child has resulted from these liaisons. I'm not positive, but I fear my son may be unable to father children. Your daughter would be as dear to me as my own child. Even if you decide not to marry Howard, I would still consider your daughter the most viable successor to Kwan Industries."

Bai thought about rejecting Jade's offer outright, but it wasn't every day a thirty-billion-dollar consortium got dropped in her lap. The prospect of leading a polynational corporation sounded intriguing. She held up a hand. "Let me just put things in perspective for a moment. If what you say is true, and I have no reason to doubt you, Howard and Jason are cousins. How does Howard feel about marrying his cousin's ex? Do they even know they're cousins?"

"They know they're cousins, but they're not close. I've been absent from my sister's life for more than thirty years, and our relationship with Jason is somewhat contentious. Only last month, Jason managed to take a casino away from Kwan Industries in Macau. We took a loss of nearly three hundred million. I wouldn't say we're on friendly terms, but he is family."

Bai felt overwhelmed. Slapping a hand to her forehead, she said, "This could get really ugly."

Jade scoffed. "I trust you'll be able to deal with two childish men. After all, I trust you to run an empire."

"I hadn't thought to run an empire. I'm still working on organizing my closet."

"You can hire someone to organize your closet, buy your clothes, and drive your car. Doesn't the thought of wielding real power appeal to you? I'm offering you a chance to live life on a larger scale, Bai. And, I'm offering you a chance to pass that legacy on to your child."

The idea of taking on Kwan Industries sounded interesting, while the thought of marrying Howard didn't appeal to her at all. But she wouldn't lightly brush aside the opportunity to pass that birthright to Dan.

"What does it mean to be Howard Kwan's wife?" she asked.

Taking her time, Jade seemed to consider her answer carefully. "Initially, marrying him will mean relocating to Hong Kong, at least for a while. You'll work with me at our corporate headquarters to learn the business. You'll work long hours, but I can assure you the work will be interesting and challenging."

"What about my children?"

"They'll be given every advantage: the best schools, private tutors, anything you want."

"And Elizabeth?"

The question eased the smile from Jade's face. "She knew she would lose you when she set you on this course. But you don't have to worry about her. Without you, she'll get her son back. As I understand the situation, the only thing standing between Elizabeth and Jason is you."

Jade's words struck home. Elizabeth wanted Jason out of Bai's life. She only now realized the lengths to which his mother had been willing to go to make that happen. Elizabeth had chosen to give up her family to ensure their safety. The thought sobered Bai.

"What about my friend, Lee?"

"The gay man? Bring him with you. You can make him the head of your security. He's perfect since there wouldn't be any talk of an illicit relationship if he's openly *tongzhi*."

"I noticed you haven't mentioned Howard. How does he feel about having a wife foisted on him? He may not want to marry me."

Picking up her tea, Jade took a sip then carefully placed the delicate cup on the table before answering. "We're both practical women," she stated, then hesitated. "Howard will marry you. He may even be an ardent lover for a short while. However, when it comes to women, my son is like his father: he has a short attention span. It won't be long before he's once again entertaining himself with whatever young girl catches his eye. You'll be free to do as you like as long as you're discreet."

Somehow, she wasn't terribly surprised by Jade's answer. Bai would be an asset to the family business, and Dan would provide an heir with Jade's bloodline. Her husband's bloodline was apparently of little concern. Perhaps, Bai considered, that would be a woman's final revenge against a husband who'd spent his life entertaining other women. She had to decide if Jade's offer was a life she'd be willing to accept in return.

"Do I have time to think about your offer?"

Jade's smiled tightened. "How much time do you feel you'll need?"

There were others who would be affected by her decision—her children, Lee, and Elizabeth. The decision wasn't one she'd be willing to make alone.

"This is all a bit daunting. I'd like time to get to know your son better. Despite your assurances he'll find other interests, marrying someone isn't something I take lightly. If I find I simply don't like him, I won't marry him."

The statement seemed to surprise Jade. She frowned but didn't say anything.

"Howard's shown an interest in dating me. I'll let that happen. If I like him, we'll go from there. That probably isn't the answer you want, but it's the best I can do."

"I'd hoped you'd be more practical. There are time constraints. At the end of next month, a new CEO will be chosen. My husband's failing health has forced the board of directors to move up the annual election. Before then, it's imperative my son announce his engagement. We need to show the world the face of a stable family man to ensure the votes we need to retain management rights."

Jade waited for Bai to meet her gaze before saying, "You have two weeks to come to a decision. That's all the time I can give you."

chapter 14

Bai discovered the door to her office unlocked. She walked through the lobby and into her office to find Inspector Kelly slouched on the couch drinking from a paper cup. Standing at the window, Lee turned to greet her with a frown.

"I see we have company," she said without enthusiasm.

Kelly smiled, an expression that did nothing to improve his appearance. "I was just telling your partner here how fortunate he is to be working with such a fine-looking woman."

"The inspector is quite taken by the curvature and inflexibility of your *gluteus maximus*," Lee stated in a flat voice.

Kelly turned on the couch to scowl at him. "I said nothin' a' the sort," he said scornfully before turning back to Bai with an ingratiating smile. "I merely mentioned—with all due respect, mind you—you have a very nice ass. But that's not why I'm here. I thought you might want to see this." He pulled a DVD case out of his pocket and tossed it to her. "It's a copy of the surveillance tape from the shooting. My friends in homicide tell me you were there. This should make everything clear."

She caught the plastic case, removed the DVD, and slipped it into the player on her laptop. Lee walked across the room to join her. When the disc started to play, her monitor showed a man in dark glasses, a baseball cap pulled low over his eyes, walking up a stairwell. He kept his head down. When he arrived at Wen Liu's room, he knocked and waited. The door opened, and his hand came up to reveal a small revolver. He pushed into the room and a few seconds later dashed out the door. Cameras caught him running down the stairwell and fleeing through the side exit of the hotel.

She looked up at Lee with a puzzled expression. He appeared to be as bewildered as she was. They both turned to Kelly, who grinned at them knowingly.

"Don't you see?" he said. "That's Chen who shot that poor woman."

"How did you come to that conclusion?" she asked. "You can't even tell if he's Chinese from this video. The man behind those sunglasses could have been Elvis."

"SFPD has determined that's Chen." the inspector repeated. He tapped his index finger into the palm of his hand for emphasis as he said, "We found drugs and money in his office. The two dead stiffs were Norteño. The dead woman was obviously linked to Chen. We found evidence at her home and in Chen's office; those two knew each other. It seems this Chen character is tying up all his loose ends, so to speak."

Leaning back into the deep leather cushions, Kelly nodded knowingly. Lee rolled his eyes and went back to the window to watch the street. He'd obviously found something of interest. Bai took a deep breath and sat down to mull over Kelly's assertions.

"How much money did you find in Chen's office?" she asked.

"The amount isn't important. The numbers on the bills matched those from the heist."

"Was there a lot of drugs?"

He waved the question aside. "What does it matter? The drugs were there. It's obvious Chen is our guy."

Money and drugs found in Chen's office, along with a couple of dead gang-bangers, sounded like too convenient an explanation. Even if Chen had kept the money and drugs at his office, he would've had ample time to retrieve them before the bodies were discovered. Something was wrong, and she suspected that "something" was sitting on her couch.

She smiled and nodded. Kelly leaned back with a grin on his face. She found his complacency insulting. "How stupid do you think we are?"

Kelly's smile dropped. "I'm not sure what you're getting at."

"You've spent so much time wrapped around a bottle you can't even come up with a convincing lie. There's no way you could identify Daniel Chen from that video. Furthermore, there's no way anybody would be stupid enough to leave drugs and money at the scene of a murder. I don't know what you're up to, Kelly, but I plan to find out."

"You just keep after Chen," the inspector said, his voice rising as his face reddened. "When you find him, you'll find the truth."

The inspector hoisted himself off the couch and staggered to his feet. A taint of alcohol and stale sweat choked the air around him. He rocked in place before he steadied himself and launched his bulk toward the door. A hand, flagging belligerently over his shoulder, served as a farewell salute. After pulling the door open, he stopped with one hand braced on the frame to mutter angrily, "I didn't always need a drink. There was a time . . ."

He shook his head as if to brush away the thought before he pushed himself off the jamb, leaving the door ajar behind him. They listened as the lobby door slammed.

"I can almost feel sorry for him." Lee remarked from where he stood looking out the window with his back to her.

"What do you find so interesting on the street?"

"That same young woman, the one following Kelly the other day, is still following him. I think I'll follow her. It seems only fair."

He turned and quickly strode from the office. Bai's cell phone rang before she could get out of her chair to follow him. The caller was Jason.

"Where are you?" she asked.

"I'm in the air, somewhere over Midway. I'll be back in San Francisco tonight."

"I didn't expect you for a couple of days."

"Plans change."

His rushing back to San Francisco left her feeling conflicted. She missed him and wanted to see him, but she had questions concerning his relationship with Wen. Since she'd found his number in the dead woman's phone directory, she'd been angry with him. She didn't want to attribute her feelings to jealousy but had a hard time rationalizing her pique any other way.

"Do you know a woman by the name of Wen Liu?"

"Why do you ask?"

She could sense the tension in his voice. As usual, he remained evasive.

"She was murdered last night. Executed. Lee had her under surveillance at the time. Someone put two bullets in her forehead. That she opened the door for her killer suggests she knew him."

There was a long silence on the line. "Wen and I had occasion to do business. Recently, she provided information proving quite valuable."

"What kind of information?"

"That isn't important." His response seemed a little too abrupt "I'm sure Wen made at least as many enemies as she did friends. It was the nature of her business."

"What business was that?"

"She bought and sold information."

"Were you an enemy or a friend?"

"Neither. If she had something I wanted, I bought it. If I had something worth selling, I sold it. Business is business."

She wanted to believe him. Jason had shown himself to be a pragmatic man and didn't, as a rule, mix business with pleasure. That wasn't to say he didn't appreciate a beautiful woman or wasn't capable of breaking the rules, but he liked to avoid complications.

"Someone didn't view her business quite so dispassionately," she stated.

"Like I said, she had enemies. Her business was secretive. I suspect her transgressions were numerous. I understand she had a partner, a man. He might know something."

"Do you happen to know her partner's name?"

"No."

"You're not being very helpful."

"I wasn't aware I was working for you." He didn't bother to hide his irritation. "I can rattle off a dozen individuals who might have wanted her dead, but what's the point of idle speculation?"

She pressed him. "Do you know a man by the name of Daniel Chen?"

"The name doesn't mean anything to me. Listen," he said, changing the subject, "we need to talk, but I don't want to have this discussion over an open line. I'll send a car for you when I arrive."

Her frustration with his secretive behavior bled through into her voice. "Call my cell when you get in. I may not be home."

He disconnected in his usual abrupt manner. He wasn't one to waste time on good-byes.

As she stared at her phone, mouthing obscenities, a shadow fell over her desk. A man stood before her. Startled, she fought an impulse to jump out of her seat while wondering how he'd managed to make his way into her office unnoticed.

A mirthless grin appeared on Daniel Chen's handsome face. He looked even more striking in person than in the grainy photograph. "Wen Liu said you could help me."

She took a moment to gather her thoughts and respond. "Are you aware she's dead?"

His face didn't register surprise. He was either very stolid or well informed. Stepping back, he settled onto her couch. His movements remained relaxed, as did his expression.

"I saw the papers," he said in a detached voice. "Do they know who killed her?"

"The police think it was you."

He smirked. "Why would I kill her? We worked together. I was very fond of her." He leaned forward and put his hands together in front of him as he stared at her. "I saw you on the news last night. You're quite the hero."

"I'm flattered you recognized me. Getting back to the point, who are you?"

"I'm Daniel Chen," he replied, looking slightly annoyed by the question.

"I've run Internet searches on Daniel Chen. Oddly enough, he appeared out of nowhere a few years ago. His paperwork must have been very convincing to have gotten him a job teaching at Berkeley." She looked at him with a questioning gaze. "So the question remains: who are you, really?"

"Forget about trying to find out who I am. Tell me who killed my friend."

Their gazes met. She wasn't fooled by his laid-back manner. The man sitting on the couch across from her was a predator. She could feel his animal presence. Her hand rested on the sleeve of her jacket. "I can do better than that. I can show you who killed Wen."

She turned the laptop on her desk so he could see the screen, then started the video from the hotel surveillance cameras. He came off the sofa in one fluid movement to bend over and stare closely at the screen. His features hardened when he saw the gunman raise the weapon.

"You!" he hissed under his breath.

Straightening his back, he stared at the screen while she studied him. His hands slowly rolled into fists. A muscle at the base of his neck twitched.

"Did you kill the two men in your office?" she asked.

He turned slowly to look at her. Eyes like blank coins regarded her in cold appraisal. "I haven't been to campus in weeks."

"What about the heist south of Market? Did you take the money and the drugs?"

He barked a humorless laugh. "I don't know what you're talking about. What money? What drugs?"

"The police have named you as their chief suspect in a cop killing, a triple homicide in the SOMA. Reportedly, you made off with a million in cash and a million in heroin."

He turned away from her and paced across the room to look out the window. "Thanks for the information. Wen was right. You helped me. I owe you."

"For what?" she asked.

"For giving me her killer."

"What good was that? Nobody could recognize her killer from that video."

As he turned toward her, a wolfish grin spread across his face. Before she could ask anything further, he turned to bolt from the room. By the time she made her way downstairs to street level, he'd disappeared.

chapter 15

Bai sat at her desk trying to puzzle out who had lied and who, if anybody, had told the truth. If Daniel Chen had nothing to do with the triple homicides in the SOMA, then who had possession of the drugs and the money? And why was Kelly so insistent on placing the blame on Chen? How did Wen Liu's murder fit into the picture, or did it? Why had Kelly come to her? None of it made any sense.

Her cell phone rang. Lee's voice sounded hesitant over the phone. "Where are you?"

"I'm still at the office. Why?"

"I need your help. I've followed Kelly and his tail north to Columbus Avenue, where he met a man. Kelly fawned all over the guy. I'd like to follow Kelly's new friend to find out who he is. If you can pick up the tail on Kelly, I can follow our mystery man. Can you meet me at the corner of Columbus and Vallejo?"

"I'm on my way," she said, getting out of her chair. "Call me if Kelly leaves before I get there."

About 800,000 people are jammed into roughly seven square miles in San Francisco. So even though the corner of Columbus and Vallejo was only five city blocks away, Bai decided the stalled traffic would make walking faster than taking a cab. She hustled past idled cars on Chinatown's narrow streets and dodged around double-parked trucks. Within ten minutes, she'd reached her destination, where she found Lee leaning with his back against a building to observe her approach.

"Where are they?" she asked.

"In Figaro's, on the other side of the street." He nodded in the direction of the popular restaurant. "The girl tailing Kelly is standing next to the bus stop. She's the young brunette wearing a jeans jacket over a red top and black denims."

"I've got her," she replied as she gazed across the street.

With her back to them, the girl seemed oblivious to anything other than her quarry inside the cafe. Following a cop, a potentially dirty one, could be dangerous—not a task suitable for a young and plainly inexperienced girl.

As Bai watched, Kelly and a man in a dark-gray suit walked out of the restaurant.

The man in gray looked to be middle-aged, clean-cut, wearing a well-tailored, expensive-looking suit. He had broad shoulders and carried himself with assurance. Wary eyes scanned the street in both directions. The man had hawk-like features beneath a deep tan that implied he'd spent a lot of time somewhere other than San Francisco, someplace where a potent sun could turn a *gwailo* chocolate brown.

The men didn't shake hands when they parted. The tan man turned left while Kelly turned right to walk toward the girl waiting at the bus stop. He wore a sour expression on his face, suggesting whatever he'd ingested at the café hadn't agreed with him.

Lee tapped Bai on her shoulder in silent farewell before walking around the corner. He used a couple of businessmen walking in the same direction as a screen between him and the tan man. She almost called him back. Something about the tan man troubled her. He seemed too aware of his surroundings, too watchful. She consoled herself with the thought that Lee could take care of himself.

Meanwhile, Kelly walked down the other side of the street. He proceeded at a considerably slower pace. His sauntering gait gave the jeans-jacket girl plenty of time to put her back to him. When the girl turned, Bai got a good look at her—a Latina, very pretty, very young. Large gold hoops dangled from her ears. Dark-red lipstick coated full, pouty lips that would never need plumping. Curly black hair dropped past her shoulders.

The girl stopped to light a cigarette as she eyed Kelly with a malevolent glare. Frowning, she inhaled deeply on her cigarette before walking lazily down the street in his wake. Her leisurely pace kept her a half block behind him. Staying out of sight didn't seem to concern her. Her attitude suggested boredom or perhaps even contempt for the man she followed.

Kelly shoved a finger up his nose as he shambled down the street. The girl stopped abruptly to shake her head in obvious disgust. Bai laughed. He continued to dig in his nose and wipe his hands repeatedly on his stained raincoat while Bai wondered distractedly what he hoped to find.

Continuing to follow the pair from the other side of the street, Bai allowed them plenty of room. The sidewalks were busy but not crowded. Around five, when office workers abandoned their cubicles, the story would be different. She hoped by then Kelly and the young Latina would have brought an end to their little jaunt.

Kelly turned right on Vallejo and proceeded to casually stroll down the street toward Powell. Before reaching the cross street, he stopped to enter the SFPD Central Station. Their little parade came to a jarring halt. The young Latina looked around in apparent confusion. Bai waited across the street, watching to see what she would do. After a while, the young woman made a call on her cell phone.

Bai grew tired of waiting. She crossed the street and walked up to confront the girl. The Latina turned away and ignored her. Bai walked around her until they faced each other again to ask, "Why are you following Inspector Kelly?"

"Check it out. I don't know you, lady. Go away."

"It's true we haven't been introduced, but you've been spotted near my office in Chinatown twice in the past couple of days. Just for your information, you're not very good at dogging people. You should try to be more aware of what's going on around you. He may be an old, drunk cop, but that doesn't mean he can't be dangerous."

"Aren't you all that?" the girl said indignantly. "You're the fuckin' danger. Are you trying to get me capped? Get the fuck away from me before I jack you up!"

While the girl sounded belligerent, her eyes darted with fear.

"Tell me why you're tailing him, and I'll leave you alone," Bai offered.

"Check it out. I'm just putting in work. He said to keep an eye on the fat *popo*, so I'm keeping an eye on the fat *popo*."

"*Who* asked you to keep an eye on the fat cop?"

"Why you wanna know?"

"I'm oddly curious that way. What can I say?"

The girl seemed scared and exasperated. When she finally spoke, her ensuing explanation sounded reluctant. "He's 'o' 'g,' *China*, Norteño."

"So this guy's an original gangster. Are you Norteño?"

"Are you *loco*, *China*?" Her attitude transitioned from frightened to disdainful without pausing to take a breath. "Girls can't be Norteño. I'm *chola*. They own me. They protect me. That's the way things are."

Bai's jaw clamped down. "I see," she reflected. "We have the same problem in my world, but being property never appealed to me. Are you sure you wouldn't be better off quitting? Life has more to offer than being somebody's bitch."

The girl looked at Bai as if she were crazy. "You don't quit. They quit you . . . with a double deuce in your fucking head," she said while pointing an index finger at her temple. "That's the way it works. Now get the fuck away from me before somebody decides I'm a hater."

On closer inspection, Bai guessed the girl's age to be around sixteen—a child. Makeup made her look older and harder. Scrape off the heavy war paint, and a teenager would surface. At a time in her life when she should have been going to school, the girl ran errands for gangsters while trying to survive in a world that viewed her as property. Her situation made Bai sad. And angry.

"I don't suppose this Norteño of yours would want to talk to a girl? Me, for instance, if you were to ask him nicely?"

"You really are trying to get me capped!"

She looked as if she might take flight. Bai calmed her by taking a step back and putting her hands up, palms out. "It was just a thought. If you think it's a bad idea, forget it."

"You gotta book now! They're gonna be here soon. If they see you, it'll be bad for me. They'll know I screwed up. Please, go away and leave me alone."

Bai took a card out of her pocket and handed it to the girl. "If you get in trouble and need help, call me."

The girl didn't look at the card. She stuffed it into the pocket of her jeans as she scanned the street anxiously.

Bai turned to walk back to the corner and cross the street. She found a doorway alcove where she could step in to watch the girl. A few minutes later a shiny black low-rider, a four-door Chevy, pulled to the curb. The girl put her hands up with one finger showing on one hand and four fingers on the other as she produced a forced smile.

Bai continued to watch as the front passenger door opened. Her old friend Rafe stepped out of the car to yell at the girl. He brought his hands up in front of her face and slapped them together. The girl shrank back and covered her head with her arms. He grabbed her by the arm and shoved her at the closed door of the car, where she slammed up against the side of the low-rider. Turning away, he got back into the front passenger seat without looking back. As the girl opened the rear door of the car, she looked up and locked eyes with Bai. As Bai started toward her, the Latina shook her head, tears on her cheeks, and ducked into the backseat of the low-rider.

Before Bai could cross the street, the car pulled away from the curb. Anger and frustration clouded her thoughts. The world could be cruel and unforgiving. She knew she couldn't save every child. She told herself that what she needed to do was to mind her own business.

Angrily, she turned to walk south on Columbus toward China-town while trying to forget about what she'd seen. After all, the girl wasn't her problem. The Latina made her own choices.

"Shit!" She spoke the word aloud and stopped in the middle of the sidewalk, her hands coming to rest on her hips. "Shit, shit, shit!"

She knew what she *should* do and what she *would* do were two different things. As she stepped to the curb to flag down a cab, she wondered why the Norteños were interested in a nose-picker like Kelly in the first place. A barely functioning alcoholic cop seemed an odd choice to keep tabs on. And why send a little girl to do the job?

"Bryant and Sixteenth," Bai informed the cabbie as she settled into the backseat.

There was no telling where Rafe had taken the girl. She'd try to enlist Boobs's help in rescuing the young Latina. He knew Rafe, and he knew the district. What she didn't know was whether or not he'd help her run a fool's errand. She had a weakness for strays. There was no use denying it.

chapter 16

The gym still smelled like dirty socks. Boobs worked with a black fighter, a tall kid who radiated intensity as he jabbed at the padded mitts Boobs held out in front of him. The slap of leather hitting leather tapped out a lively cadence as the fighter punched—one-two, one-two-three—while the kid's eyes focused like lasers on the red targets. Boobs kept moving to make the young man practice his footwork. The kid followed him around the mat like a dancer.

When Boobs spied Bai, he put his hands up to bring the session to an end. Dropping his arms and stepping back, the young fighter breathed heavily and wiped his brow with a forearm.

"Work the speed bag, Rory," Boobs said as he slipped the red mitts off his hands "Give me at least ten minutes, five on each hand. Then work the heavy bag for another twenty minutes."

Rory nodded and turned away with a backward, appreciative glance at Bai while Boobs made his way toward her with a smile creasing his face.

"To what do I owe the pleasure?" he asked.

"You may not be so happy to see me when you find out why I'm here."

His smile dimmed but didn't vanish. "Why don't you tell me and let me be the judge?"

"I want you to help me find Rafe."

The smile disappeared, and he took a deep breath. "What do you want with him?"

"I'd like to ask him some questions."

"He's not much of a talker."

Hesitant, she looked away, then back at Boobs. "There's a young girl with him, a Latina, with whom I'd like a word in private."

He stared at her and cocked his head. "I've seen that look before. There was a woman back home in Texas who would get that same determined look on her face. I learned the hard way to avoid her when she looked like that. Nothing good ever come of that look."

She smiled tightly. "You may be right. I'm on a mission. I saw Rafe rough up the young girl. He treated her like one of those gloves," she said, gesturing to the sparring mitts in his hand. "I want to take her away from him and away from the Norteños. Will you help me?"

Boobs shook his head with a look of consternation. "What are you thinking? You think if you waltz in there and ask nice, Rafe'll give you his girl?"

"What if the girl were your daughter he was slapping around? What would you do then?"

His jaw clamped tight and his eyes narrowed in anger. "She's not my daughter. My daughter died twenty years ago. She lived the life, and there was nothing I could do about it. I tried, but she liked the excitement. And she liked the drugs."

He stopped and seemed to consider a moment, his emotions calming. "Fear makes people want to be slaves—fear of being alone, fear of dying, and fear of living. That's what makes people put up with being hurt. You can't make somebody brave. They've got to find their own courage. That's the way life is."

She shook her head. "This girl's just a child. She hasn't had time to find her courage. With Rafe beating her down, I'm afraid she'll never find the nerve to break away."

He remained silent, his brow furrowed in thought. "Just assuming you get this girl, what are you going do with her? If she's running with the Norteños and living the gangster life, she sure as hell ain't no angel. You gonna take her home and make her part of your family? 'Cause right now, the only family she's got is that gang. If you take that away from her, she's not going to thank you."

"I don't know," she answered truthfully. "I just know I have to give her a chance at something better than being a gang whore. If you'd seen the look in her eyes, you'd understand. She's scared. She's just a kid."

"You should be scared, too," he said. "You go up against Rafe, you're going up against the Norteños. That's a whole lotta awful, girl."

"Then help me find a way to get her free without making trouble. You know this neighborhood and the people who live here. You're respected. Help me broker a deal."

He looked away with a scowl before turning back to face her. "Maybe I'm as big a fool as you are." He chuckled mirthlessly. "All right, I'll do what I can. Come on up to the office while I make some calls."

He led her up the metal stairs to his loft office and took a seat behind his desk. Using an old-fashioned rotary phone, he started to make calls. Most of the conversations were short as he asked to speak with a man by the name of Hector. When he finally connected, he asked for a meeting while remaining vague about what he wanted, just saying it was business. Hector seemed reluctant but finally agreed. They'd meet in an hour at a café on Eighteenth Street.

He put the phone back on its cradle and stared at her. "Hector is the lieutenant of the local Norteños. They have some kind of a military structure with generals, captains, lieutenants, and soldiers. All their generals are *Nuestra Familia*, locked up in prison just like most of their captains. Almost all of their decision makers are behind bars. That alone should tell you the kind of men you're dealing with."

"Will Hector have the authority to speak for his gang?"

"I think for what you're asking, he probably can. The girl's not a gang member, so there isn't any reason to protect her unless they're just in the mood to be assholes. It's up to you to make sure they get into the right frame of mind. That shouldn't be a problem. You seem pretty good at talking people into acting stupid."

She smiled at him. "I won't forget you helped me."

"Don't be thanking me yet. There's a good chance Hector and his boys will laugh in your face. Or worse, they won't think you're funny at all."

"Leave it to me. I'm good at motivating people to do the right thing."

Shaking his head, he was clearly unconvinced by her optimism. He stood. "I'll go with you to meet him. If things get ugly, let me handle it. Don't get in his face. These boys don't like sassy women."

Standing to face him, she replied with a smile, "I'll try to stifle my natural tendencies."

He seemed to look inward. "I'll never forget that woman down in Texas. Lord, but she was a handful of trouble." He smiled and shook his head. "I guess I'm just a sucker for sassy women."

An hour later, they sat in a booth at a diner that looked like a throwback to an earlier era. Chipped tabletops of red Formica and seats upholstered in black tuck-and-roll Naugahyde made up the decor. The smell of cumin and fried pork infused the warm air, while conversations ricocheted in rapid-fire Spanish.

Boobs ordered a Tecate *con limo*. Bai ordered the same and sipped the brew while they waited. They'd almost finished their *cervezas* when four large Latino males strolled into the café. Three of them took stools at the counter up front where they could watch the door. The fourth man sauntered back to stand next to their booth. He wore a red and white 49ers jersey with "14" displayed front and back. The tails of his shirt hung over black jeans cuffed over black work boots. Black-rimmed, dark shades covered his eyes. He wore his long black hair slicked back.

"*Ese!* You lookin' good, Boobs," the big man said as he stood in the aisle with his legs splayed and his thumbs hooked in the front pockets of his jeans.

Skittish, the patrons of the café slipped one by one out the door. Bai watched them go with interest. Not one of them made eye contact. They kept their heads down like racing turtles.

"Have a seat, Hector," Boobs said, gesturing at the empty bench across from them. "We have some business to discuss."

The man smiled but didn't sit. He gestured at Bai. "Who's your *camarada?*"

"My name's Bai Jiang," she said. "Please, have a seat."

Dropping the smile, he hesitated before sliding into the booth. Bai looked around for the waitress, but she'd disappeared. She suspected the woman wouldn't reappear until their conversation ended and Hector departed.

She smiled at Hector. "You don't seem to be very popular."

"Life at the top is lonely, *China*."

"Those of us on the bottom can only imagine."

He ignored the comment and looked at Boobs. "What's this all about?"

Boobs tipped his head at Bai. "This is her rodeo."

She tilted her head in acknowledgment. "I wanted to know why the Norteños are interested in Inspector Kelly of the SFPD and why they're having him followed."

The man stared at her behind his dark shades. "Don't know what you're talkin' bout, *China*."

"Rafe is having a young woman—a girl, really—follow him. I know because I've had Kelly under surveillance. He's been investigating the SOMA shootout from earlier this week where two of your soldiers were killed."

Mention of the drug exchange managed to get Hector's attention. He leaned over the table and removed his sunglasses, his brown eyes bright with interest. "You speakin' true, *China*?"

"I have no reason to lie."

He looked aside at one of the men sitting at the counter. "Call Rafe and tell him to bring his little *ruka* over here. I wanna talk to them."

The underling made a call. Hector got up from the booth to walk behind the counter and find a cold beer. He rejoined them in the booth, where they sat and drank.

"You know anything else?" he asked while they waited for Rafe's arrival.

"I know a lot of things," she replied. "You help me, and I'll help you."

He didn't look convinced that helping her was a good idea and frowned at her proposal. Rafe walked through the front door with the girl trailing him like a whipped puppy. They walked over to stand next to the booth.

Hector looked up at him. "This *mujer*," he nodded at Bai, addressing her with more respect, "says you're havin' your *ruka* follow a cop. Why?"

Rafe seemed taken off guard. His face looked as if he were suddenly constipated. After a long silence, he replied, "Bitch be lyin'."

Hector looked up at him and laughed. "*Vato loco!* It took you that long to come up with 'she's lyin'?" He shook his head. "You gotta learn to lie better, bro. That was terrible, man. You feel me?"

The men at the bar smiled. The girl kept her head down. Bai worked hard at keeping a straight face while Rafe stared at her with unconcealed hatred.

The smile disappeared from Hector's face. "Jet home, Rafe. I'll be by in a few. We'll talk."

Rafe looked around for some means of refusing the order but couldn't find anyone to back him up. Obviously angered, he grabbed the girl by the arm and turned to leave.

"*Chica* stays," Hector ordered.

Rafe turned. "She's mine."

"*La ruka Norteños*," Hector said tersely. "She stays."

Rafe stared at Hector defiantly before turning to storm out of the café. When he'd left, Hector addressed the girl. "Tell me everything you know about this cop and why you're watching him."

"Rafe didn't say why. He just said to follow the fat *popo* to see where he goes. He said to see if he met anybody."

"Did he?" Hector asked.

"Her," the girl said, pointing at Bai.

Hector turned to Bai with a look of interest. "What's this cop want from you?"

"What will you give me if I tell you?"

He didn't look pleased with her answer. "Maybe I'll let you walk out of here. *Yo controzzo con sotoas.*"

His claim of owning the neighborhood didn't faze her. "You couldn't stop me if I wanted to leave."

Her hand flicked, and her knife embedded itself in the upholstered bench a fraction of an inch from his ear. He ducked, after the fact, while his boys started to rise from their stools. When he looked aside at the knife and realized what had happened, he put up a hand to forestall his men.

"It's all right." He straightened upright to fix Bai with a scowl.

"*China* was just making a point." He nodded solemnly. "I probably should have asked first, but who are you, *China?*"

"My grandfather was *Shan Chu* of *Sun Yee On* triad, the head of the dragon. I'm what the FBI refers to as a 'criminal affiliate.' I've always thought the label was a little harsh."

He sat back into the cushions of the booth to study her. He seemed conflicted. "You disappoint me, *China*. I thought we were going to click up."

"We can still be friends, Hector. I think you'll find I can be a very good friend. I'll give you what you want if you give me the girl."

"Why do you want the *chica?*"

"I collect strays."

He smiled and pondered her proposal. "Don't we all?" he finally said. "The problem I got with givin' you the *chica* is it will look like I sold one of my own people."

"You're selling a girl, Hector. This is just business."

He thought some more as he rubbed his chin with his hand. Finally, he nodded slowly; the deal was struck.

chapter 17

Hector listened carefully as Bai outlined the events leading up to their meeting. He appeared especially interested when she told him about Daniel Chen.

"Do you know Daniel Chen?" she asked.

Hector shook his head. "No. I don't know anything about any *Chino* stealing our *feria* and *chiva*."

"Did you know two of your men were found dead in Daniel Chen's office?"

"I know two of my boys got wasted in Berkeley. You think this Chen guy did 'em?"

"I'm not sure. If you don't know Daniel Chen, what were your men doing in Berkeley?"

Hector rubbed his chin and looked at the three men sitting up front at the counter. His eyes narrowed as he answered. "I don't know, *China*."

His expression suggested he was troubled by how little he knew. Boobs watched and listened attentively but didn't join in their conversation.

"So, you talked to this Chen." Hector said. "What did he say?"

"According to Chen, he had nothing to do with the rip-off."

"You believe him?

She shrugged. "I'm not sure who or what to believe."

Hector seemed to consider her answer. "Then why are the cops looking for him?"

"I don't know. That's what I'm trying to find out."

Hector turned aside to the girl, who remained standing next to the table. She seemed to be doing everything in her power to make herself invisible. "You know anything, *chica*?"

Refusing to make eye contact, the girl kept her gaze directed at the floor as she responded with a quick negative flick of her head.

Hector turned to stare at Bai and asked pointedly about his money and heroin, "Since we're *vatos* now, you gonna let me know you find my *feria* or my *chiva*, right?"

"What are *vatos* for?" she replied with a smile.

Scowling, he looked over at his boys and nodded. They stood as he extricated himself from the booth. As he walked past the girl, she tried to follow him. He turned on her. "*Quedar!*"

She shook her head. He raised a hand as if to strike her, silencing her argument as she ducked away. With a sour look of exasperation, he dropped his hand slowly before turning to walk out of the café.

The girl stared after him as the door closed, then turned to Bai. "What have you done?"

Bai ignored her outburst. "What's your name?"

The girl appeared momentarily at a loss. When she answered, she sounded defeated. "Alicia Lopez." She gave her name the Spanish pronunciation, "Aleeceea."

Bai found the sound graceful and pleasing to the ear. "Do you have any family, Alicia?"

"Not anymore. *They* were my family."

"The Norteños were never your family. They just showed you they don't give a shit about you. I do give a shit about you," Bai assured her.

"Why? What do you want?"

"I'm not sure myself," she confessed. "For now, I want to go home. Would you like to go with me?"

"*Chingate!*" the girl said vehemently.

While Bai contemplated an appropriate response to being told to fuck off, Boobs stood. "It would probably be better to have this discussion elsewhere."

Nodding in agreement and getting out of the booth, Bai stopped to retrieve her knife and lay a hundred-dollar bill on the counter to cover the Naugahyde repair. As they stepped out the door, Bai noticed Rafe standing across the street staring at them. He pantomimed holding a gun, his index finger pointing at Bai. He dropped his thumb before turning to walk around the corner.

"What's that all about?" Boobs asked.

"Rafe likes to shoot me with his finger," Bai explained. "It seems to be the only weapon in his arsenal. His dick and his brain are too small to be dangerous."

Alicia laughed, a sign Bai viewed as promising. Laughter was better than cursing or tears. Before she could comment on the observation, her phone rang.

Elizabeth spoke excitedly. "Lee's been shot! He's been taken to San Francisco General."

Bai's heart plummeted. "How did it happen?"

"I don't know," Elizabeth said. "The hospital found our contact information in his wallet and called to say he was being taken into surgery. I can't leave. The girls aren't back from school yet. Go to him, Bai."

"I'm on my way." She turned to Boobs. "I have to leave. Lee's been shot. Alicia, you're with me," she commanded. "Stay close."

"Is he all right?" Boobs asked.

"I'll let you know when I know," she replied hurriedly, stepping to the curb to hail a passing taxi.

When the taxi stopped, she grabbed Alicia by the hand to urge her into the cab. The girl looked confused but complied. After giving the cabbie instructions, Bai leaned back anxiously. It wasn't until Alicia tried to remove her hand that Bai realized she still clung to the girl.

"Who's Lee?" Alicia asked.

"My friend. My family."

The girl looked confused. "Which is it—friend or family?"

"Both. There's an inane saying: 'you can pick your friends, but you can't pick your family.' I pick my family." She looked at the girl. "I picked him. And, I picked you."

"What does 'inane' mean?"

"It means stupid."

"What if I don't want to be your family?"

"That's your choice. But if I were you, I wouldn't be too quick to judge. Stick around for a while. You might decide you like it."

"I'm not Chinese," Alicia stated.

"Really? I hadn't noticed."

The girl looked away. Bai picked up her phone to call Jason. She feared he'd still be in transit. He picked up on the third ring and started talking before she could say anything. "I'm just going through customs. I'll be back in the city within the hour."

"Lee's been shot. I don't know his condition. I'm on my way to San Francisco General."

"I'll meet you there," he said and ended the call.

She dialed again, this time to the hospital's information desk to find the surgical floor where Lee had been taken. He was on the fifth floor, north wing, but they couldn't tell her anything of his condition. They didn't know. She stared at the phone as her stomach churned.

"*Mia padre* got deuced a year ago," Alicia said in a soft voice. "He was *tecato*. When Bai stared at her she explained, "He liked to shoot heroin. A Sureño capped him while he was slinging rock to support his habit. The cops let him lie in the street for hours while they picked up the shell casings and took pictures. They treated him like shit. I guess maybe he was."

"Did he claim Norteño?"

Alicia nodded. "Um." She seemed to reflect. "He wasn't all that. But after he was gone, no one protected me. My mother ran away when I was little. My father's asshole friends passed me around and used me until Rafe claimed me. He kept the others off of me, but he wasn't any better. He's hard, likes to hit." She looked at Bai. "I'm a whore. I'm not the kind of person you want for family."

"People are more than their history, Alicia. I got pregnant at seventeen, and I'm still not married. Some think I'm trash, though they're afraid to say it to my face. You can't let other people decide your worth. Stay with me, at least for a while. Take some time to find out who you are. I'm offering you sanctuary. Take it."

Alicia stared into her eyes before shrugging and turning away. The girl snuffled and dug into her purse, leading Bai to believe she'd been moved to tears. Instead, she brought out a pack of cigarettes and a lighter.

Bai reached around and grabbed the pack away from her. "Sorry to act like your mother, but that's part of the package. You can smoke when you're eighteen if you still want to. Until then, you're going back to being a teenager."

Before Alicia could respond, the cab pulled to the curb in front of the hospital entrance. Bai paid the cabbie and opened the door. Looking glum, the girl followed her out of the cab. Bai had enough experience with teenagers to know the battle of wills had only just begun, but she had more important issues to deal with. Thoughts of Lee consumed her.

They walked through sliding glass doors to the hospital lobby. Patients and visitors packed the hallways leading to the elevators. Cramming into a crowded lift, they proceeded up to the fifth floor, which had been split into four wards. Each had its own waiting room, imaginatively designated by its geographical location: East, West, North, and South.

With a reluctant teenager in tow, Bai made her way to the nurse's station in the north quadrant of the building, where she identified herself as Lee's sister. A harried-looking nurse informed her Lee hadn't come out of surgery, and they had no way of predicting how long he'd remain there. His condition had been listed as serious with multiple gunshot wounds. Bai would be paged as soon as the surgery ended or when they had more information.

She turned to Alicia. "Have you eaten today?"

"This morning," the girl replied without enthusiasm.

Bai pulled a roll of hundred-dollar bills out of her pocket and pressed one into Alicia's hand. "There has to be a cafeteria in the building somewhere. Get yourself something to eat and bring me back a black coffee when you're finished. I'll wait here."

Alicia looked at the bill then at Bai. "Are you rich?"

"Yes," she said. "It just so happens I am."

The girl seemed to reflect for a moment then smiled with a look of glee. "Boo ya!"

"Yeah, 'boo ya!' Now, go get yourself something to eat. And buy some nicotine patches if you think you're going to need them."

Frowning, Alicia turned around to wave the hundred-dollar bill over her shoulder in reply.

Bai found an unoccupied chair in the waiting room next to a rotund man with skinny legs. He wore red shorts and matching suspenders over a bright-yellow shirt. His attire led her to believe he was either color-blind or unusually festive.

The gentleman's head bobbed in greeting as she took her seat. Tears brimmed, then overflowed slowly from his eyes. She looked away, giving him privacy.

Left to her thoughts, she carefully put all of her emotions into a box and closed the lid. Until she could come to terms with Lee's injuries without completely losing it, her feelings would stay locked away. The thought of losing him terrified her. The thought he might die because of her insatiable curiosity filled her with contempt and remorse. *Why couldn't she mind her own business?*

chapter 18

"My name is Larry Boil," said the plump man in the colorful clothing.

"Bai Jiang," she replied as she suffered a limp, damp handshake.

"Why are you here, Bai?"

"My friend was shot."

"Was it an accident?"

"That seems unlikely."

"I see." Larry seemed to think about her answer. "What kind of work do you do, Bai?"

"I find lost people," she explained.

He nodded and showed interest. "Is that lucrative?"

"Not so much," she reflected. "The money is lousy, and I seem to really irritate people."

"Then why do you do it?" he asked.

She produced a wan smile. "I've been wondering that myself."

He nodded but appeared baffled by her answer. She looked aside and saw Alicia walking toward them with a large paper cup in her hand. She stopped in front of Bai and held out the coffee.

Bai accepted the caffeine gratefully. "Thanks."

"Is this your daughter?" Larry asked.

Bai looked at Alicia and smiled. "Yes, isn't she beautiful?"

"She looks like you."

"She does. Doesn't she?"

Alicia looked at Larry then at Bai and made a face suggesting all adults were idiots. Bai sipped her coffee and patted the empty seat next to her. Alicia sat.

"Did you eat?" Bai asked her.

She nodded. "Mmm."

"What did you have?"

"Hamburger."

"Was it good?"

She shook her head.

"Hospital food never is."

The girl nodded but didn't reply. Bai left Alicia to her thoughts. She'd turned the girl's life upside down. It would take time for Alicia to sort through the changes. She'd open up if and when she felt ready.

A voice called Larry's name over the intercom. He got up and, with a farewell nod to Bai, walked toward the nurse's station. Time ticked slowly by until Alicia's voice interrupted her reverie. "You didn't ask for your change."

She turned blankly to look at the girl. "I don't want it. Keep the change for pocket money."

"I've decided to go with you," Alicia said. "It'll be interesting to see how long your family puts up with having a Mexican whore around the house."

Bai met the girl's gaze. Alicia chewed her lip, showing her apprehension.

"Be yourself," Bai said. "They'll love you."

Alicia didn't look convinced.

Jason walked into the waiting room with Martin and another enforcer at his back. He waved his two bodyguards back as he walked over to speak with Bai. A tense smile set his features as his gaze shifted to Alicia then back again. "Sorry it took so long to get here. There was traffic."

"He's still in surgery. I haven't been able to find out anything," Bai replied.

He nodded toward Alicia. "Who's your friend?"

"This is Alicia."

As Jason gazed more earnestly at the girl, she seemed to melt under his scrutiny—not a good sign.

"My name is Jason, Alicia," he said, holding out his hand. "It's a pleasure to meet you."

She took his hand timidly.

"Jason is family, Alicia," Bai informed the girl, "but that doesn't mean you shouldn't count your fingers when you get your hand back."

Alicia smiled; Jason frowned.

When he spoke, his words were for Bai's benefit. "I've talked to a contact inside SFPD. Lee was shot twice in the back at close range with a small-caliber handgun. They think it was a silenced twenty-two. No witnesses came forward even though it happened in broad daylight on a crowded sidewalk. No exit wounds, so the paramedics made the assumption the bullets were still in him. Other than that, they couldn't tell me anything. There wasn't much blood, and nobody heard or saw anything suspicious. Pedestrians who stopped to help him thought he'd fainted until they noticed the holes in his back."

"He was following a man in a gray suit—about six feet tall with broad shoulders and a dark tan," Bai informed him.

"Do you know who he is?"

"No, but Inspector Kelly does. He met the tan man at Figaro's on Columbus Avenue this afternoon."

"The man who came out of the restaurant?" Alicia asked.

Bai turned to her. "Yes. Do you know him?"

She shook her head. "No. But the fat *popo* met him once before. I saw them come out of the police station, the one on Sacramento Street, yesterday. They were arguing."

"That's good to know," Bai said, putting her hand over Alicia's. "Thanks for telling me."

Jason turned to the girl. "Where did Kelly go when you followed him?"

"He hangs out at a bar down in the Tenderloin called the Sand Dab on Twenty-Third. He's a real boozer. He's always there."

Jason's eyes narrowed in thought as Bai watched him closely. She knew he loved Lee like a brother, and she suspected he had his own ideas about how to deal with Inspector Kelly.

"Let me talk to Kelly first. He knows me. I may be able to get more out of him by asking nicely."

He seemed to consider her argument, then nodded slowly, which she hoped was a sign of assent. If he decided to beat the truth out of Kelly, she knew there would be no stopping him.

Bai heard her name over the intercom. A disembodied voice asked her to come to the nurse's station. She turned to Alicia. "Can you wait here for me? I'll try not to be too long."

The girl nodded, and Bai got up to walk toward the nurse's station with Jason at her side.

"So, you found another stray," he said.

"Don't take my feelings lightly," she warned. "I'm committed to that young woman."

"I see." His tone sounded serious.

Turning aside, he motioned at Martin to watch Alicia, pointing at his eyes then at the girl sitting in the waiting room. Martin nodded in understanding. She would be guarded.

A surgeon in green scrubs waited at the nurse's station to update Bai on Lee's condition. Appearing at once impatient and exhausted, the doctor's eyes searched the room as he stood behind the kiosk. Upon spying Bai, he stepped around the enclosure to take her by the elbow and draw both her and Jason aside. Her stomach knotted as she searched the doctor's face for signs of bad news.

The doctor introduced himself then guided them down the hallway. "Your brother is out of surgery and in intensive care. I removed two bullets from his chest cavity. One of them hit a rib. The bullet snapped the bone and fragmented like shrapnel. That's why the surgery took so long. We were looking for small bits of lead that proved difficult to find. The other bullet collapsed a lung and lodged against his sternum. I believe we got everything. His injuries will take time to heal, but with luck, I expect a full recovery."

Bai let out a deep breath and almost cried with relief. "Can we see him?"

"Yes. I doubt he'll know you for the next several hours, but there isn't any reason you can't see him. If you'll follow me, I'll show you where we're keeping him in intensive care until we're certain he's stable. Once he's moved onto the floor, you can spend as much time as you want with him. In ICU, we like to keep the visits short."

The doctor led them through a set of double doors where he

instructed them to wash their hands and don white surgical masks before leading them through a second set of doors. Subdued lighting revealed a row of cloth-screened cubicles lining each side of the room. Gowned and masked nurses worked in the midst of medical apparatus. Green displays surrounding the hospital beds glowed to impart an otherworldly feel.

Lee was in the first cubicle lying on his back with tubes running out of each side of his chest and wires hooked to little round pads attached to his sternum, neck, and temple. His skin looked pale. Bai's eyes filled at the sight of him.

The doctor glanced briefly at the data displayed on the machines before busying himself checking the drains on the sides of Lee's chest. He nodded briefly toward Bai and Jason, "Don't worry about the tubes and wires; they're all temporary. He's conscious but heavily sedated. He'll be addled until the drugs wear off—a good three or four hours from now. If you don't have any more questions, I'll be on my way. I have another surgery."

They both nodded, and the doctor left them alone with Lee.

Seeing Lee in his present state, Bai felt tears flowing from her eyes. Jason put an arm around her shoulders and drew her to him. She didn't resist and quietly sobbed against his chest.

"It's all right," he said. "It'll take more than a couple of little bullets to kill Lee. I expect he'll be really embarrassed when he wakes up and finds out someone ambushed him. His pride will be wounded worse than his back."

She wiped her eyes and tried but failed to smile. Lee would be furious when he realized what had happened, and rightfully so. Only a coward shoots someone in the back. He'd want retribution. From the look on Jason's face, Lee would have to stand in line.

She could read Jason's thoughts. "He's my partner."

Jason frowned as he met her gaze. "Lee's not an amateur. Whoever did this is either very lucky or a professional. Let me handle this."

"You can watch my back."

His mouth fell into a hard line. "You have children to care for."

He might have been right, but that didn't alter her obligation to Lee.

"I have to do this," she replied without emotion. "Like I said, he's my partner."

His features softened when he realized he couldn't dissuade her. "If you're intent on finding the shooter, you're going to have to make some concessions, the first one being adequate protection. I'm going to arrange for security on the house and the kids. You'll have to inform my mother and the children of the necessary precautions. We'll be as subtle as possible, but bodyguards are bodyguards. There's no way to hide them."

"I understand."

He smiled. "How long has it been since you've worn a Kevlar coat?"

He referred to a protective overcoat with bullet-resistant panels on the chest and back. The outer shell of the coat could be made of anything from microfiber to oiled canvas. The coat could be a little confining. She didn't relish the idea of wearing one. "There's got to be another way."

"When you go to war, go prepared," he said emphatically. "Kevlar has saved my life on more than one occasion. The coats today are lighter and more comfortable than they used to be."

"It just seems so retro."

"This isn't about fashion. It's about staying alive."

"If you were a woman, you'd understand."

"And if you were a man," he replied tersely, "we wouldn't be having this conversation."

chapter 19

Before checking Lee's vital signs on the bedside monitor, a stern-looking nurse peered over her glasses at Bai and Jason. She shot them another look after seeing to her patient's needs, implying their visit had come to an end. Lee remained semiconscious, so they wouldn't accomplish anything by staying longer. Bai reluctantly left his side.

Jason took her arm to lead her from the ward and walk with her toward the surgical suite's waiting room. "Where did you find the girl?"

"The Norteños had her. They were using her to run errands and just using her in general."

"Why get involved?"

"There was something about the way she looked at me. I couldn't turn my back on her. I tried." She smiled at the thought. "She refused to ask for my help. She's stubborn. I guess I saw something in her that reminded me of me."

"You're telling me they just gave her up?"

"I cut a deal. I traded information."

"Information about what?"

"The drug exchange in the SOMA that went bad. I had some information Hector wanted."

"So you've met Hector?" He looked surprised and worried at the same time. A scowl pulled at the corners of his lips.

"We're buds." She crossed her fingers to show him. "We're like this."

"You'd better start sleeping in Kevlar," he advised. "With friends like Hector, you don't need enemies."

"Hector will be my friend as long as he needs me. Right now we have a common interest—finding the money and the drugs."

"Why do you care about finding the money or the drugs?"

She thought about Jason's question. "I've been lied to and used. I know that. What I don't know is why. I have the feeling if I can find the drugs and the money then the rest will fall into place, including why the police want Daniel Chen, why Wen Liu was murdered, and why Lee was shot."

Jason's silence hinted at his thoughts on the subject. Her inclination for pursuing the truth had led her into trouble before. With Lee's having been shot, Wen Liu murdered, and the two Norteños killed, it was pretty obvious somebody was playing for keeps.

Waiting where Bai had left her, Alicia stood as they approached. "Is your friend all right?"

Bai put a hand on Alicia's arm. "He's in intensive care. The surgeon expects a full recovery."

Alicia nodded with a frown. "So we can leave? I don't like hospitals."

Jason addressed Bai. "I'll give you a lift home. I have a car."

She nodded a curt assent.

He turned aside and inclined his head to Martin, who stood watching them from the entrance to the waiting room where he could keep an eye on the corridor. Martin acknowledged the signal with a subtle nod then made a call on his cell. As they walked out of the waiting room, Martin preceded them to the elevators, where he held an empty lift open. After they entered, he followed them inside to place himself in front of the doors as a human shield. As they exited the lift in the lobby, two more enforcers waited to follow at their backs.

Alicia turned around nervously as the black-suited men fell in behind them. Bai put an arm around her shoulders to assure the girl. "They're friends."

"Big muthuhs," Alicia observed.

Bracketed by two black SUVs, a matching limousine waited with its engine running in front of the hospital. Martin held the rear door open for them. Entering first, Bai tugged Alicia's hand to pull her into the car. They sat on a bench seat facing the rear. Jason followed to sit facing them. Alicia, meanwhile, ran her hands appreciatively over the black leather interior. Her eyes got big as she admired the trappings of the big sedan.

"Nice ride," Alicia said to Jason. "Yours?"

He smiled. "The car belongs to the business."

"Business must be good. What's your thing?"

"Jason is a gangster," Bai informed her. "He just happens to be a very accomplished gangster."

"I prefer 'entrepreneur,'" Jason said with a hard-edged smile. "What I do doesn't differ appreciably from what every businessman does. 'Killing the competition' is the capitalist's credo."

"What's a credo?" Alicia asked.

"A credo is a system of beliefs," Bai answered. "Capitalists believe fair competition will lead to a better life for everyone. Unfortunately, the 'fair' aspect of competition is open to interpretation. Like most businessmen, Jason doesn't mind fudging the rules a bit."

Alicia nodded her head but appeared confused by the answer. Jason remained stoic, his face an unreadable mask. Bai suddenly realized she was tired—not physically, but emotionally. Her eyes closed momentarily as she mentally relaxed her guard.

"Are you all right?" Alicia asked.

Bai opened her eyes to see the girl's concern. The overture surprised her. She smiled to set Alicia at ease. Despite her bluster, the girl revealed a vulnerable side. The hard shell she presented to the world already showed signs of cracking.

"I'm fine," Bai said, reaching out to hold the girl's hand. Alicia didn't resist. "We'll be home soon. I think you're going to like my family. They may take some getting used to. If you're patient, I think you'll eventually come to like living with us."

Alicia nodded but looked skeptical.

Jason interrupted. "What are your plans tonight, Bai?"

It took a moment for her to gather her thoughts. "I'm going to get Alicia settled and have dinner. Then I hope to have a hot bath and a cold scotch, followed by about eight hours of sleep. Whether or not any of that takes place is purely speculative. Not unlike the rest of my life, nothing today has gone as planned. Why?"

"I thought we might go out. I have something to discuss with you in private."

"I'm still recovering from our last date. Did we by chance ... ?" She fluttered her free hand in front of her like a spastic mime.

He smiled. "No. I don't have rigid requirements when it comes to consensual congress," he stated obliquely while casting a glance at Alicia to see if she followed the conversation, "but both parties' being conscious is the absolute minimum."

She smiled. "Sorry about that. I didn't get a chance to thank you properly for the lovely evening."

"You can thank me tonight, if you're really sincere."

"Tonight is a bit hectic."

The teen watched their interplay with interest. Jason noticed but didn't offer Alicia an explanation. Bai might have been inclined to clarify her relationship with Jason if she'd had a better understanding of it herself.

"Can I call you later?" Bai asked. "We can talk then."

He nodded but didn't look happy with her response.

The car pulled to the curb in front of her house. Jason stepped out of the car first. By the time Bai and Alicia exited the vehicle, triad soldiers in black suits stood outside to report to Jason.

Bai drew Jason's attention away from his soldiers. "Would you like to come up and say hi to the girls?"

He shook his head. "No. That would be overstepping the boundaries."

Jason hadn't interacted directly with his mother in nearly three years, though the breach remained outwardly cordial. Elizabeth wanted him out of Bai's life. He refused to go. The two remained at an impasse.

"Thanks for everything," she said, moving closer to him.

She went up on her toes to give him a kiss on the cheek. He turned at the last moment to catch her lips with his. Alicia's giggle brought Bai back to the real world. She turned to put a hand on Alicia's back and push her up the steps to the lobby of her building. She glanced back at Jason, who continued to watch her from where he stood on the sidewalk. Not until she'd made her way inside the door did he return to the limousine, which then pulled away from the curb. The SUVs and the triad enforcers stayed.

She placed her thumb against the sensor plate on the elevator to open the doors to the lift. She ushered Alicia in then pushed the button for the third floor. The girl turned to her. "How many families live in this building?"

"Just one. I own the building. We live on the top floor. Lee has an apartment on the first floor. The second floor is a gym. I'll have the girls give you a tour as soon as you've been introduced."

"Who are the girls?"

With her mind occupied by Lee's assault, she'd completely forgotten to fill Alicia in on her family. "Dan is my thirteen-year-old daughter, and Jia is my fifteen-year-old. Elizabeth is my mother."

Alicia's brows knitted together as she appeared to draw in on herself. Bai took her hand again. "It'll be all right."

The girl nodded and took a deep breath as the doors to the lift opened. Elizabeth, Dan, and Jia stood in the entry with anxious expressions. When they saw Alicia, their expressions morphed from anxious to curious.

"How is Lee?" Elizabeth asked before Bai could exit the lift.

"His surgeon expects him to make a full recovery."

"That's good news," the older woman stated, her eyes shifting to Bai's companion.

Dan and Jia seemed reticent to speak in front of a stranger, their usual boisterous behavior on hold.

"This is Alicia," Bai informed them as they stepped out of the elevator. "She's going to be staying with us. Alicia, these are my daughters—Dan and Jia—and my mother, Elizabeth," she said, indicating each in turn.

Alicia nodded silently, and the girls nodded in return.

Dan asked, "When can I see Lee?"

Dan only had two friends: Lee and Jia. She developed fiercely loyal attachments to those she loved. Bai could see the tension and strain in her daughter's face.

"We'll have to wait and see. He's still in intensive care. He's going to be all right. I promise."

Dan's expression remained doubtful despite Bai's assurances.

"Jia, I thought Alicia might stay with you in your room for now, if you don't mind," Bai said, changing the subject. "You're about the same age and the same size. I was hoping you could loan her whatever she needs tonight. Tomorrow, we can go shopping to buy clothes and necessities."

Jia smiled and walked forward to take the newcomer's hand. "Having a roommate will be fun," she said. "Would you like to see our room? It's really nice."

Alicia turned to Bai with a questioning look.

"Go ahead and get acquainted. I'll be here if you need me," Bai assured her.

Jia led Alicia to the back of the house. Dan looked at her mother in cold appraisal before turning to follow the girls, her gait stiff with tension.

"Will she be staying long?" Elizabeth asked.

"That's entirely up to her. I hope so," Bai replied.

Elizabeth took the news gracefully. "I'll set another place at the table. Dinner will be ready in about an hour. I imagine you've had a difficult day. You can fill me in on Lee after you've had a chance to catch your breath."

Bai followed her into the kitchen, where the older woman continued to prepare dinner. Bai filled a crystal tumbler with ice before pouring two fingers of Yamazaki scotch into the glass. She took a stool at the breakfast counter to sip her drink while watching Elizabeth tend to the stove. "*Sun Yee On* soldiers are keeping an eye on the house."

"I'm aware," Elizabeth replied. "Tommy called an hour ago to let me know. He's just back from Hong Kong. He said to tell you he was sorry to hear about Lee."

Bai thought of the rift between Tommy and Lee. Lee had been Tommy's favorite while Jason, Lee, and Bai were growing up. "Men are stupid," Bai proclaimed, more loudly than intended.

Elizabeth turned to look at her with a smirk. "You're just figuring that out?"

She waved a finger at Elizabeth. "I've always suspected as much. Now it's confirmed."

Turning back to tend the stove, Elizabeth ignored the outburst.

"Stupid but indispensable," Bai continued. "I worry when Jason's around, then find myself worrying when he's not around. Someone should start some kind of loaner program where a woman can check out a man then simply return him when he gets on her nerves. That would solve the problem."

"I imagine men feel the same way about women," Elizabeth said, busy at the stove. "Relationships are difficult under the best of circumstances."

"I'm not really sure I have a relationship with Jason."

"You have a child with him. That's one relationship that won't ever go away."

"True."

"Tell me about Lee."

"Someone shot him twice in the back with a small-caliber gun. We don't know why. He doesn't have any enemies I know of. That's why we're taking all the precautions. We don't know whether Lee was the target, or if someone wants to hurt me."

"The chances you and Lee take frighten me. Have you considered finding a safer occupation?"

"I like being a *souxun*. Lee and I are careful. This is the first time one of us has gotten seriously hurt. The problem is I don't even know why."

Elizabeth turned with a look of concern. "Have you given any more thought to dating Howard Kwan?"

Bai's mind blanked. Howard was the last thing on her mind.

Elizabeth pursued the matter. "Marrying him would put an end to gangsters' sitting on your doorstep. It's a chance to lead a respectable life."

Bai lifted her glass to her lips and sipped scotch as she thought over Elizabeth's assertion. She let the cold liquor roll over her tongue and warm in her mouth before swallowing. "I always find respectable people suspect," she replied. "Those who preach the loudest always seem to have the most to hide."

Elizabeth stared at her with a sad expression.

Bai suffered the stare until she realized Elizabeth wasn't going to give up. "All right," she finally relented. "I'll give him another chance. But if he calls me 'old' one more time, I'm going to beat the crap out of him."

chapter 20

A reserved atmosphere presided at the dinner table. Alicia ate the Chinese food without comment. Everyone spoke in hushed voices, as though fearful of breaking something fragile. Later, all three girls decided to sleep in the same room to get acquainted. Bai suspected by tomorrow morning she'd be facing three bleary-eyed teenagers.

Later, as she soaked in her much-anticipated bath, the thought of the three brought a smile to her lips. She held an icy tumbler of Yamazaki to the side of her face, the cold glass pressed against her flushed cheeks. Steam from the bath surrounded her while Lee's condition occupied her mind. He still hadn't been moved from ICU. A nurse there had informed her he would have to stay in intensive care for an additional twenty-four hours. He'd spiked a temperature, and they feared infection.

The door opened, and Jason stepped into the room. She tilted her head to look at him with a quizzical expression.

"We need to talk," he explained.

"First, let's talk about how you got in here."

He waved her question aside and sat on the edge of the tub to take her drink from her hand. "How is Lee?"

Bai knew Jason was just making conversation, stalling. He could get an update on Lee's condition as easily as she. His reticence made her curious. "He's running a temperature, still in intensive care. They're giving him antibiotics. Why are you here?"

He ignored her question. "I'll stop by the hospital later tonight and check on him."

"Don't you ever sleep?"

"Sleep is a terrible waste of time."

He slept only one or two hours a day. Working day and night, he personally managed his teams around the world, regardless of the time difference. He drove himself as if he had something to prove.

He took a sip of her scotch. She considered protesting but didn't have the energy to rally any righteous indignation, forcing her to acknowledge she was glad to see him. "Fine," she capitulated. "What do you want to talk about?"

He hesitated before answering. "The Kwan family."

"What about the Kwan family?"

"Stay away from them."

"Why?"

"They're dangerous."

"You're talking about your aunt and your cousins."

"They don't see me that way, at least not my aunt. I'm her enemy. That makes you and Dan her enemies, by default."

"She's asked me to marry Howard."

"You can't trust her. I'm telling you, she's poison."

She held out her hand and gestured for her drink. He handed the glass back to her, so she could take a sip while contemplating his words.

"What about Howard?" she asked.

Contempt infused his voice. "What about him?"

"Do you think he considers you his enemy?"

"I don't have any idea. I've never come up against him either in business or personally. Jade's ruled Kwan Industries with an iron fist for thirty years. I imagine she runs her family the same way."

"He didn't seem like a bad man. His attitude toward women is a bit jaded, but his having an overbearing mother would explain that."

"You're not seriously considering marrying him are you?" His tone suggested he found the thought repulsive.

"I'm not considering anything. I'm just asking questions."

He stared at her with a contemplative look. "I know you. You're up to something."

She smiled and took another drink. The cold scotch and hot bath improved her mood. "What business did you have with Wen Liu?"

She wanted to find out if Jason had had a relationship with the woman. He held out his hand for her glass. She suspected he was stalling and shook her head.

"Stingy," he quipped.

"If you don't want to tell me, I'll just assume you have something to hide."

"Everyone has something to hide," he said. "But Wen isn't one of those things. I bought information from her. We had a business arrangement. That's all."

"What kind of information?" she asked.

"She had the names of men who held gambling markers for Samuel Kwan."

"Samuel would be Howard's older brother?"

"Yes. He owned a casino in Macau. He likes to gamble and ran up a sizable debt. He'd passed out founders' shares in his business as collateral. That way he wouldn't have to tell his mother about his losses. Samuel, as you might guess, is something of an idiot."

"So what did you do with the information?"

"I bought up the shares. The company is privately held. The individuals holding the markers were more than happy to get cash for stock they couldn't sell."

"How much did you pay for the shares?"

"About fifty million dollars."

"That's a lot of money."

He smiled and shrugged. "For fifty million dollars, I ended up with controlling interest in a casino worth five to ten times that amount. I booted Samuel out of the executive offices and sent him running home to Mommy. My management team has turned the business around in less than a month, and we're seeing a profit that will pay back the initial investment in less than a year."

"And that's why Jade Kwan hates you?"

"That's one reason."

"What's the other reason?"

"It gets a little complicated," he explained. "I wouldn't have moved on the casino if Jade hadn't decided to delve into *Sun Yee On*'s line of business. She fired the first volley."

"What do you mean?"

"The casino in Macau was being used as a distribution center. She formed an alliance with a consortium of individuals who move heroin out of Afghanistan. Had she not decided to enter the drug trade, I'd have left her alone. The choices were either to take away her distribution center or put a bullet in her head. Tommy was impatient to resolve the problem. If you look at it from my perspective, I saved her life."

Bai smiled. "I doubt she sees it that way. Who was she in business with?"

"There were a number of people involved. Warlords in Afghanistan grow the product. Government agencies provide transport. Arab investors provide financing. From Macau, the product was supposed to be packaged and flown worldwide on a fleet of private jets used to ferry whales to and from the casino. Transporting the high-rollers was a front. The heroin distribution was a major operation in the making."

"You probably made a lot of people unhappy."

"I'm not in business to be popular."

"You have little to fear in that regard," she said before changing the subject. "Have you ever had anything to do with Inspector Kelly of the SFPD?"

"Isn't he the cop who took the report at Dan's school? Does this have something to do with the drug heist you were looking into?"

"Yes and yes. Kelly's the cop who approached me. He came to my office and asked for my help on behalf of the police department."

"I'm surprised you said yes."

"Kelly told me a Chinese by the name of Daniel Chen was the bag man, and the police take deadly exception to cop killers. I was moved."

"So you decided to rescue him."

"Yes. Was I wrong?"

"Not wrong, just predictable."

"Anyway, this Daniel Chen turned out to be a professor at Berkeley. I went to his office and found two dead Norteños. The police sent Lee and me to his home where we met Wen Liu. Did you know she likes to walk around naked?"

"I wasn't aware of that. What does that have to do with finding Chen?"

"Nothing. I just wanted to make sure you didn't know she liked to walk around naked."

He frowned. "Did you find Chen?"

"Not then. Lee and I followed Wen to the Grand Hotel where she was gunned down in her room."

"But you eventually found Chen."

"No. He found me. Wen had obviously called him with my contact information before she was murdered."

"Where did he find you?" He sounded concerned.

"He showed up around noon at my office."

"What did he want?"

"He wanted to know who killed Wen."

"What did you tell him?"

"The truth. I didn't have a clue. But I did have a copy of the surveillance DVD showing the killer. When he saw the murderer, he seemed to know who the shooter was, which was strange because the killer wore a baseball cap and sunglasses."

"Do you still have the DVD?"

"It's at the office."

He nodded and drew a deep breath. "I'd like to see it tomorrow. Maybe there's something of interest the police didn't notice."

"That's not a problem. It's still in my laptop sitting on my desk." She hesitated before continuing on her train of thought. "Howard and his security detail were at the Grand when Wen was killed. I don't think he'd have met me there had he planned to have her murdered. I don't see his doing that."

Jason eyed her speculatively. "I don't know what he's capable of, but I wouldn't put murder past his mother. Her presence in San Francisco is troubling."

She shrugged. "I'll keep that in mind. Is there anything else I should know?"

"You're beautiful, and I want you."

His words brought a smile to her lips and heat to her cheeks. She was embarrassed that he could electrify her so easily. She put the cold glass to her cheeks to stop the burning. He smiled, recognizing her condition, and leaned over to kiss her gently. She opened her mouth to accept his tongue as his hand brushed her breast.

She broke the kiss.

"Hand me a towel," she said, standing to get out of the tub.

He stood to oblige, handing her a bath sheet. She wrapped the towel around her waist and walked out of the bath and into her bedroom. She drew down the covers on her bed, dropped the towel, and slipped between the sheets. He stood in the doorway watching her.

"It's a big bed," she said.

He smiled and loosened his tie. Disrobing, he placed his clothes neatly on a side chair. He took his time. She watched him, admiring the flat muscles on his stomach and the butterfly effect of his back muscles when he flexed. She counted the scars on his back, shoulders, and stomach from where bullets had ripped into his body or blades had sliced him open.

He walked over to the bed and pulled the sheets aside to reach for her hungrily. She drew his head down as she wrapped her legs around him to tumble him down on top of her. They used their strength against each other like two wrestlers fighting for dominance, their kisses fierce and demanding until he forced her legs apart. Their struggle ended when he entered her; the rhythm of their bodies moving together with familiar ease. Long, lingering kisses accompanied by strong, gentle hands brought her to climax again and again. She was lost as her body responded, mindless and adrift. When sated, they fell asleep in a tangled embrace.

She woke in the middle of the night—alone. No longer tired, she got out of bed. Her closet door stood ajar. When she entered and switched on the light, she could see Jason had left her another present. A long, black coat hung from her dressing chair.

Pulling a clean black tee over her head, she grabbed black jeans off the shelf and slipped them on. Black socks and black trainers completed her outfit. Picking up the coat to inspect it, she found the garment surprisingly light. Kevlar panels padded the chest and back of the coat. A compression holster had been clipped onto the back panel, low near the waist. Two short throwing blades with matte-black finishes were sheathed inside the cuff of each sleeve.

She opened her wall safe to retrieve her Beretta Compact. More modestly sized than a regular Beretta automatic handgun, the Compact fit her hand though it still carried thirteen bullets in the clip and one in the chamber. She jammed the gun into the compression holster at the back of the coat then slipped the garment on, fastening the overlapping front panels with reinforced zippers.

She opened the front-flap pockets of the coat to find a *shuang dao* sheathed under each flap. Jason knew she favored the long single-bladed knives. Each looked like a pirate's cutlass with a hollowed round grip used for spinning the blades.

Wrapping a long, red silk scarf around her neck, she let the ends of the fabric drape down her front. She glanced in the mirror and found her outfit to be unexpectedly chic. Her lips lifted into a smile at the thought she might set a new fashion trend.

chapter 21

Bai stepped out of her building and walked down the front steps to the sidewalk. Street lamps shed pools of light along the damp, dark asphalt. A predawn quiet encompassed the street. She turned and came face-to-face with two *Sun Yee On* soldiers. Their implacable expressions lent them a stern demeanor.

"I'm going to work. I don't need an escort," she informed them.

"We have our orders," the larger of them replied with a deferential bow.

She considered arguing with them but realized the effort would be wasted. They took their orders from Jason. "Fine," she relented with as much grace as she could muster. "Stay back a half block and give me some space."

She patted her coat to show she wore protection. They nodded in unenthusiastic acceptance of her condition and stood aside to let her pass.

Two all-night coffee vendors plied their trade between her home and her office. Always rooting for the underdog, she chose the one that wasn't a franchise to buy coffee for herself and her escorts. They gratefully accepted her peace offering and seemed to become more comfortable in her presence.

"What are your names?" she asked.

The big one replied, "I'm Bo, and this is Song."

They both stood over six feet tall and weighed in excess of 250 pounds each. As a courtesy, Bai exchanged cell phone numbers with them, promising to let them know in advance of her movements.

"If you'd care to follow me, gentlemen, my office is only a few blocks from here."

Exiting the coffee shop, she sipped the bitter brew as she strolled toward her office while enjoying the warmth of the cup held between her hands. A heavy mist haloed the street lamps and softened the harsh outlines of the city. The damp air smelled of ocean. She found herself smiling as she walked, the solitude of the slumbering city providing a serene comfort.

She reached her office and went upstairs to flip the lights on. Her bodyguards remained outside. The room appeared undisturbed. Her laptop rested on her desk with the lid still open. The papers sitting next to the computer were just as she'd left them. She looked around the empty room and suddenly missed Lee with an unexpected emotional wrenching that verged on physical pain.

Taking a deep breath and swallowing her anxiety, she took a seat in her office chair and turned on her PC to watch the DVD of Wen Liu's killer. She sipped slowly from her cup and watched the digital pictures through tear-filled eyes while fighting to put her emotions back in the box.

Nothing that might have provided a clue to the assassin's identity jumped out at her as she watched. The second time through was the same, as was the third and the fourth. On her fifth viewing, she saw something she hadn't noticed before. As the killer raised his gun outside Wen Liu's doorway, for a brief instant, something peeked from beneath the jacket on his extended arm.

She played the scene over and over again, pausing the recording as she worked to pick out the details of the object. The grainy pictures strained her eyes and blurred her vision. The more she looked at the brief glimpse in the video, the more convinced she became that she was looking at the head of a snake. But she couldn't be sure.

She sat back in her chair. From Chen's reaction, she felt sure he knew Wen's killer. Unfortunately, the head of a snake, or whatever the object was on the killer's wrist, wouldn't provide her with the killer's identity. Her efforts had come to nothing.

She pulled her cell phone from her pocket to check the time. The display read nearly five in the morning. By six, the sidewalks would start to crowd with day-shift workers. Trucks would rumble through the streets to make their rounds, filling the shelves and bellies of the metropolis. She wanted to visit Lee before the city stirred and spilled its inhabitants into the streets.

Her bodyguards waited patiently for her outside her office building. They stood on the sidewalk drinking coffee and smoking in an unsuccessful attempt to look inconspicuous.

"Smoking will kill you," she said to them.

Song flicked his butt into the street. "Anything happens to you," he grumbled, "Jason will kill us. And that," he said while exhaling with a wry grin, "isn't just blowing smoke."

"Your concern is duly noted," she replied. "As a special favor to you, I'll try not to get killed. Do you have a car?"

Bo nodded and turned to walk down the sidewalk to a black SUV parked in a red zone. When he brought the vehicle forward, Song opened the rear door for her then took a seat up front next to Bo.

"Take me to San Francisco General Hospital, please," she said.

Bo put the car in gear and pulled away from the curb. The trip took about ten minutes on the nearly empty streets. When they arrived, Bo stayed with the car while Song escorted her into the hospital. She turned to him when they reached the intensive care unit on the fifth floor. "You can wait here, or you can go for coffee. I'll be a while. I plan to spend some time with my friend."

He nodded and turned to stand with his back to the wall next to the door while she walked through the threshold that employed a negative air system to repel germs. On the other side of the door was a small room with scrub sinks, gowns, and masks. She stopped to wash her hands and put on a face mask.

As she walked through the second door to enter the ward, she noticed a physician in a white lab coat standing next to Lee's bed. Lee lay on his back with his eyes closed. With his back to her, the physician reached into his pocket to extract a syringe. He lifted the hypodermic to test the plunger. Bai noticed a tattoo of a snake's head peeking out from beneath his white coat. Her reaction was instinctive and swift. She reached for a knife inside her coat cuff and snapped the blade at the man's back.

The assassin must have sensed her presence. His arm thrust up as he turned to face her. Her blade sliced through the sleeve of his white coat to lodge deeply in his forearm. His hand spasmed and he dropped the syringe. Ignoring the knife sticking out of his arm, he quickly moved toward her. A surgical mask covered the lower half of his face, leaving only the brown, crinkled skin around his glaring eyes to identify him as the tan man.

Meanwhile, two nurses who'd noticed the commotion ran toward them.

Bai reached inside her coat pockets to pull out her butterfly knives and flip them once by their circular grips before holding them up defensively. When he saw the knives, the would-be killer suddenly snatched the knife from his forearm and changed direction. He grabbed one of the frightened nurses by her hair and yanked her head back to expose her throat. The deadly throwing knife rested against the woman's neck as he turned to face Bai. She could sense the smile beneath the surgical mask.

"Your choice," he stated, indicating the knives held in her outstretched hands.

"Fine," she replied in a resigned voice.

She let the knives clatter to the linoleum floor.

His eyes registered triumph.

Unzipping her coat, she reached behind her back to pull out her Beretta and point it at him. "I'd rather shoot you anyway."

His eyes wildly darting, he looked around the ward. "I'll kill her."

Pricking the nurse's neck, a trail of blood quickly stained her white uniform. She sobbed hysterically and screamed.

Bai shrugged. "I've always found nurses to be officious and bossy."

"DO YOU THINK I'M KIDDING?!" he shouted.

"Do I look like *I'm* kidding?" she replied calmly.

He dragged the nurse with him as he started to back away.

In response, Bai pulled back the hammer on her Beretta and in a harsh voice said, "If you take one more step, I will put a bullet in your head. Your demise will be swift and permanent. But," she said more coolly," a hospital ward is a poor choice of battlegrounds. If you drop the knife, I'll let you leave, providing you assure me you won't hurt anyone on your way out."

"How do I know I can trust you?"

"If I'd wanted to kill you, you'd already be dead."

Her words seemed to surprise him. "Who are you?"

"That's just what I was going to ask you." She nodded at Lee. "Why are you so intent on killing my friend?" She saw him hesitate for the first time, momentarily unsure. Lowering her gun, she stepped aside to give him a clear path to the door. "Leave my knife at the door as a professional courtesy."

He seemed to think about her offer as he eyed the door before again turning to meet her gaze. Shoving the nurse aside, he sprinted toward the door. The knife clattered to the floor. Three nurses seemed to materialize out of nowhere to congregate around their hysterical coworker while Bai rushed over to check on Lee. He seemed to be sleeping peacefully. His pulse and respiration registered normal on the monitors.

She pulled her phone from her jacket and dialed. "Bo, there's a man leaving the hospital in a white doctor's coat with a bloody left sleeve. If you see him, follow him, but don't try to stop him."

"What's this about?"

"There's no time, Bo, just do as I ask. If you see a tan man in a white doctor's coat, follow him. I've got Song with me, so I've got protection."

Ending the call, she reached down to pick up the dropped syringe by the edges of the plunger, being careful not to smear any prints. The hypodermic was still full. When she straightened, she noticed Song standing at the foot of the bed. He held her knives.

"You have a wonderful sense of timing," she told him.

He stared back at her with a confused expression.

After holstering her gun, she took the butterfly knives from Song and placed them in their pocket sheaths. Grabbing a plastic bag off Lee's nightstand, she placed the syringe in the bag then slipped the whole thing into her pocket. When Song retrieved her throwing knife, she wrapped the blade in Kleenex before dropping it into the same pocket.

No sooner had she finished than three hospital guards charged into the room with their guns drawn. They wore stylish light-blue uniforms with darker trim. Their weapons swung from left to right in wide arcs as they looked for someone to shoot. Seeing that everyone else in the ward either wore a hospital uniform or was hooked to a monitor, they cleverly narrowed down their suspects to Bai and Song.

"The man you're looking for is wearing a white physician's coat and has a cut on his left forearm," she said while pointing in the direction of the exit.

The men looked from her to the group of nurses nearby. The nurses' prodding gestures proved sufficient to send all three guards scurrying out the door in pursuit of the tan man. Bai hoped they didn't have the misfortune to catch up with him. She doubted they'd survive the encounter.

"What are your orders?" Song asked, looking sheepish.

"Go back outside, wash your hands, and put on a mask then come back here. You're going to watch over this patient until I can arrange for private security and a private room. Can you do that?"

"So long as you don't leave," he replied. "I go where you go."

She'd expected as much and nodded in acknowledgment. She took out her phone to make a call. Jason picked up on the second ring.

"Where are you?" she asked.

"I'm sitting at your desk watching the DVD from the Grand. Why?"

"You're wasting your time. The man who killed Wen is the man in the gray suit with the dark tan that Lee followed. He has a snake head tattooed on his wrist and a hole in his forearm where one of my throwing knives took a bite out of him just five minutes ago. He just ran out of San Francisco General after trying to inject Lee with a hypodermic."

"Is Lee all right?"

"Yes. And before you ask, I'm fine too. My two shadows are with me. What I need from you is the name of a competent agency to provide around-the-clock protection for Lee. I won't leave his side until I know he's safe."

"I can manage that," he replied. "Give me about an hour."

"It'll take that long to get him moved to a private room and sort out the mess here. I'm sure someone's going to want to report the assault. I'm going to try to head off any publicity."

"Understood. Anything else?"

She wanted to ask him why he'd left in the middle of the night, but she didn't. She'd decided long ago that she'd never cling to a man. The sentiment didn't leave her any less lonely or any less resentful, but the gesture did leave her pride intact.

"No. Nothing important," she lied, ending the call in frustration.

chapter 22

Bai called the phone number on the card Inspector Kelly had given her. The connection rang several times before being answered. "Whaat? Uhhh, who...?" Then the line went silent long enough for her to wonder if she'd been disconnected. A croaky voice finally asked, "Who is this?"

Kelly sounded like someone had kicked him in the gut.

"Sober up, Kelly, and haul yourself down here to San Francisco General. I need your help."

"Who the hell are you, and why are you telling me what to do?"

"It's Bai Jiang. If you don't get down here fast, I'm going to spill the beans on the friend you met yesterday at Figaro's. He tried to kill Lee. Unless you want this story to go public, get your ass down here and fix this mess."

"Hold on," he said. "Let me clear my head and get this straight. You say he tried to kill Lee?"

"Twice."

"That doesn't make any friggen sense," he replied. "Listen, don't do anything stupid. I'm on my way. Don't talk to anybody. And fer Christ's sake, don't say anything about the man you just mentioned. You got that?"

"I hear you, but make it fast. Your friend hasn't been subtle in his attempts to kill Lee. This time, he had a lot of witnesses. This mess won't go away on its own."

She closed the connection and dropped her phone into her coat pocket. As she looked around, she could see the intensive care unit was starting to fill with concerned doctors and bewildered guards. Nobody seemed to be in charge.

"If you don't have a mask on, go put one on. If you don't have a good reason to be in here, get the hell out," she ordered in a loud voice.

140

Several people turned around to look at her with stunned expressions before heading for the exit. Song passed them en route from the opposite direction with his surgical mask in place. A man in a white lab coat stepped over to check on Lee while Song took up a position at the foot of the bed to watch. She recognized the doctor as Lee's surgeon from the night before.

He talked calmly as he fidgeted with the drains and checked Lee's catheter bag. "I heard there was a ruckus in here."

"Yes," she replied. "I've called the police. They're on the way. How is my friend?"

"He's doing much better. His fever is down, and there's no blood in his urine. The drains are clear. We should be able to take them out later today."

"How long before he can be discharged?"

"I'd like to keep him another day or two to make sure there aren't any more complications or infections. His wounds were deep. He's going to be in a lot of pain for the next couple of days."

"I'd like him moved to a private room where he can be guarded."

The doctor looked speculatively from her to Song standing at the foot of the bed with his back to them. "That shouldn't be a problem. Frankly, I'd be surprised if administration doesn't insist on it."

A man in a dark suit, accompanied by a uniformed hospital guard, approached the bed. Both wore surgical masks. The suit spoke but didn't offer his hand. "My name is Walter Flag. I'm a hospital director. This is our head of security, Captain Saunders."

A portly man of about sixty with graying temples and manicured nails, Flag wore an expensive suit. Saunders seemed about the same age but taller and leaner. He had somber brown eyes that scrutinized her closely. Their masks concealed their expressions.

Saunders picked up where Flag left off. He spoke in a guarded tone. "We'd like you to explain what happened here. We understand from the nurses a confrontation between you and a gentleman occurred where you brandished knives and a gun."

"Inspector Kelly of SFPD is on the way. I won't waste time telling the story twice. I will tell you someone masquerading as a doctor attempted to kill one of your patients. With that in mind, I think it's probably best to handle this quietly."

The two men looked at each other as the surgeon quietly slipped away, obviously wanting no part of their problem. Flag spoke to Saunders in a voice pitched loud enough for eavesdroppers who stood nearby to hear. "I'll leave this in your capable hands, Captain Saunders. If you need me, I'll be in my office."

The captain's eyes hardened. Flag turned on his heel and strutted from the room while Saunders watched him leave with poorly concealed contempt.

"Some days are just like that," she said in sympathy.

He looked at her in stark appraisal. "Do I need to worry about whether or not this counterfeit doctor is coming back?"

"In a word . . . yes."

His arms crossed defensively as he looked at Lee and then at Song. The surgical mask made it difficult to determine his disposition, but "unhappy" seemed the most likely candidate.

"While we're waiting for the police," she asked, "whom do I see about having my friend moved to a private room? I'll provide security for him. That'll be one less problem for you."

Saunders turned to meet her gaze. "We have VIP rooms, if you don't mind paying."

"Done," she replied.

He nodded in response and pushed a button on a square, black communication device attached to an epaulet on his shoulder. He gave instructions to prepare a VIP room for Lee and to refer any issues with the change of rooms to Director Flag.

As Saunders finished his conversation, Inspector Kelly crashed through the doors and into ICU. Song reached inside his jacket. Bai stepped forward and put out a hand to restrain the triad soldier. The notion of allowing Song to shoot Kelly proved tempting, but she needed the inspector.

"Who's in charge here?" Kelly blustered while rocking back on his heels.

She could plainly see he was still drunk. Reeking of alcohol, he obviously hadn't had time to cast off the dregs from the night before. She nodded at Song to stay put then gestured to Captain Saunders to follow her. She walked toward Kelly while pointing out the door. "Let's take it outside, Kelly. There are sick people in here, and you're carrying enough germs to bring an army to its knees."

Kelly raised a hand in protest as he turned to follow her. He appeared exasperated. "Don't bother asking what I think," he mumbled. "I'm only the friggen police."

They walked through the double doors and into the hallway with Saunders bringing up the rear. Once in the corridor, she removed her mask and turned to confront Kelly angrily. "I don't know what you've been swilling, but it seems to have addled your brain. I'm not even a little bit interested in what you think. I'm worried about Lee. I want to know what's going on, and I want to know now!"

He threw up his hands in frustration. "We can't talk here. This place is too public."

Saunders removed his mask, so Bai could clearly see the deep scowl etched on his face. He asked a pointed question of Kelly. "Do you know who the assailant is?"

Kelly waved his hands frantically and shook his head. "You don't understand," he replied in a defeated voice. "I don't have the slightest idea who he is. I swear on my mother's grave I don't know. That's assuming you're talking about who I think you're talking about. What I need to know is did anyone get hurt? Do I need to file a report?"

"A nurse received a superficial neck wound," Saunders answered. "She seemed pretty badly shaken by the incident. I'm willing to downplay the event as violent behavior by an unstable individual." He turned his gaze on Bai. "We don't want any rumors being spread about doctors trying to kill patients."

"That's fine with me," she said, "as long as Lee is protected and gets the best of care. That's my only concern."

"We'll get him moved immediately to a private room," Saunders said. "While that's taking place, I'll interview the nurse myself. There's no sense in subjecting her to even more trauma."

Kelly turned to Bai and asked, "So why am I here? Did you get me out of bed to run down here so you can call me a drunk? You could've done that over the phone."

"Your job is to make sure that SFPD doesn't show up to interrogate anyone."

"I am SFPD," Kelly countered in frustration.

"That's exactly my point. You're my personal SFPD. I can reason with you. If some newbie detective were to show up and sniff out a chance to make a headline, we'd all have our pictures in the paper. Nobody here wants that. Right?"

Two heads nodded in agreement.

"So we keep a lid on this assault. It's better for everybody," she said.

"How is it better for you?" Kelly asked.

She glared at him. "I don't want the tan man to know I'm coming for him."

"Jeezus!" Kelly cried. "Why can't you just leave well enough alone? You pick at a scab, and it'll bleed. You keep pickin' at that man, and you'll be the one bleedin'," he said as he shook his head in frustration.

"Why don't you get some coffee and wait for the report from Captain Saunders?" Bai suggested. "Make your call downtown or whatever you have to do to bury this fiasco. I'll stay with Lee until he's settled. Then you and I, Kelly, will sit down to have a nice little chat."

"Fine, fine, fine . . ." Kelly replied. "You do that."

She frowned at Kelly, who nodded in acquiescence while waving her away with a flick of his fingers. With misgivings, she left the two men standing in the corridor and walked back to the intensive care unit. Still standing where she'd left him at the foot of Lee's bed, Song scrutinized anyone who came into the ICU. Nurses chanced nervous glances in his direction but quickly averted their eyes.

Two orderlies wearing blue scrubs followed Bai into the room. The attendants unhooked Lee from the monitors, then she and Song followed his bed up to the sixth floor where a pristine suite of rooms waited. The main room boasted a good view of the city through picture windows. Blond furniture and a big-screen television on the wall provided a comfortable setting for both the patient and his visitors. The orderlies rolled the bed over to the window, where they hooked Lee up to another set of monitors. A nurse marched into the room to make sure everything was in order. She checked his vital signs and output bags before nodding deferentially to Bai then leaving.

Bai walked over to stand next to his bed and pressed her hand against his cheek. He looked peaceful but pale. "May all your dreams be joyful," she whispered, "and may all your angry shades be gentled and laid to rest."

She kissed him on the forehead and smoothed his hair back, grateful he lived.

chapter 23

Four very large men wearing black suits over black tee-shirts walked into Lee's private room. Hardware bulged under their suit jackets. Bai reached into her pockets, and Song tensed with his hand inside his jacket.

About six feet tall, the shortest of the men spoke. "We're from Axis Security to see Bai Jiang. Jason Lum contracted for our services— a four-man detail for around-the-clock protection."

"All four of you came to guard him at once?" Bai asked curiously.

The men smiled.

"No ma'am," the original speaker said. "This is just a meet and greet, so you'll know who we are. We'll rotate on four six-hour shifts. Two of us will be in the room at all times. If there's a reason one of us can't make a shift, you'll be notified in advance."

"I see."

The speaker turned to his team and nodded. Two of the men turned to walk out of the room, while he opened his jacket to move away from the door and place his back against a wall. Standing with his hand inside his jacket, he had a clear shot at anyone coming through the entry. The other guard assumed a similar stance on the other side of the room.

Bai walked back to Lee's bed to put her hand on his forehead. His skin felt cool to the touch. As she withdrew her hand, his eyes blinked open.

A moment or two later, he recognized her. "Where am I?"

"You're in San Francisco General."

"What am I doing here?"

He reached for one of the drains on the side of his chest. She stopped his hand.

"You've been shot," she said softly. "The tan man put two holes in your back. Don't worry. The doctors say you're going to be fine. You just need a couple of days to rest and take it easy."

"Who's the tan man?"

"The tan man in the gray suit you were following."

He seemed to have difficulty remembering. Meeting her gaze, he asked, "Water?"

She poured water from a plastic pitcher and put a straw in the cup before holding the plastic tube up to his lips. He sipped slowly then shook his head.

"It hurts," he complained.

"I imagine it does. The good news is the shooter used a twenty-two, so the scars will be small."

"I guess that's good news," he said half-heartedly. "What are the tubes for?"

"They're drains. The doctor is going to take them out later today. It'll be something to look forward to."

"For you or for me?"

She smiled.

"I dreamt a naked man jumped up and down on my chest," he said.

"Why was he naked?"

"All the men in my dreams are naked."

She smiled at his attempt at humor. "I can tell you're feeling better."

"Do you suppose you could get them to give me some more drugs?"

"Why? Are you in pain?"

"I could be if that's the right answer."

"I'll see what I can do."

She pushed the call button for assistance. When the nurse came into the room, she glanced warily at the men standing around with their hands in their jackets. The woman had a pinched face with hair parted in the middle and drawn back into a ponytail at the nape of her neck.

"He wants drugs," Bai told her.

"He isn't due for his morphine for another two hours." She looked at Lee. "Where does it hurt?"

"Where doesn't it hurt?"

The nurse looked at Lee a long moment before caving in. "I'll get you something and be right back."

He looked at Bai when the nurse had left. "What do you think she means by 'something'?"

"From the look she gave you, I'd bet on Tylenol."

Lee frowned. "I thought the same thing. She has an Amish look, doesn't she?"

"Don't worry. We'll have you out of here in a day or two. Just hang in there a little longer."

"Like I've got a choice?" Becoming more aware of his surroundings, he looked around. "What's with all the muscle?"

She nodded at the security team near the door. "Those two are around-the-clock protection for you. This one," she indicated Song, "is mine, compliments of Jason."

"What did we do to deserve all this attention?"

"I'll explain later. Do you remember anything from before you were shot?"

"I remember I was following him, and he disappeared. Then it's a blank. Who is he?"

"That's the part I'm not sure about. He's the one who 'did' Wen Liu."

"Do we know why?"

"No."

"We don't know much, do we?"

"No, but we're not going to let a little thing like ignorance slow us down. We're too stupid to let that happen."

His smile made her feel better.

She confided in him "The tan man tried to kill you again about two hours ago."

"Here, in the hospital?"

She nodded. "I put a knife in his arm. I knew you'd want me to."

"Why didn't you shoot him for me?"

"My first instinct was to kill him. The feeling was almost euphoric.

I had to stop myself. I wonder, sometimes, if I'm not more like my grandfather than I'd ever imagined."

He looked at her with concern. "This isn't the time to have second thoughts, Bai. A moment's hesitation could mean your life."

"I know. I realize I should have shot him, but the thought of taking another life frightened me, Lee. My instincts to kill frighten me. I'm afraid of what I'll become."

He frowned. "Fill me in on what's happened since I got shot."

She took a deep breath and collected her thoughts. "I had a meeting with the Norteños. They don't know anything about Daniel Chen. Rafe showed up to pick up the girl tailing Kelly, so I made a deal and bought her from the Norteños. She's at home with Elizabeth and the girls. That's why I have to leave soon."

He looked at her, then chuckled, then grimaced. "Don't make me laugh. It hurts. I can't believe you've collected another stray. You're worse than a cat lady."

"The pain serves you right for making fun of me."

"You sound like Nurse Ratched. Where is that nurse anyway?"

Just then, the nurse came back into the room carrying a paper cup in one hand and a covered dish in the other. She put the dish on the tray next to Lee's bed and handed him the cup.

He looked inside at the clear liquid. "What is it?"

"Liquid Tylenol," she replied. "Take your medicine then you can have some Jell-O. As soon as you're cleared for solid foods, we'll bring you a tray."

He turned aside to stare at Bai with a stricken look on his face. She smiled and held out the cup and straw.

"Save me," he pleaded.

"Take your medicine, and eat your Jell-O like a good boy," Bai encouraged him. "When you get out of here, we'll find a steak and a bottle of really good wine to make up for all your suffering."

He took the Tylenol but refused the green Jell-O. "I've suffered enough."

"Is there anything you need me to do while you're in here?" Bai asked "Feed the fish? Water the plants? Do your laundry?"

"Tell Elizabeth to water my plants. You're not to go near them."

She shrugged, aware of her reputation for having a black thumb.

His expression became somber. "Bai?"

"Yes?"

"Be careful. I didn't see the tan man coming. He was there one moment—gone the next. Before I had time to backtrack, he had me. Don't play with him. If you see him again, shoot him."

She nodded somberly. "I promise."

"Go home and see to the kids. I'll be fine."

"I'll be back later."

"Do what you need to do. I'm not going anywhere. I think I might sleep for a day or two."

She pressed a hand against his cheek and leaned over to kiss his forehead. "I'm glad you didn't die. I'm not sure what I'd do without you."

"Get out of here before you have me in tears. I'll bet crying hurts as much as laughing."

She smiled and squeezed his hand in parting. As she walked toward the door, Song preceded her. He opened the door and checked the hallway before allowing her to leave the room. She gave one last wave to Lee as she walked through the doorway then opened her phone to call Kelly. She wanted a word with the inspector before leaving the hospital. Her call went unanswered.

She called Bo. He immediately picked up her call. "No sign of any tan man in a doctor's coat, Bai. I circled the block but didn't see anyone fitting that description."

"Thanks, Bo. Song and I will be down shortly. I just have one more stop to make."

She got directions to the hospital's security office and found Captain Saunders there. Song waited for her outside the door. The captain stood as she entered. "Is everything satisfactory with the private room?"

"The room is fine," she replied. "In case you haven't been informed, we have security in place. I was wondering where Inspector Kelly has gotten to."

"Your inspector scurried out of here as soon as I handed him the incident report."

Saunders looked as if he'd swallowed something bitter. She sympathized; Kelly had that effect on people.

"Did he say where he was going?"

"No, but I don't think you'll have to look farther than the nearest bar. He seems to have a problem."

"You noticed, huh?"

"Hard not to notice. He smells like a distillery."

She changed the subject. "Did your men find any sign of the fake doctor with the knife wound?"

"No. I put an alert out to local medical facilities to be on the lookout. A wound like you described would benefit from stitches, but if he's smart he'll just use butterfly bandages and take a broad-spectrum antibiotic."

She nodded and put out her hand. "Thanks for everything. I appreciate your cooperation."

"I suspect I'm the one who should be thanking you," he said as he took her hand. "You prevented a murder inside my hospital then put a lid on the story. You have my gratitude."

"If you really want to show your appreciation, keep an eye on my friend. I'd feel better knowing he has backup for his security detail."

"I've got a man dedicated to watching the corridor camera around the clock. Nobody will get into that room without being scrutinized. You have my word."

"Thanks again, Captain. I'll let you know if I find out anything more about our assailant. I want him put away as badly as you do."

Song fell into step with her as she exited the captain's office. Walking through the lobby of the hospital, her phone rang.

"Where are you?" Elizabeth asked. "Do you have any news of Lee?"

"I'm just leaving the hospital now. Lee is conscious and feeling much better. I've had him moved to a private room, and I'm on my way home. Is everything all right?"

"Yes, we're fine. I'm fixing the children breakfast. Should I send them to school?"

"No. Tell them we're going on holiday. We'll talk about it when I get home, but I think this might be a good time to get some country air."

Ominous silence greeted her from the other end of the line. "Are you thinking of sending us away?"

"No. I'm thinking the girls might like to spend some time lying around a pool and learning how to ride horses. Spring in the wine country is beautiful."

"Where will you be while all of this is going on?"

The question forced Bai to consider. The house in the country was only an hour away by car, and spending nights with the family would ease Elizabeth's fears. She could sleep in Healdsburg and still work in the city. Skirting the truth, she replied, "I'll be staying with you and the girls."

Her answer seemed to calm Elizabeth. "In that case, I think a trip to the countryside is a wonderful idea. Once we're settled, perhaps you'd like to invite Howard to spend some time with the family. That would give you a chance to see how he responds to the children."

"Sure, why not?" she replied with as much enthusiasm as she could rally. "Spending time with Howard would just about make my day perfect."

chapter 24

Bo fidgeted behind the wheel of the SUV as they sat in morning rush-hour traffic. More than half a million people commuted to work in the city. Bumper-to-bumper, cars lined Bush Street, a major thoroughfare.

Resigned to the crawl of heavy traffic, Bai leaned back into her seat to relax and wait with her eyes closed. When she reopened her eyes, the SUV had come to rest in front of her building. Song held the rear door open for her. She smiled in apology for her drowsiness. He bowed as she swung her legs out of the vehicle.

The doors to the lift opened on the third floor to the aroma of fried bacon. She found the girls sitting at the dining room table finishing a late breakfast with Elizabeth. On the table rested bowls of rice, scrambled eggs and potatoes, along with plates of bacon, sausage and toast. In anticipation of her arrival, a place setting waited for her at the head of the table.

"Good morning," she said cheerily.

The girls turned to her as Elizabeth said, "I've already given them the good news concerning Lee."

Bai nodded and took her seat to spoon eggs and potatoes onto her plate before topping the pile with bacon and sausage. The girls remained quiet. From their expressions, no one had slept much the night before. After taking a few bites of bacon, she poured a cup of coffee from a carafe sitting on the table next to her. "Has Elizabeth explained we're going to the country for a few weeks on vacation?"

The girls turned to her with expressions ranging from confusion to delight. Elizabeth responded first. "I thought I'd let you surprise them. From the looks on their faces, you've succeeded."

Bai smiled. Everyone but Dan looked happy. Dan put her fork down and stood. "I won't leave Lee. He's hurt. He needs me. He's my *shifu*."

"Your *shifu* is doing fine," Bai replied, secretly pleased Dan saw Lee as her mentor. "I've just come from the hospital. He'll be released in a few days to join us. He's the reason we're going someplace nice to recuperate. We'll prepare everything for when he arrives. As a matter of fact, Dan, we'll be staying at the estate your father bought for you as an early inheritance. He wanted you and the family to have a place outside the city where you could enjoy your summers."

Dan sat down to stare at her mother skeptically. Bai's little girl showed signs of growing up. A time would come far too soon, she feared, when spinning the truth to her daughter would no longer suffice. She dreaded that day. She wanted to shelter Dan from the harsh realities of life as long as possible.

"The house has acres and acres of vineyards as well as a swimming pool," Bai continued enthusiastically. "I understand horseback riding lessons are also available. That is, if anyone is interested."

She dangled the bait and waited to see who would take the line.

"When are we leaving?" Jia asked with a smile splitting her face.

"We'll leave as soon as we're packed. You won't need much. We'll shop for Western wear and bathing suits on the way. Just take the essentials," she advised, sensitive to the fact Alicia only possessed the clothes on her back.

Jia didn't wait to finish breakfast. Excusing herself, she dashed to her room to pack. Dan looked suspicious but resigned. Alicia looked uncomfortable.

"Dan," Bai said, "if you're finished, would you see to packing? I'd like some time with Alicia."

Dan looked aside at Alicia and smiled in encouragement. Bai could see that a bond had already formed. Dan left the room, and Elizabeth stood to excuse herself.

"Please stay, Elizabeth. This is just girl talk," Bai said.

Elizabeth took her seat and sipped tea from a porcelain cup.

Bai continued. "I know everything is new to you, Alicia. I just want to make sure you're doing all right and you're not uncomfortable. I want you to think of this as your home. You don't have to feel like a guest. You can be sad when you're sad, angry when you're angry, and happy when you're happy."

The teen looked at her and nodded wordlessly.

Bai wondered where the cocky Latina from yesterday had gone. She worried. "Is there anything you need?"

Alicia shook her head. "Everyone's been really nice. That's the problem. I'm not sure how to act."

"You don't have to act. Just be yourself."

The girl smiled wryly, obviously amused by the thought. "I'm not sure that's a good idea. I'm not sure I like who I am."

Bai tried to comfort her. "Everyone tries to be the best person they can be. We don't always succeed. All we can do is keep trying to be better by being kinder, gentler, and more forgiving. Just remember you're not alone. Everyone struggles to find themselves."

Alicia's expression remained doubtful.

Bai added, "I'm here for you. We all are. You're not alone anymore unless you want to be."

Alicia nodded. "I like Dan and Jia. I'd like to stay, at least for a while."

"Good," Bai replied. "Liking is a good start," she said, standing. "On a lighter note, I think we should hurry these ladies along so we can hit the road. We have a million things to do today, not the least of which is to buy you a wardrobe."

She pulled the girl to her feet. "Let me change my clothes then we'll go spend some money. Nothing cheers a girl up like shopping."

In less than an hour, a caravan of cars rolled across the Golden Gate Bridge headed for Healdsburg. Two triad soldiers led the procession in a black SUV. Behind the lead car, Bai drove her MINI Cooper with Alicia in the passenger seat next to her. Elizabeth, Jia, and Dan followed in Elizabeth's black BMW, chauffeured by Song. In the rear trailed a black SUV driven by Bo.

They stopped at a mall in San Rafael to shop. Outfitting the girls for a vacation took longer than expected. In addition to a wardrobe for Alicia, they bought Western riding boots and outfits for everyone with the exception of the triad soldiers, who seemed content with their black suits. Alicia needed a phone and tablet to match those Dan and

Jia carried. Conscripted as bearers, their bodyguards carried armloads of packages.

When Bai's credit card started to show signs of fatigue, they all piled back into the cars to drive north another forty minutes.

They pulled into the long drive leading up to the house on top of the hill. She'd called ahead to let the Corazons know they were coming. The couple met them in the parking court with smiles and waves.

As soon as they disembarked, Bai conducted the necessary introductions. Fausto and Coleta seemed to take special delight in the children, whom they helped with luggage before showing to their rooms. As everyone finished unloading the cars, a very long, very sleek motor coach rumbled up the drive to park on the edge of the property. A black limousine followed the coach to stop next to the black SUVs.

Jason stepped out of the limo with a sober look on his face.

"What's this?" Bai asked.

"Delighted to see you, too," he replied. "When I heard you were leaving the city without notice," he hesitated to emphasize what he'd said, "I realized my men would need a place to sleep. The bus has bunks and communications. This way they won't be imposing on you."

"Thank you," she muttered, not completely sure she wanted the presence of bodyguards.

"I want to make sure Dan and the girls are safe. My men will stay until I know there's no danger."

Coleta stepped out of the house to beam at Jason. "Will you be joining us for lunch, Mr. Lum?"

Jason's expression changed like a flipped switch as a smile brightened his features. "I'm sorry, no, Coleta. I have business back in the city."

Bai understood Jason wouldn't stay because of Elizabeth.

Not privy to the family rift, Coleta naively pursued the matter. "When you phoned to say you were coming, I sent Fausto to get ribs. I thought we'd have a barbecue. We have plenty for everyone. I planned for a dozen big appetites."

At the mention of barbecue, the triad soldiers lit up like Christmas trees. Bai determined she needed to find the tan man quickly, or she and her bodyguards might end up looking like Coleta's husband, Fausto, with stomachs large enough to provide shade for their boots.

Coleta beamed at Jason. "Lunch will be ready in an hour."

"Another time, perhaps, Coleta," Jason said, turning to face Bai. "I'd like a chance to show you the communications inside the bus, if you have a moment."

She looked sharply at him. "Fine."

They walked to the edge of the drive. He stepped around her and held the door to the motor coach open. She walked past him and up the two steps to the interior.

The front section of the bus, behind the driver's console, held a table and four high-backed chairs secured to the floor on round swivels. Backing the table and chairs were cabinets holding electronic equipment bristling with cables. A command chair had been secured in front of the cabinets facing three flat-screen monitors positioned in a semicircle.

Jason sat in the chair and pushed a red button to the left of the screens. A low hum emanated overhead. "That's the satellite dish on the roof deploying. If your cell phones are blocked, the direct satellite link will provide secure communications. Once the satellite is up, push this switch," he said, indicating a green toggle. He did so then picked up the receiver of the desk phone next to the screens and held it out to her.

She put the phone to her ear and listened to a dial tone.

He nodded. "That's all there is to it."

She handed him back the receiver. "Is this why you called me in here?"

"Not really," he said. "I want to know what happened this morning. I'm trying to keep you and the family safe. You're not making it easy."

"I probably should have talked to you first before moving the family here. I thought we'd be safer away from the city."

"You may be right. Nonetheless, I want my men here as insurance. We still don't know who this tan man is or his motive for killing Wen and shooting Lee. His actions might be directed at me, and you just happened to get in the way."

"I don't know what to think anymore," she admitted. "Lee had never seen the man before yesterday. He obviously realized Lee was following him. But killing someone on a crowded street for being nosy seems a little extreme. I can't help thinking a game's being played we know nothing about, a game with very high stakes."

"Did you get any indication he knew you?"

"No. As a matter of fact, he asked me who I was, so I asked him who he was. Neither of us volunteered an answer."

Jason shrugged. "Did you get anything? A scar? An accent?—anything we might use to identify him?"

She took the syringe in the plastic bag out of her pocket along with the tissue-wrapped throwing knife. "I have his prints and his DNA. I didn't see any point in giving them to the police. The tan man and Kelly seem to already know each other. I don't know whom to trust."

He held out his hand with a smile. "If he's on file, we'll find him. I have contacts inside law enforcement who can run the prints and the DNA for a match."

"I did good, didn't I?" she said with a smile.

"You did good," he admitted. "And, in case you're wondering, you do know whom to trust. You're just too stubborn to admit it."

chapter 25

Afternoon and evening passed in a blur of activity. The girls swam and ate before Fausto and Jason's soldiers rounded them up for a trip to the local equestrian center, where they arranged riding lessons. Elizabeth and Coleta, meanwhile, put their heads together to sort out how to provide meals for everyone. The four bodyguards demonstrated awe-inspiring appetites. Their party now numbered eleven. They'd have an even dozen to feed when Lee arrived.

Pleading work, Jason returned to the city. He took the limousine with him. Bai spent the afternoon sleeping. Providing an encore to the huge lunch, dinner turned out to be a blend of Chinese and California cuisines: barbecued salmon steaks and fried rice.

Exhausted after their all-night slumber party and an active day, the girls fell into bed without being prodded. Elizabeth followed them soon afterward, leaving Bai free to do as she pleased. She took a shower and dressed for work in basic black before donning her Kevlar coat to sneak out of the house quietly. Her date, Inspector Kelly, waited at the Sand Dab.

She didn't make it past Bo and Song. Both men wore night-vision goggles. They caught her trying to sneak into her car.

"Seems like cheating," she said as they intercepted her.

"Jason told us to expect you," Bo said with a resigned air.

"What else did Jason tell you?"

"To be more afraid of him than of you," Song replied. "So far that doesn't seem to be a problem."

After a bit of negotiating, they resolved that Song would follow her into the city and provide backup. Bo would stay with Jason's other two men in Healdsburg to guard the children. And Jason would be kept apprised of her activities.

Traffic remained light as she approached the Golden Gate Bridge.

Fog enveloped the orange girders to form a hazy obscurity as the dense mist softened the edges of certainty. Headlight beams refracted off tiny beads of moisture in a lustrous glare that slowed traffic to a crawl. Cars groped their way across the metal span like moles.

On the other side of the bridge, fog held the city in a moist embrace. She drove slowly through hazy streets where drivers edged along at a snail's pace.

A solitary bulb suspended from an arced metal tube cast a muddled glow over the entry to the Sand Dab. Barely legible letters spelled out the name in faded blue-on-white over the door. Plate glass, painted black, fronted the street to shield those inside from curious stares and the depredations of light.

Bai stood on the sidewalk outside to check her weapons. She lifted her butterfly knives to ensure they moved freely then reached around to the small of her back to check the grip on her pistol. She didn't know what to expect. Her faith in Kelly, the little she'd had to begin with, had disappeared along with the tan man. Nonetheless, Kelly had information she wanted. She was determined to make him talk, one way or another.

Song stood at her back. She turned to him. "I want to talk to the inspector privately."

"I go where you go."

She smiled tightly. "Like I was saying, why don't you join me? Just stay out of the way."

He nodded. "Not a problem."

She stepped inside and waited to allow her eyes to adjust to the gloom. Song followed her and took a position just inside the door.

Acrid smoke hazed the silent room. Sconces along the walls emitted barely sufficient light by which to navigate. Empty, high-backed booths lined the right side of the room while the left wall remained bare. The smell of cheap cigars and damp mold permeated the air. In the back of the room curved a long wooden horseshoe bar with stools, half of them occupied.

She approached the bar and saw the broad back of Kelly's stained trench. He sat with his shoulders hunched and his head down. She needn't have worried about sneaking up on him. He wouldn't have noticed an elephant slipping onto the stool next to him unless the pachyderm had tried to steal his peanuts. She took the stool next to him as men, or what was left of them after a lifetime of drinking, turned to eye her blearily. A skinny fellow with pockmarked skin and long, limp hair stood behind the bar polishing a glass while scrutinizing her.

"What?" Bai asked. "You've never seen a woman?"

"Not recently," he replied with a gap-toothed grin. "You're a little high-tone for this place. Are you with him?" he asked, nodding at Kelly.

Kelly raised his head and slowly turned to look at her. He managed to make the effort appear exhausting. When he recognized her, he scowled and went back to studying the drink sitting on the bar in front of him.

The bartender smirked and continued to polish the same glass, the rag in his hand stained an unhealthy shade of brown. "What can I get ya?"

She looked at the rag, then at the man. "A tetanus shot."

"You want that over ice?"

She ignored the question. "Is your back door unlocked?"

The man scoffed. "I'd be outta business in a week if it was. Do I look stupid?"

"That's a loaded question," she replied. "What time did Kelly come in today?"

"Around one," he answered then seemed to catch himself. "Kelly who?"

"No. But I do look a little like her, don't you think?"

The bartender stared at her vacantly.

She smiled. "Apparently not."

His expression remained blank.

She threw a thumb over her shoulder toward the men's room. "I feel a sudden urge." Pulling Kelly up by the collar of his coat, her firm grasp steadied him as he stumbled to his feet to stare at her blearily.

She addressed the bar. "If anyone feels compelled to follow me, I won't be pleased."

The bartender didn't look happy but nodded. "Knock yourself out."

She didn't get any reaction from the dissolute patrons at the bar, who were probably too immersed in their own despair to take notice. Pushing Kelly toward the men's room, she followed him inside where they could talk in private.

The men's room held a single stall and a stained urinal shoved up against the wall next to an equally brown sink. Grime-gray tiles covered the floor. Fragrant eau d'sewer discouraged loitering.

She shoved Kelly up against the wall. "You can't hide forever, Kelly," she said in exasperation. "Talk to me. Tell me what you know about the tan man."

"You might be surprised what I can and can't do," he mumbled sullenly. "If I was you, I'd be gettin' the hell outta' here before I lose patience."

"If you were me, I'd kill myself. That not being the case, tell me what you know while I'm still asking nicely."

He sneered at her, his voice full of contempt. "What's a sweet little piece of ass like you gonna do?"

Without thinking, she punched Kelly in the gut. Her hand sank into soft belly flesh nearly to her elbow. The big cop folded like tissue as she stepped back. He gasped for breath and slowly sank to the floor with his legs splayed out in front of him.

"Jeezus!" he swore while taking short breaths. "I didn't know girls could hit so hard. Are you sure you're a woman?"

She dropped on her haunches to talk to him. "You really bring out the worst in me, Kelly. I don't know what kind of hold the tan man has on you, but we can work this out. Like you said in my office, you weren't always a drunk. You were a good cop once. Tell me what you know. Let's quit tearing each other apart and start working together."

His gaze met hers, and the bravado seeped away, his shoulders slumping and his features becoming haggard. "It's too late for that. The truth is ... I'm not really sure who your tan man is." His head tilted back and he took a deep breath. "He's connected. That much I know. I was told by brass to help him and not ask any questions. He wanted to find Chen on the QT. I thought you could find him for me. I don't know why Lee got shot. Shit happens."

"Shit happens, all right," she acknowledged. "It usually happens to me. Are you sure you don't know anything more about the tan man?"

"I know he's a prick, and a scary one." Kelly shook his head slowly and sighed. "I really don't know how I ended up like this. I was human once." He stared at the dirty tiles between his splayed legs.

She looked at him and couldn't help feeling sorry for him, already regretting the impulsive punch. "I'm sorry for hitting you, Kelly. Come out, and I'll buy you a drink. Not here, of course. I'm not that brave. Let's go someplace and talk where it doesn't smell like shit."

He waved a hand listlessly. "Save the apology. I had it comin'." He remained quiet for a long time. "I need a little privacy to take care of business. Wait for me outside. This won't take but a minute. Then we'll have that drink."

She looked at him and hesitated.

"It's all right," he said. "I just need to take a piss and pull myself together."

She stood reluctantly. "Don't take all night. This place gives me the creeps."

He nodded his head and waved her away. She turned to walk out the door and toward the bar. As she rounded the corner, she heard the gunshot. The bartender met her gaze with a scowl.

She ran back and slammed the bathroom door open. Kelly sat where she'd left him. His gun lay in his hand at his side. Blood and gore dripped from the ceiling. The smell of cordite overpowered the bathroom stench.

She leaned back against the bathroom door and sighed. "Kelly, what have you done?"

She didn't wait for the police. Despite having a concealed carry permit, the butterfly knives would be a problem. Too, she didn't want to have to explain why she'd been looking for Kelly. The story didn't even make sense to her; she'd have been hard-pressed to explain it to someone else.

She walked out of the bar and into the fog to find her car. Song followed her to her car and waited patiently in the black SUV behind her. She started the ignition, uncertain of her destination, and found herself heading straight for Chinatown and home. Her mind seemed as cloudy as the mist, while the windshield wipers slapped back and forth like forced applause.

When she arrived at her building, she got out of the car to explain to Song she'd be spending the night at home, then ran up the steps of her building. Pressing the elevator sensor, she stepped into the lift.

"'If you were me, I'd kill myself,'" she repeated as tears welled. She brushed at the errant drops with her hand. "'If you were me, I'd kill myself?' When are you going to learn to muzzle your fucking mouth? What kind of crazy bitch says shit like that?!"

She cried and couldn't stop. She dropped to the floor of the elevator as sobs racked her body. When she ran out of tears, she lay curled on the floor, too emotionally spent to get up.

Eventually forcing herself upright, she pushed the button on the lift to take her back to the lobby. There was no sign of Song as she got into her car. She headed west toward the hospital. She needed to get a sanity check. She needed to lean against the rock that was Lee. She needed her friend.

The elevator ride to Lee's floor garnered a number of stares. She could only imagine what she looked like: a tall Asian woman with short hair and mascara tracks running down her face, wearing a crimson-red scarf and a long black coat like an anime character. A smirk formed on her lips at the thought.

Automatic pistols swung up to greet her as she walked into Lee's room. She froze. Recognition slowly dawned on the faces of the two bodyguards as the pistols slowly dropped to be holstered again.

"Sorry," one of the men said. "You surprised us. It's a little late for visitors."

"I know," she replied. "I need to see my friend. Can we have a few minutes alone?"

The two guards exchanged looks then opened the door. "We'll be right outside if you need us," the speaker for the pair said. "Take your time."

The door closed, and she turned toward Lee's bed. Awake, he studied her warily. She walked over and sat on the edge of the mattress. His drains had been removed. His color looked better.

His eyebrows lifted in a question. "What's wrong?"

"I just needed to see you."

"This is me, remember? What's wrong?"

"Kelly ate his gun."

Her statement surprised him. He seemed to think about the idea. "I'd be lying if I said I'll miss him."

"I was with him, Lee. I told him if I were him I'd kill myself. Then he pulled out a gun and blew his brains all over the ceiling."

She started to cry again.

Lee's face contorted with anger. "It's a good thing he's dead, or I'd kill him myself, the useless shit."

Pulling her forward so she could lay her head against his shoulder and cry, he patted her like a child. She rested against him and snuffled.

"It's not your fault," he assured her. "Kelly didn't die because of you. He killed himself because he got tired of being a useless drunk. You were just the last witness to a selfish existence. He died the way he lived—without a thought for anyone but himself."

"He said the tan man was looking for Daniel Chen. Kelly was just his gopher. He came to us so we could do his job for him. Maybe you got shot because the tan man thought you were Chen."

"Do I look like Chen?"

She wiped her eyes, looked at him, and shook her head. "We all look alike to a *gwailo*. I think you look a little like Cary Grant."

He smiled. "You're an idiot, but I love you."

She put her head back on his shoulder. "Just a little longer, then I'll be all right."

He put his arm around her. "Take all the time you want. If you're a good girl, I'll share my Jell-O with you."

chapter 26

Around two in the morning, Bai drove from the hospital to Chinatown, where, for the first time in days, she didn't have to pass triad soldiers to get to her door. Her car slipped into its familiar parking spot in the garage. When she reached the third floor, the flat stood dark and empty.

After turning on a light in the kitchen, she poured three fingers of scotch and took the crystal highball glass with her into her bedroom. She kicked off her shoes and shucked her coat onto the floor.

As she sat down on the bed, her phone rang.

"You're late getting home."

She didn't bother to ask Jason how he knew her whereabouts. "You don't have to worry. I have Song with me somewhere. I had business in town."

"What kind of business?"

"The kind of business that isn't any of your business."

"Aren't you interested in finding out *who* the tan man is?"

He had information for her. She could tell by the tone of his voice. "That was fast. I only gave you his prints yesterday."

"I don't have a name for him. My contact inside law enforcement ran his prints. His identity came back as a classified file with a federal hold, which means your tan man either was or is a federal agent. Or he's in witness protection."

She appreciated his efforts but felt a sudden urge to go to sleep. Her head lolled as she tried to think. Her brain refused to work. "I'm too tired to think about this tonight. Can we talk tomorrow?"

She took a drink of scotch in an effort to numb herself.

"Do you want company?" he asked.

"Not tonight."

"Are you all right, Bai?"

"I've had a bad night. I confronted Kelly. He blew his brains out.

I feel like it's my fault, even though, rationally, I know that's not true. I think I've had as much as I can handle for one day. I have to rest."

"If you need anything, call me."

"I will. Thanks for the information. I'm going to sleep now."

She ended the call then downed her drink before sprawling on the bed and wrapping the coverlet around her like a cocoon. There didn't seem to be any need to undress. She pulled her knees up until she curled into a fetal position. Her dreams were filled with blood and guilt.

Morning came much too soon.

Her phone woke her at eight. She looked at the display but didn't recognize the caller. When she answered, a surly voice greeted her. "This is Howard. I've been expecting your call. Why haven't you called me?"

"Good morning, Howard. Yes, I've been doing well. Thank you."

She snapped her phone shut and pulled the covers over her head.

"Jackass," she mumbled.

A minute later her phone rang again. Howard changed his greeting. "Good morning, Bai. How are you? I hope you're doing well."

"I feel like dog shit," she mumbled and hung up on him again.

A minute later her phone rang. When she answered, he blurted, "What does it take to have a conversation with you?"

"Take me to breakfast."

"When would you like me to pick you up?"

"An hour . . . in front of my building."

"I'll be there."

She hauled herself from the bed to the shower, got dressed, and waited in the lobby until a limo pulled to the curb. A chauffeur stepped out to hold the rear door open. She exited her building to walk down the steps. She'd dressed, as usual, in black jeans and a leather jacket. Throwing caution to the winds, she'd left her Kevlar coat lying on the bedroom floor.

Howard didn't step out of the car to greet her. She found him working feverishly on a laptop inside the rear compartment. He didn't look up when she entered. His fingers flew across the keyboard for another minute before he closed the laptop and turned to her.

"Sorry," he said. "Memos had to go out immediately. A great deal of money was at stake."

"I understand. Business is business."

"Where would you like to go for breakfast?"

"The Cliff House. I'd like to see the ocean. I find the sea calming."

"Did you get that, Jan?" he asked his driver through the open glass partition.

Jan answered without turning around. "Yes, sir. I'll see to the reservation."

"So, this is your idea of a private conversation?" she asked.

Howard leaned forward to push a button that raised the glass partition. "Is that better?"

"Much. Thank you."

"I understand you met with my mother," he said glumly.

"I did."

"What did you discuss?"

"Bloodlines."

"Yours or mine?"

"Ours, as it turns out. Were you aware your cousin Jason is the father of my child?"

He looked surprised. "No. I wasn't."

"Your mother is very aware. She sees my daughter as the heir to Kwan Industries. How do you feel about that?"

"How old is your daughter?"

"Thirteen."

He smiled. "For a minute, I thought I was already being replaced."

"That doesn't speak well of your mother."

"You should take that up with my two older siblings. I suspect they feel the same way after being replaced."

"How do you feel about marrying a woman who comes to you having had your cousin's child? Won't that bother you?"

"Not nearly as much as I suspect it will bother Jason," he replied with a self-satisfied smile.

The thought of his cousin's displeasure seemed to delight him.

She didn't consider his glee a mark of good character. Moreover, she didn't want to become embroiled in a bitter family dispute, especially one involving Jason. He and she hadn't always agreed, but they'd always cared for and protected one another.

"Do you want to marry me, Howard?"

He seemed to ponder the question. "I have to marry someone. It really doesn't matter to me whom. I imagine I'll go on living as I always have, devoted to my work and traveling from country to country. You should know being married to me will be a lonely affair."

He stopped and pursed his lips. "Having said that, I also have to admit I'm attracted to you. I don't quite understand my feelings. I find you entertaining and unpredictable, and annoyingly honest. I'm not saying I'm in love with you, but I wouldn't mind giving a relationship a try. It would be a first for me."

"What do you mean by 'relationship'?"

"A real marriage isn't what I'm suggesting. You have to understand I don't have much experience in these matters. My parents' marriage is more of a business contract than a union. The only thing they have in common is a company that consumes them and three sons they've spent their lives ignoring." He hesitated. "I'm not proposing monogamy or anything that confining."

She studied his features. He seemed to be serious. His expression appeared thoughtful, though his concept of a relationship was vague, at best. What he'd described barely qualified as dating, let alone a marriage.

She tried a different tack. "What do you think your mother is looking for?"

"That's an interesting question. To tell you the truth, I'm not sure."

"Your mother hinted she wanted to train me to take over as chairwoman of Kwan Industries when she retires."

"That's not entirely implausible," he said, smiling. "My mother's motives have always been a mystery to me. If what you say is true, it would definitely be advantageous for me to marry you. I've always suspected I'm the Prince Charles of Kwan Industries. I fear I may reach old age without ever plucking the crown from my mother's head. Perhaps together, we might wrest control from the old girl."

Though he smiled, she got the feeling he wasn't joking. A glint of hope, or perhaps greed, slipped past his cool demeanor, giving her the impression he craved the helm of Kwan Industries and wasn't sentimental about how he achieved the position.

"I don't think your mother would be easily displaced," she observed. "She's a formidable woman."

"Then it should be interesting. You're also a formidable woman. Let the jousting begin," he said, throwing his arm out for emphasis.

She smiled, letting him think his nonchalant attitude fooled her. He obviously sought allies in his bid for power. Her concern centered on whether or not he could be trusted. He joked about opposing his mother for control of the family business. Two brothers had already been set aside. The pattern of deceit and betrayal within the family disturbed her.

They reached the Cliff House and walked into the Bistro to have breakfast. Their table rested next to a window where they had a view of the Pacific. Held at bay, a gray bank of fog roiled a few miles offshore. The churning water below reflected the same dreary shade as the overcast sky.

She sat and enjoyed the view while savoring the welcoming smells of coffee, baking bread, and frying bacon inside the warm café. After lots of coffee and a Dungeness crab omelet, she felt almost human again. Howard appeared reluctant to leave. He sipped his cappuccino as he studied her from across the table.

"You're really quite stunning. The short hair and black clothing work to hide how beautiful you are. A practiced eye can see beyond your tedious apparel. You have amazing cheekbones and beautiful, full lips. Your body is long, shapely, and well-muscled. You're quite the specimen."

"Don't get yourself all worked up, Howard. And just for your information, women don't like to be referred to as 'specimens.' It really takes the shine off of the compliment."

"I didn't mean to flatter you," he stated. "I merely wondered what you'd look like after a day at the spa and a complete makeover. I see real potential."

"What you see is what you get. Don't assume I want to change to make myself more attractive for you. You'd be wrong. I like the way I am."

"I like the way you are, too. I just don't think a woman with thoughts of becoming the head of a conglomerate can afford the luxury of dressing like a ninja. The jobs may, for all intents and purposes, be the same, but you don't want to advertise that fact."

He was probably right. She hadn't given thought to what kind of image she'd need to project if she were to become a public figure. Her dress and mannerisms would certainly have to change. The way she talked would definitely have to become more circumspect.

"What kind of look would you recommend?" she asked out of curiosity.

"I'm not sure. Would you like to go shopping? I think it would be fun, and the excursion would give us a chance to get to know one another better."

She played with the idea. He seemed enthusiastic. He could also be quite charming, when he wasn't being an ass.

"Could we make a date tomorrow? I need to get my partner released from the hospital today."

"Tomorrow's fine with me. I look forward to it. What happened to your partner?"

"Someone shot him in the back."

"Really?" His eyebrows shot up. "I hope he'll be all right. Do you know who did it?"

She nodded. "Given time, he'll be fine. I have a pretty good idea of who shot him, but not why." She frowned. "Finding out why is proving much more difficult."

chapter 27

Lee sat in an armchair looking bored. A Giants game played on the large flat-screen television with the sound turned off. His two security men flanked him with their hands resting inside their jackets. They each had one eye on the door and one eye on the game. They nodded to Bai as she walked into the room.

"Gentlemen," she responded to the guards. And, to Lee, "I see you're up and around."

"And ready to get out of here," he replied. "Nurse Ratched came in a half dozen times last night to wake me up and ask if I was resting comfortably. I've had all the recuperation I can stand. I want out."

"They're filling out your discharge papers now. We'll be leaving soon."

"That's good news."

He seemed to want to say more but stopped himself. He looked toward the men standing guard. She got the hint. "Would you gentlemen be so kind as to step out of the room? We'd like a moment in private."

The men silently left the room and pulled the door closed behind them.

"What's up?" she asked.

"Jason came by to see me last night. He told me what he'd found out about the identity of the tan man."

"What else did he have to say?"

"He's worried about you. He's afraid you'll do something rash."

"He worries too much."

"He cares about you."

She brushed the comment aside with a flick of her hand. "He has his own problems to worry about. He should let me worry about mine."

"You seem angry."

"I am angry . . . and impatient. That's my fault. I've always wanted more from him than he's willing or able to give."

"What are we talking about?" he asked.

"I've been offered a marriage to Howard Kwan of Kwan Industries. His mother wants me to continue expansion of their thirty-billion-dollar business. I'm toying with the idea."

"More important than the money, what do you think of Howard?"

"I've only met him twice. He's hard to know. From what he's told me, I'm not sure it really matters what I think of him. The marriage would be more a matter of convenience."

"Don't you think it would be nice to be in love with the person you're marrying?"

"Look where love has gotten me!" She stopped to take a breath and look away for a moment, letting her emotions settle. When she continued, her voice softened. "To be honest, I'm not sure what I want anymore."

"That's a pretty cynical perspective. For the sake of argument, let's say you accept this proposition. Why rush into a marriage?"

"Howard's father is in poor health. His parents want to install Howard as CEO before his father passes to ensure a smooth transition of power. His mother, Jade, is chairman of the board. She feels his being married would be a big mark in his favor with the other board members. A marriage would demonstrate he's settled down and more stable in his personal life."

"What do you think?"

"I think when one door opens, another closes."

"You're thinking of closing the door on Jason?"

"I'm just thinking out loud."

He remained quiet.

"What do you think?" she asked.

"I don't know, Bai. I don't have an unbiased opinion. Jason's my friend. Have you talked to the girls about getting married?"

"No. I'm pretty sure I know how Dan will feel. She loves her father. But this change wouldn't be just for my benefit. She would be the heir to Kwan Industries. The girls would have their futures ensured."

He smiled. "I don't believe there's such a thing as an ensured future. Getting shot made that perfectly clear. One moment you're here and the next . . . gone—*finito*. The end of life is uncompromising and inevitable. Everyone dies."

"Don't you think it's better to die rich?"

"Unhappy people strive for money thinking wealth will solve their problems. That rarely seems to be the case."

A muscular-looking blonde nurse backed into the room pulling a wheelchair. Bai and Lee turned to her.

"Your release papers are processed, Mr. Li. You're all set to go."

Lee stood unsteadily with Bai's help, still numbed by pain medication. He sat in the wheelchair while the nurse swiveled the foot platforms around before releasing the brakes on the wheels. Bai had already collected Lee's valuables. There wasn't any clothing to pack. The police still held it as evidence in the attempted homicide.

As they exited the room, one of Lee's bodyguards preceded the wheelchair while the other followed. The procession secured an elevator and descended to the lobby without incident. Bai pulled her car around to the front entrance where the two bodyguards assisted Lee into the passenger seat. She released the security detail and pulled away from the curb with a farewell wave.

Lee turned to her with a weary smile. "Thanks for breaking me out."

"I'm taking you to the summer house in Healdsburg."

"I'll need my things from home—clothes, shaving kit."

"Already packed and in the back of the car. I also brought along your lab computer and Wen's cell phone in case you get bored."

"Good thinking. There are a lot of files I haven't opened yet. It might be interesting to see what other information she sold and to whom she sold it. The tan man could be an agent working for an unhappy customer, or even a victim of data theft bent on revenge."

"Maybe," she said, turning the thought over before changing the subject. "What do you remember about the day you got shot? Where did the tan man go after we split up?"

He closed his eyes a moment then spoke slowly as if he were pulling one memory out after another. "I followed him over to Montgomery Street. He'd backtracked south a few blocks to the Business District. I held back about a half block to stay out of sight. The sidewalks were pretty congested. That part of town is always busy."

He stopped and shook his head as if to jostle a memory. "I saw him go into a high-rise office building south of Jackson Street. By the time I made it to the lobby, he'd disappeared. I remember looking at the registry in the building. None of the business names meant anything to me. I'd lost him, so I walked across the street to a coffee shop where I could keep an eye on the front entrance. He came out of the building about a half hour later. I followed along behind him on the other side of the street. He didn't appear apprehensive. I felt confident he didn't know I was tailing him."

"Where did he go then?" she asked.

"He walked back up Leavenworth and around to Sansome. I crossed the street at the light. By the time I reached the corner, he'd disappeared again. Walking up Sansome, I remember a stinging pain in my back as if I'd been burned. I couldn't seem to catch my breath. I vaguely remember dropping to my knees. My chest hurt. Then, nothing."

"Do you remember the address of the building where you lost him the first time?"

"It was 645 Montgomery. The front was faced with polished black granite. The lobby was nice, clean, and done in black granite as well. There wasn't an information booth inside. A lot of big buildings have receptionists. This one didn't."

"I'll take another look at the building. I'm curious about who owns it and who leases space."

"I can do an Internet search on the building and see what there is to find." Lee closed his eyes a moment. "Maybe I missed something. The building seemed innocuous. There were security cameras, but nothing out of the ordinary."

"Can you remember anything else?"

"The coffee at the coffee shop was really bad and really expensive. I don't mind paying more for coffee, but I expect it to be good. When I get time, I'm going back to have a word with the manager."

She looked at him and shook her head. "You were almost killed, and you're worried about a bad cup of coffee?"

"It's the principle of the matter."

"What principle is that?"

"There's no excuse for bad coffee."

"I wasn't aware that was a principle."

"It's listed under the code of the 'righteous bitch.'"

"I thought that was me."

He smiled. "And, so it is, Grasshopper."

Bai managed to get Lee situated before leaving Dan in charge of his care. Jia and Alicia returned from riding lessons and greeted him. The encounter was the first time Alicia had met Lee. She acted uncharacteristically shy. Bai left as he kept the girls spellbound by telling stories while high on pain meds. When she last saw him, Lee held court with three beautiful handmaidens in attendance.

She almost made it out the door before Elizabeth caught up with her.

"Bai, do you have a minute?"

"Certainly," she replied with a smile on her face as she turned in the doorway. "I was just on my way back to the city to run some errands."

"We missed you at breakfast. Will you be home in time for dinner around seven?"

"Yes. I'll be here. I had a breakfast date with Howard Kwan this morning and didn't want to wake you."

Elizabeth smiled. Her shoulders visibly relaxed. Bai's date with Howard clearly managed to deflect her concern. As long as Bai kept seeing Howard, Elizabeth appeared content.

"If something comes up," Bai added. "I'll be sure to call. He mentioned something about shopping and getting to know each other better. He thinks I should change the way I dress if I'm to assume the role of a public figure."

"Really?" Elizabeth nearly chirped with excitement. "So, Howard is talking about marriage. That's wonderful. I'm so happy for you."

"Don't get too excited. I'm just trying on the notion to see if the idea is a fit. Being his wife means changing my lifestyle and my behavior. I'm not even sure that's possible."

Elizabeth lectured. "You can do anything if you set your mind to it. Did he say anything else?"

"He didn't know Dan was Jason's daughter. He seemed to like the idea Jason wouldn't be happy with the marriage. His reaction seemed childish. I'd like to avoid turning a marriage with Howard into a defeat for Jason."

"That may not be possible," Elizabeth warned. "If you're the prize, only one can be the winner."

"I'm wondering when I became a prize. I'll have to give my new status more thought. Maybe there's a way to leverage being a trophy."

"Don't get carried away. You need to focus and be proactive to make the most of this opportunity."

"What are you suggesting?"

"I think a new wardrobe is a wonderful idea, one long overdue. You need to present a more feminine face to the world. I can hardly imagine the impact you'll have."

"The impact will be my butt hitting the floor when I fall off my shoes. I've never mastered high heels. I'm not even sure I want to."

"We'll practice," Elizabeth enthused.

"Won't that be fun?"

The sarcasm seemed lost on Elizabeth, who appeared captivated by the prospect of a feminized Bai. "We should probably hire a makeup consultant. I'll make some calls. We'll talk tonight and arrange time in your schedule for a wardrobe consultation. As soon as possible, I'd like to make appointments at the major department stores."

She stared at Elizabeth and wondered how she'd inadvertently opened the gateway to hell. From the determined expression on Elizabeth's face, Bai was about to join the ranks of the well-coifed, whether she wanted to or not.

chapter 28

Bai felt a sense of relief, a feeling of homecoming, as she passed through the bridge tollbooth and entered the city proper. The vineyards and rolling hills of Healdsburg were nice, but she never really felt comfortable amid all the fresh air and wide-open spaces.

She'd lost Song in traffic and had called to let him know she had a meeting at *Sun Yee On*'s headquarters. He'd naively agreed to meet her there. She stopped at her building long enough to change clothes and create a disguise. The result was a navy-blue cashmere blazer with matching pants and closed-toe navy flats topped by a beige Hermès raincoat. The outfit made her indistinguishable from thousands of other women in the Business District.

To complete the disguise, Bai donned a pair of large plastic-rimmed sunglasses and a brown wig, giving her shoulder-length hair. Her reflection in the mirror resembled someone a bit stuffy and bookish. The glasses helped to camouflage her Asian ancestry. With a quick nod in the mirror to bolster her courage, she was on her way.

Walking to the Business District took about fifteen minutes. When she reached the corner of Montgomery and Clay near the coffee shop where Lee had waited for the tan man, she stopped to watch the flow of traffic on the sidewalk. Most of the buildings did a brisk business. 645 Montgomery didn't appear to be an exception. People entered and left the building in a steady flow. Perhaps as a consequence of serving bad coffee, very little activity took place at the café across the street.

She walked toward the coffee shop while looking a little lost. Standing in front of the café, she looked up and down the street before pulling out her cell phone to look at the display. She shook her head and frowned as she thrust her phone back into her coat pocket and marched into the café.

The man behind the counter smiled at her. "May I help you?"

"What do you recommend? I have an appointment in a half hour and could use something to perk me up. The audit could take all afternoon. I don't want to be drowsy."

"A double espresso should do the trick as long as you're not sensitive to caffeine. It's pretty strong."

"That sounds exactly like what I'm looking for."

Bai smiled affably while looking around. Small tables rested against the wall on her right. A couple more tables provided a view out of the front window. She was the only customer.

"That'll be eight dollars."

She paid that and a tip then took a seat at a small table along the back wall where she could see the shop as well as the street. The barista delivered her coffee and returned to his newspaper, ignoring her.

She noticed a number of oddities as she sipped her coffee. A camera under the front awning pointed out, not in. The blinking red light on the camera faced the street and 645 Montgomery, the building across the way. The cameras inside the café faced the window seats and not the counter, where any kind of dispute would likely occur. More importantly, the café provided the only convenient vantage point from which to watch the entrance of the high-rise across the street.

She sipped the espresso slowly. Lee had been right about one thing. Their coffee tasted like old cigarette butts. The only customers they could possibly hope to attract would be strangers to the area and anyone wanting to surveil 645 Montgomery.

She'd seen enough. Taking an alcohol wipe from her pocket she made a show of wiping her hands before surreptitiously wiping her cup to remove prints and DNA. Standing abruptly, she walked toward the front door. Stopping to look back and wave at the camera with her middle finger, she then turned to walk quickly back to Clay Street. Once around the corner, she ducked into the first entryway that provided concealment.

A man in a suit and trench coat dashed past her while looking furtively about. His eyes locked onto hers as he turned his head and spied her in the doorway. Smiling, she watched as he came to a sudden halt then turned around and walked toward her.

When he reached the alcove where she stood, he stopped and nodded. "You were expecting me."

"I expected someone."

He wore a smile that never reached his eyes. "Who are you?"

"You first."

The smile fell away. "That's not the way it works."

With fingers flexed rigid like a spade, her hand shot out to catch him in the throat. The sudden attack took him off guard. He reached inside his jacket with one hand as he gagged for air while grasping his throat with the other hand. She trapped the hand inside his jacket as she pulled him close to knee him savagely in the groin. He dropped to his knees as his face turned purple.

She knelt next to him on the sidewalk as people gawked. Looking as if she were trying to revive him, she slapped his face with one hand while she slipped her other hand inside his jacket to lift his wallet.

"Call an ambulance!" she cried as she slipped the wallet into her jacket pocket. Pulling his jacket open and tilting his head back, she could see the shoulder holster and the Glock semiautomatic he'd been reaching for. As the man turned blue and started to lose consciousness, she felt his windpipe and pushed down to compress the sides and open the airway. He immediately drew a deep breath.

In one fluid motion, she stood and turned to walk away, swallowed by the gathering crowd. She headed back to Chinatown in a tactical retreat. The enemy had been flushed. Now she needed to make a clean getaway.

She walked home quickly and dropped heavily onto the leather sofa in her living room. Tossing the wallet she'd stolen on the coffee table, she went through its contents and found credit cards under two separate identities: a Thomas Walsh and a Thomas Gregory. Walsh had a key card identifying him as an employee of Hader, Incorporated.

Hader, she recalled, was the largest private army in the world. The multinational corporation contracted with the United States military and other NATO nations. They specialized in handling missions too politically awkward for legitimate armies to handle. Their ranks were filled with ex-military and cast-offs from clandestine organizations.

While the government boasted of downsizing the military, the privatization of war had grown at a corresponding pace. Hader had become rich and powerful at the taxpayers' expense.

As she sat to think about what to do next, Jason walked in. He wore a black silk suit and a white shirt with a red tie. His apparel bespoke power. She looked at him and couldn't help but feel a little intimidated—and more than a little attracted.

"Interesting look," he said, noting her appearance. "I think I like you better with short hair."

"Are you here to critique my fashion sense?"

"No. We need to talk."

"About what?"

"About ignoring your security. Your bodyguards can't keep track of you if you keep ditching them."

"I'm not ditching them."

He looked at her.

"OK, maybe I did ditch them. But I'm sleuthing. That's what I do—I sleuth."

"Your sleuthing worries me." The look on his face changed. He sobered. "I'm sorry about Kelly."

"Why are you sorry?"

"I'm sorry his death affected you. It couldn't have been pretty."

"Death never is," she said, then changed the subject. "I'm onto something. I need to move fast and stay mobile. I can't be bothered with bodyguards. Leave your men in Healdsburg to keep the children safe. I'm fine on my own."

"I wouldn't worry so much if Lee were with you. He seems to have a calming effect."

"I miss him, too, but I can do this on my own."

He gestured at the wallet and the pile of cards on the table. "What are you looking at?"

"I flushed out one of the people I think ambushed Lee. He works for Hader, Incorporated."

"How did you get the wallet?"

"I let one of them follow me."

"Did you kill him?"

"No, but he's going to be talking and walking funny for a while."

"You should have killed him. If he can identify you, you'll be fighting an army. If that's the case, I'm not sure even I can protect you."

"I'm not asking for your protection."

He looked frustrated. "I wish you'd be more careful."

She paused to look at him before continuing. "Just to let you know, I'm thinking of getting married."

He spoke in a soft voice. "That would be a mistake."

"Why?"

"Howard is a little off. He seems normal, but there's something wrong with him. I wish I could be more specific, but I can't. It's just a feeling."

"Your calling someone abnormal seems a little ironic. You kill people for a living."

"I didn't say I was perfect. But I do have ethics."

She smiled sweetly. "Your ethics seem quite flexible."

He nodded his head. "True, but I do have them. I'm not so sure about Howard."

"He seems nice enough."

"He does, doesn't he? I'm sure you'll consider anything I say about him suspect. So I'll leave it to you to find out what kind of man he really is. At the moment, I'm more worried about the Hader Corporation than Howard Kwan. Howard will make your life miserable; Hader will kill you."

"I'm going to assume Hader is running operations out of 645 Montgomery," Bai said. "That's where Lee followed the tan man. I suspect he's either an employee or a government agent working with Hader. Either way, I need access to that building."

Jason looked at her and scowled. "A high-rise building isn't easy to break into. If Hader has offices there, they'll be secure and heavily guarded. They run around-the-clock operations and never sleep."

"There has to be a way in."

"If the tan man is coming and going from the building on Montgomery, you'd have a better chance of grabbing him off the street."

"He does seem comfortable walking the streets," she said as she considered his suggestion. "When Lee followed him, he didn't resort to riding in cabs, which may suggest he actually prefers walking. But assuming he's a professional, he won't walk a reliable route to or from anywhere since the first rule of evasion is to avoid patterns and schedules. So, grabbing him off the street will require a team."

Jason interrupted her. "I'll snatch him for you if you'll do me a favor."

His offer sounded tempting, but there was always a catch. She regarded him warily. "What do you want?"

"If he turns out to be either a government operative or an employee of Hader, I want you to back off. I'll make him pay for what he's done because Lee's my friend. That will finish it. I don't want you to declare war on the government or on Hader. Those are battles you can't win."

She stuck out her lower lip and considered his offer. That he was probably right made accepting his offer more difficult. Doing so would mean admitting she was wrong. In the final analysis, however, she really didn't have any other options. She didn't have the manpower or the equipment to kidnap the tan man.

"You win," she finally said.

He looked at her and frowned. "That's one way of looking at it. If Hader gets wind of what I'm up to, they'll kill me. I'll save the victory dance for later."

chapter 29

Jason departed with a stern warning to be careful. She forced herself to get back into her car for the drive back to Healdsburg. She'd promised to be with her family for dinner. If she hurried, she could beat the commuter traffic leaving the city.

Arriving at the house in Healdsburg, she met Bo in the motor court.

He opened the car door for her with a frown, obviously unhappy with her activities as he said, "Everyone is in the kitchen."

He looked like he wanted to say more, but he gritted his teeth and held his counsel.

"Tell Song I'm sorry when you see him," she said as a peace offering.

He nodded and closed the door of the car.

As Bai entered the house, the sound of laughter guided her steps. She walked across the living room to observe her family through an open doorway. Lee walked a short distance from the kitchen to the dining room and back again while Dan hovered behind him like a hummingbird. Jia and Alicia helped Elizabeth and Coleta prepare dinner. Bodyguards stood around looking useless but content.

When she walked into the kitchen, Jia descended on her with a hug and a smile, a welcome that made the long drive worthwhile. Dan stood back to stare at her mother with a wary expression. Alicia observed the interplay with apparent interest.

Jia grabbed her attention. "You wouldn't believe how much fun it is to go riding. The horses are really big. There's a white horse named Lucky I really like. And, there's this guy who says we can ride for free when we're better riders. They have all these horses people bought who don't ride them, so we can exercise them and even get paid to ride them. Is that cool or what?"

"That is cool," Bai replied.

"The people at the stables are really nice," Alicia added. "They take really good care of us. So far, we only ride in the arena, but with the bodyguards that's probably a good idea. Nobody's figured out how to get one of these guys on a horse."

Shifting uncomfortably, those same bodyguards avoided eye contact.

Bai smiled at the girls' dilemma. "The bodyguards are temporary. They won't be with us for more than a week or two. It's looking more and more like Lee's assault was a case of mistaken identity."

"Is that right?" he said as he made his way gingerly into the kitchen. He looked around for a place to sit. Dan turned to run into the dining room to retrieve a chair she placed behind him.

"Thank you," he said as he lowered himself into the seat.

"Can I get you anything?" Dan asked him.

"No. I'm fine. Why don't you rest? I'll stay here for a while."

She nodded and turned to leave without looking at her mother. Bai shot an inquiring look at Elizabeth, who shook her head as a sign questions could wait until later.

Lee captured her attention by saying, "There's something of interest you should look at when you have time."

"Can it wait?"

He nodded in response.

Elizabeth interrupted before Bai could speak. "I've made appointments for you and the girls to get facials, manicures and pedicures at a local spa on Friday afternoon. I thought the outing would be a good bonding experience."

Bai looked at her, perplexed. "What day is today?"

Elizabeth stared at her in obvious dismay. "Today is Tuesday."

"Will you remind me on Thursday, so I don't forget?"

Elizabeth smiled tightly. "Don't worry. I'll see that you remember."

"Thanks," she replied. "It sounds like fun, doesn't it, girls?"

Two heads bobbed, though the girls' expressions suggested they were as clueless as Bai about the scheduled primping.

"Is there anything else scheduled this week?" Bai asked.

"Nothing you need to concern yourself with," Elizabeth replied cryptically.

Bai turned her attention to Lee. "Would you like to join me on the terrace for happy hour?"

He replied with a wan smile. "I thought you'd never ask."

"Will you need assistance?"

"I can make it to the terrace on my own if you can carry the drinks."

"Your usual?" she asked, meaning a dry vodka martini.

"Yes, and make it a double."

She went into the great room, an expansive room off the terrace where a small bar with a mini fridge resided. She made a double martini for him and a scotch rocks for herself before taking the cold drinks to the terrace. Lee stretched out on the chaise longue where he looked every bit the country gentleman.

As she handed him his drink, she asked, "How are you feeling?"

"Like somebody beat me with a two-by-four. I've weaned myself off the drugs."

"Don't push yourself. It will take time to heal."

"This isn't a good time for me to be disabled. The man who shot me is still out there. You need me to watch your back."

"Jason has agreed to help me. Before long, we'll have a better idea of who the tan man is and why he shot you."

"Then you don't believe my being shot was a case of mistaken identity?"

"No," she said emphatically. "I just want to set Elizabeth and the girls at ease." She hesitated a moment before continuing. "The tan man is a pro. There's little chance he mistook you for someone else."

He looked interested. "What have you found out?"

"You remember the café with the bad coffee?"

"Yes. What about it?"

"That's where you got fingered. The place is wired. Anyone interested in the building across the street gets their picture taken. While you were watching them, they were watching you. You were right about the coffee, by the way—terrible."

"So you went there?"

"Yes. That's where I was this afternoon."

"Did you find out what the tan man was doing at the Montgomery address?"

"Not exactly. A man followed me after I left the café. It turns out he works for the Hader Corporation. I suspect that's the reason the tan man was on Montgomery Street."

"So . . . this man who followed you just offered you this information?"

"I'm sure he would have, had he been able. Sadly, he was incapacitated at the time."

Lee nodded his head knowingly. "I hope they haven't figured out who you are. What you did was risky. You need to be more careful."

"That's just what Jason said. You may be right; however, I feel if I don't keep chipping away at the lies, we'll never find the truth."

"The people you're looking for aren't gentle souls. Hader runs revolutionary governments all over Africa, Central America, and the Far East. They think nothing of killing thousands of people. The death of one nosy Chinese woman wouldn't even make a blip on their ethical radar."

"That's what has me puzzled. Why would they go to all the effort of shooting you? Coming after me makes even less sense. They have nothing to gain."

"Maybe the tan man thought I'd made him."

"The only person the tan man appeared to be interested in was Daniel Chen. Chen seemed to recognize the tan man from the hotel surveillance footage, which suggests they know each other."

"What do we really know about Chen?" he asked.

"He's Chinese, and he seems to have worked with Wen. He's elusive. Even the tan man can't find him. I'd bet he's a player."

"Exactly! A clandestine agent, but who is he playing for?"

"That's what we don't know. But one thing we do know about Hader is they're a for-profit company. If they're looking for Chen, someone paid them to look, or he has something of value they want. They're not a charity."

"Maybe when Kelly couldn't produce Chen, the tan man went

to Hader for assistance," Lee speculated as he chewed his lower lip in thought. "I've been going through the files on Wen's phone. I found a spreadsheet with names and encrypted data. Most of the information is in a code I haven't been able to decipher, but there are some generalities that I've been able to infer. Since we know Jason purchased information, I was able to sort out some of the entries by columns . . ." He saw her eyes start to glaze over. "Anyway," he continued with a look of consternation on his face. "To make a long story short, there were a couple of entries for Howard Kwan."

Bai shrugged. "What did you find out?"

"It seems Howard Kwan didn't buy information. He sold it."

"So what does that mean?"

Lee shrugged in return. "I have no idea. I just thought you should know what I know."

She sighed. "I'm starting to feel like the blind man feeling the elephant. What we know could mean any number of things. The scenarios are endless."

"Closer to home, you have a bigger problem."

"What do you mean?"

"Dan overheard Elizabeth gushing on the phone about your marriage prospects with Howard. She's at that awkward age where she wants to be an adult but still has the insecurities of a child. I think the thought of her world changing so radically scared her. And like you, when she gets scared, she gets angry. I've watched her simmer like a little teapot all day. It won't take much to set her off."

"Thanks for the warning. Elizabeth is on a quest to get me married. Howard is the first candidate with potential to pop up in years. I think she's decided to pull out all the stops. The strange part is Howard seems just as adamant. I hang up on him; he calls right back."

"He sounds like a glutton for punishment."

"I wonder," she said thoughtfully.

"Where are you at in your relationship with him?"

"I'm not sure. I'm going shopping with him tomorrow to buy a new wardrobe. He wants to make me socially acceptable."

Lee chuckled. "No small task."

"The problem I'm having with this makeover is I like the way I am. I don't feel any need to change. Who's to say what a successful woman is supposed to look like?"

"Obviously, that would be Howard and Elizabeth. Why don't you just go along with the program? If you absolutely hate the new you, nothing's stopping you from returning to your old wardrobe."

"That's true. The real issue from my perspective is that people seem determined to change me. What's the matter with 'me' just the way I am? You like me. Jason likes me sometimes. Elizabeth used to like me."

"She still loves you. I think she feels your dead-end relationship with Jason is her fault. He's her son. She raised the two of you together. She couldn't get you into a dress when you were younger, so maybe she feels she's failed you. Maybe this is her way of making amends."

"What's between me and Jason is between me and Jason." She'd grown tired of repeating her argument. "No one else can take responsibility for the attraction between two people. The chemistry we have is volatile and dangerous. We both know that and still can't seem to stay away from each other. That's our problem!"

"What a terrible fate: to have an attraction so strong your love defies convention! I'll save my tears for all those who've never suffered the way you have."

Bai looked at him sourly. "You're obviously feeling better."

"The martini helps. Perhaps I should have another," he said with a smile as he held out his glass.

chapter 30

Howard's concept of shopping was to have Bai try on countless dresses while he sat drinking champagne and passing judgment on the apparel. After two hours of playing mannequin, she'd reached the end of her patience. She stood in a sapphire-blue cocktail dress. Billowing satin gathered around her waist over a tight black sheath underskirt that constrained her gait to tiny steps. She minced around like a trained poodle.

"What kind of masochist came up with this dress?" she asked plaintively.

Howard stared at her appreciatively and motioned with a twirling finger for her to turn around. She stared at him and twirled one of her fingers to show him what she thought of the idea.

"We'll take it," he declared to the pandering saleswoman standing next to his chair.

"That's nearly a dozen dresses, Howard. Let's call it a day."

"We're just getting started."

"I generally avoid telling someone when they're wrong because it's rude. I'm going to make an exception in your case, Howard. You're wrong. We're done shopping."

He frowned and pursed his lips. "You're not being very cooperative."

"Two hours of strutting around in dresses that squeeze me as if I were an olive in a press is enough for one day. If you want, I'll sit in the chair and drink champagne while you prance around on three-inch heels. I suspect we'd both enjoy the experience more."

He looked angry; she didn't care. His fascination with designer clothes and branded accessories annoyed her. She wanted to tell him what she thought, but in consideration of Elizabeth, she held back. She'd promised to give him a chance. The task wasn't proving easy.

His pique quickly disappeared to be replaced by a rigid smile.

"You're right. I'm being selfish. Let's take a break and have lunch. What do you feel like eating?"

"I want comfort food. Let's go to the Tadich Grill for a lobster casserole."

She selected the restaurant because she knew he'd hate it. The Tadich had been in business nearly a century and didn't acknowledge food trends, serving traditional fare and generous portions. Table service was first-come, first-served with an emphasis on efficiency, not obsequious behavior. Waiters in white shirts and white linen aprons hustled plates full of hot food. A long, busy lunch counter set the mood for the eatery.

Bai and Howard were lucky and arrived before the noon rush. Seated at a table where wood worn smooth by thousands of diners reflected a warm shine, they perused the menu. The place filled up fast, and the noise level ratcheted up to keep pace. They ordered a lobster casserole for her and a wild salmon steak for him. He selected a bottle of white wine, a Napa Valley chardonnay, to accompany the seafood.

"What do you think?" she asked, spreading her arms to encompass the surroundings.

He smiled weakly. "Marvelous. I love the rustic feel."

She could tell he hated everything about the restaurant. His discomfort seemed small compensation for the morning she'd endured trying on dresses.

She waited until the wine had been served before satisfying her curiosity. "Do you know a woman by the name of Wen Liu?"

He stopped to consider the name before answering. "I don't believe so. I've met a lot of people in business, but that name doesn't sound familiar. What does she do? Perhaps if I can put her name in context, it will jog my memory."

"She buys and sells information. I should say, she bought and sold information. She was murdered at the Grand Hotel the night of our first date."

He looked shocked. "What a terrible coincidence. But, no, I'm sure I'd remember someone of that nature. She sounds like a shady character."

She smiled to hide her disquiet; Howard had lied to her. The question was why.

"Shady? Perhaps," she equivocated. "Wen was definitely a character. But that's not reason enough to kill her. Yet someone did. I'm trying to find out why."

"Why?" he asked, seemingly perplexed.

She leaned back and took a sip of wine. "Wen's killer shot my partner. I need to find out why people around me are being hurt. It's become personal."

"Do you make a habit of meddling in other people's affairs?"

The tone of his question indicated disapproval. She reined in her temper and answered in a barely civil tone. "I have an inquisitive nature."

He looked unhappy with her answer. "When we're married, I hope you'll curb your inclinations."

She smiled and chewed the inside of her cheek. "They say there's nothing like marriage to stifle one's interest."

Taking a sip of wine, he seemed to work at deciphering her reply. Luckily, the food arrived before he had a chance to question her further.

He picked at his plate as he studied her quietly. She devoured the lobster casserole along with a green salad and a half loaf of sourdough bread with butter. She thought of ordering chocolate cake for desert. Howard's lips continued to smile, but his eyes continued to observe her coldly. She decided to forego desert in order to be rid of him sooner.

"Where to next?" he asked.

"I'd love to spend the day with you, Howard, but I have errands this afternoon. And this evening I have a prior commitment."

His face showed a flash of resentment before quickly recovering. "Dinner tomorrow?"

She couldn't think of a graceful way out. She wanted to shut him down and be done with the dating charade, but the thought of Elizabeth's disappointment made her hesitate. "Sure. Dinner tomorrow sounds great."

"I'll pick you up at your place at seven."

She smiled and nodded.

"Can I drop you anywhere?"

"No. I prefer to walk," she quickly replied.

He stared at her a moment before standing. Hesitant, he acted as if he wanted to say more but decided not to. "Tomorrow then," he said, nodding to her. "I'll have the packages dropped at your place this evening."

Jaw tight, he turned and left.

"That was awkward," she mumbled to no one in particular as she watched his retreating back.

Shaking her head as she got up to leave, she tried to understand her aversion to Howard. He was an elitist, an attitude that many rich people seemed to have. He thought his money could buy him respect and he flaunted his entitlement, all of which flew in the face of her Buddhist training. Enlightenment couldn't be purchased, nor could respect. Character had to be earned through effort.

Dismissing thoughts of Howard, she took her phone from her pocket to make a call. The phone rang several times before being answered. "This is Bai Jiang. I owe you a date. Are you free tonight?"

Michael Chin, the waiter from the Grand, replied, "You're not much for small talk, are you?"

She felt combative after her morning with Howard. "No. Is that a problem?"

"Not at all," he replied. "I like assertive women."

"That doesn't answer my question," she said.

"I'm free tonight." He quickly replied. "Tell me where and when. I'll be there."

"This is your date. You tell me."

"Fine," he said in an accommodating voice. "Would you like me to pick you up, or do you want to meet me?"

"Tell me where and when. I'll be there."

He laughed. After a morning spent in an atmosphere of feigned gaiety, she liked the sound of his honest laughter. "Let's meet at the Durango Club in the Mission at eight. They have a good band and a crowded dance floor. Is that all right?"

She replied in a less surly voice. "Sure. I haven't danced in a long time. I hope I don't embarrass you."

"Are you kidding? Every guy in the place is going to wish he were me."

"I somehow doubt that, but you're sweet to say so. I'll see you at eight."

She closed the phone and drew a deep breath. A deal was a deal. She'd promised Michael a date. She'd deliver on her promise.

Idling away the afternoon alone in her apartment, she found the solitude refreshing. Around seven in the evening, her packages from the shopping spree arrived via Howard's chauffeur. The bags and boxes filled the elevator as she ferried them upstairs.

Looking through the purchases for the least objectionable of the dresses, she picked out a short black tube dress with an asymmetrical neckline adorned with crystals. The dress stretched to allow her freedom of movement and still managed to look stylish while covering all of her girl parts.

She called a cab to take her to the Mission District. She didn't see any sign of her bodyguards, but that didn't mean they weren't nearby. Despite their bulk, Jason only employed professionals. If they didn't want to be seen, they'd be difficult to spot.

The Durango Club pretended to be a Mexican tequila bar. Other than the name and the tequila, the only thing Mexican about the place was a smattering of furnishings. The interior exemplified an odd blend of techno-Mexicana. Stainless steel furnishings of the easy-to-clean and almost indestructible variety dominated. *Sombreros* and *serapes* hung high on the walls for their own protection.

Patrons crowded the bar at the entrance. Men stared appreciatively when she walked in. Michael stood just inside the door waiting for her.

"Have you been here long?" she asked.

"A while," he said with a deprecating smile. "I'm trying to impress you with how cool and mature I am. I got here an hour early because I was anxious to see you."

He wore a black dress shirt and jeans that showed off his trim build. His warm smile and gentlemanly manner set her at ease. She put her arm through his to let the watchers know she was with him. He beamed with pleasure. She almost laughed at his transparent joy.

"Are you going to buy me a drink?"

"I'd buy you the bar if I could. What would you like?"

"Scotch. Anything will do," she said, mindful of his youth and his budget.

Grabbing her hand to lead her toward the bar, he wended his way through the crowd with her at his back. Clubbing was a new experience for her. She'd been seventeen when she'd given birth to Dan. Afterward, life with a child consumed her time and energy. Nostalgia swept over her while she thought of the passing years.

After ordering their drinks at the bar, he turned to her with his hands full and a big smile on his face. Retreating from the bar through a three-deep crowd with her following, they found a table next to the back wall where the room was almost quiet enough to have a conversation. He pulled out a chair and handed her a highball glass.

She accepted the drink and raised her glass. "Thank you."

"*Salud*," he replied, tipping back a Tecate.

"Tell me about yourself," she said after taking a sip.

"I'm twenty-five and have a bachelor's degree in business from San Francisco State. My mother is Japanese; my father, Chinese. Both of them were born here. I'm adopted, as are my seven siblings. I work as a waiter at night, teach aikido at the Japan Center during the day, and run an online business in motorcycle parts the rest of the time."

"You sound like a busy man. Your father is Chinese, yet you don't speak Chinese. Why is that?"

"My parents were missionaries in China. I was adopted there. We returned to America when I was three. My father worked, and my mother raised us. She took us with her when she taught her aikido classes. As a result, I speak fluent Japanese."

"Your parents sound interesting, socially conscious."

"They are. My father is a devout Christian who doesn't believe in proselytizing. He says actions speak louder than words. My mother is a

pacifist who has a black belt, seventh dan in aikido. They're living con-
tradictions. What about you?"

"I'm older," she stated bluntly. "I have children but never married.
I barely finished high school and never made it to college. I work as a
souxun, mostly finding lost people. I was born in San Francisco and
raised in Chinatown. There isn't too much more to tell."

"Your date the other night seemed like an intimidating man. His
security cleared the bar, so you could talk in private. Are you in some
kind of trouble, Bai? Maybe I could help."

She reached across the table to put her hand on his and smiled.
"You're sweet, but I can take care of myself. You can do one thing for
me, though."

"What's that?" he asked eagerly.

"You could ask me to dance."

chapter 31

Dancers shuffled elbow-to-elbow as they moved to the rhythm of the music. Bai and Michael let the crowd sandwich them until their hips pressed against each other. They danced for hours to the beat of techno jazz and R&B.

The temperature went up as the crowd thickened. Around eleven, they took a break to sit at their table and lick salt off their hands while downing tequila shots. Sensing something out of place, Bai looked up to find Rafe and three Norteños standing in front of the table.

Rafe smiled wickedly. "You just can't stay away, *China*. You and me, we got some business. You feel me?"

He slapped a fist into his palm and smirked at her. She recognized the men standing behind him as Hector's men. They fanned out to make sure she couldn't get past them.

"Where is Hector?" she asked.

Rafe shrugged. "He decided to court out. Somebody had to take the blame for the lost *chiva* and *feria*," he shrugged, dismissing the heroin and money. "His bad."

"Was it you who dropped the dime on him?"

He shrugged again. "Payback for dissing me. Now it's your turn to pay, *China*."

Michael looked up from his drink. "We don't want trouble. Walk away and do yourself a favor."

Rafe laughed and pointed at Michael. "All you got is one little buster to back you up, *China*? I think you got a big problem."

She should have tried to defuse the situation, but alcohol fueled her frustration. Anger had been building in her for days. Being remade by Elizabeth and Howard, Lee's getting shot, Kelly's suicide, and now Hector's demise at the hands of an idiot like Rafe sent her over the edge. She kicked off her heels under the table and stood to face the

Norteños. She looked at Rafe and smiled. "I've had a bad week. You're not helping."

Rafe and his crew smiled.

"You got a big mouth, *China*," Rafe sneered.

Standing up alongside her, Michael put an arm out to usher Bai behind him. "Let me handle this, Bai." Turning to Rafe, he said, "We're not looking for trouble. Just walk away."

Rafe threw the table aside with one hand as he drew his other arm back. Michael leapt into the air to land a spin kick to the side of Rafe's head as the thug lunged forward. Rafe plummeted to the ground with his eyes rolling back as his face met the floor. Continuing his leg sweep, Michael pivoted around again to catch another gang-banger with a boot to the face.

Bai ducked under the swinging fist of a large Latino and kicked her attacker in the side of the knee with a crippling blow that elicited a shriek of pain. He rolled on the ground in agony. The last Norteño reached for her while pulling a flicker knife from his back pocket. Michael slapped the back of the Norteño's head with a beer bottle to drop him to his knees.

Pandemonium erupted. Fights broke out randomly and spread like a wildfire. Fists and bottles flew through the air. Bai stopped to grab her shoes while Michael fended off panicking clubbers stumbling toward them. He grabbed her by the hand and ran toward the back of the club against the flow of the surging crowd.

Crashing through a fire door in the rear, they set off alarms that shrilled as he pulled her into the alley. They ran the length of the narrow lane to the sidewalk, where he drew her to a halt next to a row of parked motorcycles. He grabbed a helmet off one of the bikes, a black, low-slung racer that looked like a rocket, and handed it to her. Straddling the bike, he turned to her as she adjusted the helmet on her head. She climbed onto the bike behind him.

"Where to?" he asked.

"Chinatown," she replied and leaned forward to put her arms around his waist.

He kicked the starter, and the motorcycle roared to life.

The crowd parted as the bike wove through fleeing clubbers. Song stared at her as they flew by. Sirens wailed. Lights flashed as fire trucks and police cars passed on their way to clear the thinning throng.

Once free of the crowd, Michael opened up the throttle, and the bike screamed. They sped between lanes of stalled traffic. He avoided lights and seemed to know the city well as he careened around corners to fly down alleys and side streets. She laughed out loud as the bike soared through the night.

The motorcycle slowed at the sidewalk in front of her building. The snarl of the engine subsided to a loping idle before Michael turned a key to kill the engine. She slipped off the back of the bike and removed her helmet, feeling suddenly shy.

"Can I see you again?" he asked.

Shaking her head, she handed him the helmet and put her hands on his face to kiss him. The kiss lingered. She had difficulty making herself pull away.

"I had a wonderful time," she said breathlessly.

"I did, too. Let's do it again," he insisted.

"The kiss?" she teased.

He smiled. "I was talking about the date. The kiss was nice, too."

"I think I'm too old and too jaded for you, Michael. We live in different worlds. But it was fun. I enjoyed the date. Thank you."

"You don't feel too old when I kiss you."

His words almost thawed her resolve. She could feel the heat rising from her chest. With a meek wave and a shake of her head, she turned and ran up the steps to her building. She didn't trust herself to speak. At the top of the steps, she turned to wave again before bolting through the door and running for the elevator.

She exhaled with a sense of relief as the doors closed on the lift. A tinge of regret confused her as she rode to the third floor. A part of her, the part that yearned for a normal life, wanted to see him again. He was fun and charming and handsome. His youth and innocence appealed to her.

She thought of him as she pressed her fingers against her lips while remembering the feel of his when they kissed and the feel of his hips as they'd danced, sending new waves of heat to flush her face. But he was just a boy, and a civilian.

Her phone rang. It was Jason. "I hear you're a biker girl now."

"When does surveillance turn into stalking?"

"When there's no longer a threat."

He had a point.

"Have you scooped up the tan man?" she asked.

"No. I've got eyes on the building on Montgomery Street, but he hasn't been sighted. I'm wondering if you scared him off."

"He didn't seem like the type to scare easily."

"He's drawn a lot of attention. He might be waiting for things to cool down. That's what I would do."

"I'm going to take another crack at finding Chen. He seemed to know the tan man."

"Whatever you do, be careful. And stay off the back of motorcycles."

"Why?"

"Because it makes me anxious."

"That hardly seems reason enough."

"Maybe not to you. It seems like a perfectly good reason to me."

"Good night, Jason."

"Good night, Bai."

After she'd ended the call, she suddenly felt lonely. She'd been drinking and was in no condition to drive to Healdsburg. Instead, she slumped off to bed alone and wondered again why she hadn't asked Michael to stay. As her head hit the pillow, the handsome young man continued to occupy her thoughts.

Morning dawned with a pounding reminder of the deferred pain that inevitably accompanied tequila shots. She guardedly tested the vision in her right eye before making the decision to open her left. She tried raising her head. A dull ache behind her eyes informed her she wasn't as young as she used to be. Her tongue tasted like burnt rubber and seemed to be glued to the roof of her mouth.

The rest of the world's problems would have to wait until she'd had a cup of coffee. Her stumbling gait carried her toward the kitchen, where she found Jason sitting at the counter reading the morning paper.

"You're looking spritely this morning," he said in reference to her nakedness, "and quite perky."

"Did you make coffee?" she asked, ignoring his lewd comment.

"It's sitting on the counter."

"When did you get here?"

"About an hour ago. I thought it best to let you sleep."

"Thank you."

She wasn't sure why she thanked him for invading her privacy. Thanking him just seemed like the polite thing to do, one of those automatic responses she'd learned as a child.

"You should either put some clothes on, or I should get naked," he suggested.

She pointed in the general direction of her bedroom. "Go find me a robe."

Shrugging, he did as she requested and returned with a silk robe.

"Thanks," she said as she pulled on the garment.

"Add a pair of fluffy house slippers and a cigarette, and the picture would be perfect," he taunted.

She looked at him tiredly. "Why are you here?"

"We have a lead on the tan man."

She looked up and attempted to focus her sluggish thoughts. "What do you mean, you 'have a lead'? Help me out here."

"He's been sighted in the Business District. We just haven't yet pinned down his location."

"And you're here because . . . ?"

"I wanted a cup of coffee."

"You can get coffee anywhere."

"Not and see you naked."

"Next time, I'll text you a picture."

"It's not quite the same, but I appreciate the gesture." He hesitated a moment before asking. "Will you be in town today?"

"Yes. I'm having dinner with Howard tonight. I'm telling you, so you don't feel compelled to have me followed. He has his own security. I'll be well taken care of."

"You're a very busy woman these days. Years without a date and now men seem to be everywhere."

"Are you jealous?"

"Perhaps," he admitted dourly. "I'm not entirely sure."

"I'm sorry," she said.

"Why?"

"I don't know. It just seemed like the polite thing to say."

"You've always been overly polite."

"That's your mother's influence. I'm surprised it never rubbed off on you."

"Are you sure you're not sorry because you love me?"

"I'm definitely sorry I love you."

"That's not what I meant."

"I know what you mean. You don't have the right to guilt me, Jason. You had your chance and made your choice. You didn't choose me."

His face fell, all pretense gone. "I know. I'm sorry."

"Why? Would you choose differently now and pick me over the Brotherhood?"

"No," he replied. "I'm sorry I've hurt you."

She looked at him and pointed toward the exit. "Call me when you find the tan man. In the meantime, stay out of my kitchen."

He stood and pointed to his phone. "Don't forget to send me the picture."

Staring at his back as he walked away, she wondered if she should laugh or cry. Her muddled brain couldn't come to a decision, so she did a little of both.

chapter 32

Bai picked up the phone to call Jefferson Boob. She was curious whether or not he'd learned anything of Daniel Chen or the tan man.

"Boobs's Gym, how may I help you?" he asked in his Southern drawl. His Galveston twang reminded her again of his gentlemanly Southern manners. She wondered, not for the first time, why all of the really good men were too young, too old, or too married.

"It's Bai, Lee's friend. I'm calling to see if you've heard anything of Daniel Chen or a man who might be looking for him. The man looking for Daniel would have a dark tan. You need to be very careful if you see him."

"It's always a pleasure to hear your voice, Bai. I'm just finishing up here. Do you suppose you might stop by so we can talk?"

"Sure. What time is good for you?"

"Is now convenient? I should have my business wrapped up by the time you get here."

She wasn't sure why Boobs wanted to talk to her in person, but she didn't see any reason not to accommodate him. "I'll be there in about fifteen or twenty minutes."

"I look forward to seeing you."

Taking the elevator to the lobby, she walked out onto the sidewalk where Song sat in a black SUV watching her house. An overcast day carried the scent of ocean as a cold breeze blew inland. She wore her Kevlar coat over her black tee and jeans. Her Beretta rested in the compression holster at the small of her back.

She opened the door of the vehicle and slid into the passenger seat. "I need to see a man at Boobs's Gym on Sixteenth near Bryant."

Song nodded and pushed the start button on the SUV.

When they arrived at the gym, she walked down the squalid alley and eased open the green door of the gym. Stopping just inside, she gave instructions to Song. "Stay here and keep your eyes open. I've got business upstairs with the owner."

He nodded and put his back to a wall. She turned to face the cavernous room, which stood empty and silent. Walking to the back of the gym, she stepped up the stairs and opened the door to Boobs's office. He sat at his desk and looked at her with a welcoming expression. As she took a step toward him, an arm wrapped her neck from behind. A hand reached around to clamp onto her gun as she pulled the pistol from her coat. She kicked and twisted, but the arm remained locked around her neck like a vise, choking off her screams. She fought until she felt the gun fall from her hand as her vision dimmed. Nothingness enveloped her.

Spikes of pain shot through her temples as she slowly regained consciousness. With her eyes still closed, tiny points of light flashed in her mind's eye. She thought she might throw up but suppressed the urge until the vertigo passed.

It was several moments before she opened her eyes and only then realized she couldn't move. She'd been stripped down to her underwear and lay face-up on one of the weight benches in the gym. Her hands had been taped to the legs of the weight bench behind her head. Barbell stanchions in front of her held her taped ankles with her legs raised and spread as if she were a turkey ready for stuffing. She lifted her head and saw herself in the mirrored wall in front of her. Duct tape held her firmly in place.

"Scream all you want, bitch. It won't do you any good. Nobody's gonna hear you."

Rafe walked over to stare down at her with a satisfied smile. Bruises on his face showed where Michael had kicked him unconscious the night before. He leaned over to run a finger up her thigh. As he played with her panties, he laughed.

"What have you done to Jefferson? Where is Song?" she asked.

He stopped to look up toward the office. "You don't have to worry 'bout the old man. He's not gonna bother us. Song the guy you left guarding the door? He's not as tough as he thought. Weight bar up against his head and it was all over."

"What do you want?"

Rafe dropped the smile. "I want payback, bitch. Made me look like a fool when you stole my woman. Then, your little buster kicked me in the head. I thought I'd have some fun with you then maybe give you to my boys. Gonna teach you a lesson, *China*."

"And, after that?"

He pointed his finger at her and dropped his thumb.

"Wouldn't you rather have money? I have lots of money," she said, trying to distract him.

He seemed to think about her proposition before shaking his head. "Can't trust you. You'll promise me money then bring the cops down on me. Best I just have some fun with you. After, I'll let you join Hector."

"There will be people looking for me. Lee will find you. When he does, he'll kill you."

He scoffed at her. "You talk too much."

He reached into his back pocket to pull out a flicker knife. With a flick of his wrist, he twirled the blade as he studied her.

"Let's see what you got."

He reached down and slid the blade under the center strap of her bra. The fabric gave way to expose her breasts. A beefy hand reached down to squeeze her nipple roughly. She cried out and tried to flinch away. He grabbed her other breast and squeezed. She screamed in pain.

"Like that, *China*?" he asked as he twisted and pinched her flesh. "Just wait. There's lots more where that came from.

He slapped her hard across the face once, then again. Her head rocked. Bending over, he put a hand around her throat and squeezed. She gasped for air as he slapped her again and again.

She almost blacked out before he let go and stepped back. His eyes glazed over, and his chest heaved. Reaching down with both hands, he grabbed her panties to rip them apart and toss the pieces aside. She fought against the restraints.

While she struggled, he unbuttoned his trousers and let them drop around his ankles. He pushed his skivvies down around his knees and took his erect penis in his hand. He stroked his swollen member with one hand as he slipped his other hand between her thighs.

"You're gonna love this, *China*," he said as he forced his fingers inside her.

As she lifted her head to spit at him, she saw him look up with a smile on his face. The smile slowly turned to a frown.

An earsplitting explosion made her start. A black hole appeared on Rafe's tee shirt. The mirror behind him cracked, and blood splattered its surface. Dismay etched his features as he dropped onto his butt and panted, taking quick, shallow breaths. Then he stopped breathing. His dead eyes stared at her while his hand gripped his rigid penis like a toddler's favorite toy.

In the splintered mirror, she could see Boobs staggering toward her unsteadily. Breathing heavily, he dropped next to her.

"Are you all right?" he asked.

He was doing his best not to embarrass her by looking away.

She trembled. Silent tears rolled down the side of her face. "I think so. Scared and embarrassed but alive, thanks to you."

"Give me a minute, and I'll cut you free. I just need to catch my breath. That boy near did me in with his choke hold."

"Maybe you could just cut one hand free, and I'll do the rest."

He nodded and pulled a six-inch switchblade from his pocket and flicked it open. He turned around far enough to slice through the binding on her wrist then handed her the blade behind his back. Taking the proffered knife, she shakily sliced the rest of the bindings then, trembling, carefully folded the knife and handed it back to him.

"Your clothes are in my office. I didn't take the time to stop and get them. I'll wait here while you get dressed."

She tried to stand only to find her shaking legs wouldn't hold her and sat down again.

"There's a bottle of whiskey in my desk drawer," he said, taking notice of her condition. "Holler down when you're ready, and I'll come up. Take your time, missy. I'm not going anywhere."

It took a few minutes before she felt confident enough to try standing again. She wobbled toward the metal staircase at the back. By clutching at the railing, she managed to haul herself up the stairs. Her clothes were in a heap just inside the door. She dropped to the floor and pulled on her clothes as tears rolled down her cheeks. After a while, she managed to pull herself together enough to stand up.

The whiskey in the desk drawer was cheap and burned her throat as she took a swig. She thought about it, then took another.

Walking to the office entrance, she yelled down, "It's all right. You can come up now, Boobs."

He came slowly up the stairs with the gun still in his hand. A frown dragged at the corners of his mouth. He looked tired and embarrassed as he entered the office. She was reminded again he wasn't a young man.

"I'm sorry that happened to you," he said. "Rafe came in here right after you called. I told him you were on the way over, thinking he'd take the hint and leave. I didn't know he had it in for you. After he choked you out, I tried to stop him; he put me out too. It's just lucky I came around when I did."

He placed the gun on his desk with a shaky hand. "I found your gun in your things. I didn't know what else to do."

"It's all right," she said. "You did the right thing."

She handed Boobs the bottle. He took a long pull before sitting down at his desk with a used-up look.

She pulled her phone from her pocket to call Jason.

"I need a cleaner."

He took down the address she gave him without asking any questions. When she'd ended the call, she turned to Boobs.

"I need to find Song. There will be men here soon to take care of Rafe's body. You have to understand, Boobs. As far as anyone is concerned, this never happened."

He met her gaze and nodded before repeating, "It never happened."

Below, they found an unconscious Song trussed with duct tape. The blood from a deep cut on the side of his head soaked the white collar of his shirt.

As they worked his bindings free, Bai questioned Boobs. "Do you remember what I asked you over the phone?"

He shook his head. "The only man with a tan around here is me."

"Have you seen anything of Daniel Chen?"

"No, but then I don't suppose I would. If he's on the run from the Norteños, he wouldn't be hanging out in the Mission. This is their turf, and Chen's no fool." He hesitated a moment. "How is Lee? Do you know what happened?"

"I think the tan man shot him. I'm not sure why."

"Is he going to be all right?"

"In time," she said. "Right now, he's resting."

"Knowin' him, he's madder'n a flea on fake fur."

She smiled weakly. "He is. He can't wait to get well enough to find the shooter and return the favor."

Their conversation reminded her of their earlier phone call. "What did you ask me over here to talk about?"

Boobs looked confused for a moment before he spoke. "I heard that inspector who came here asking about Daniel Chen committed suicide. I was wondering if you knew anything about that. I thought his death might be connected."

She shook her head somberly at the memory. "Kelly died from despair."

Before she could elaborate, her phone rang. The cleaners had arrived. She went to the door with Boobs to let them in. Three Chinese men dressed in black suits waited at the door. Jason, thankfully, wasn't with them. Her first concern was Song. The cleaners carried him out to see to his medical needs before returning.

After showing them the body, she collected her shredded underwear and used her knife to pry the bullet from her gun out of the wall. She didn't want to leave any evidence behind. The bullet would serve as a grim reminder of how close she'd come to making orphans of her children.

Two of the men hauled the corpse out in a wheeled moving crate and shoved the box into a plain white van. The third man sprayed the surrounding surfaces down with some kind of cleaner to remove any trace evidence. The men didn't utter a word the entire time.

They left as silently as they'd arrived. As if nothing had happened.

chapter 33

Bai drove home alone.

She experienced a sense of dislocation as she rode the lift up to her flat, feeling as if she stood outside her body and watched herself as if she were a stranger. After drawing a hot bath, she peeled off her clothes and slipped into the steaming water without registering the heat. She felt numb to the world around her.

Her phone, sitting on the edge of the tub, rang. It was Jason.

"Are you all right?"

"Yes."

"You don't sound all right. Did you kill the Norteño?"

"No. Somebody did me the favor. Is Song all right?"

"He'll be fine. He has a thick skull. Do you want me to come over?"

He sounded concerned. She didn't want his comfort.

"No. I'm fine. I have a date with Howard tonight. I don't want to be late."

She spoke the words but didn't feel them. She didn't feel anything.

"Fine," he replied, sounding angry as he ended the call.

"Fine!" she said to the empty bath, mumbling to herself as she leaned back and tried to let go of the horror.

The experience with Rafe terrified her. She found the feeling profoundly unpleasant and wanted to forget what had happened. Her head slipped under the surface of the hot water as she attempted to wash away the memory. Eyes open, she stared through the rippling water at the light on the ceiling. She stayed submerged until aching lungs forced her to the surface. Taking a deep breath, she slid beneath the water again, determined to shake off the fear holding her hostage.

When she emerged from the tub, she felt more in possession of herself. She dried her pruned skin and walked into her closet to stare at the pile of dresses, high heels, and designer bags still lying on the floor.

Her bare foot toed the packages. Casual toeing turned into kicking as she suddenly vented her anger. Once she'd thoroughly trounced the frilly frocks, she felt better.

Ignoring the designer clothing, she chose to wear her standard black tee, jeans, and trainers. Her asymmetrical leather jacket with the knife sleeve completed her outfit. When she was dressed, she felt like her old self, not someone else's idea of who she should be.

Howard's limo arrived at seven. He wasn't in it. One of his security guards ushered her into the rear compartment, where she sat alone. The car proceeded toward the Embarcadero. She was surprised when they stopped under the portico of the Grand Hotel.

Her escort ushered her out and silently led her to the bank of elevators, where he selected the top-floor lounge. She smiled at the thought of her first meeting with Howard and then frowned. She still hadn't found a way to like him. Tonight she would end the charade and tell him she had no interest in marrying him.

The elevator opened to a silent room. Her guide ushered her across the empty lounge to where six bodyguards stood in a cluster. Howard sat in a chair nearby with a smug expression. He silently gestured for her to have a seat in a chair facing him a few yards away.

When she'd taken the seat, he spoke. "I brought you here, Bai, to teach you a lesson."

She thought the comment odd. "What lesson would that be, Howard?"

He smirked. "People should know their station in life."

He flicked his fingers. His bodyguards moved aside so she could see Michael Chin held down on his knees with his arms pulled up behind his back by two of Howard's bodyguards. Blood from a split lip stained his chin.

"Imagine how disappointed I was to find you'd turned down my offer of a date to go out with a waiter—a servant. Do you have any idea how you made me feel? The humiliation? You turned me down to go out with this?" he said, pointing at Michael.

Michael raised his head to look at her then looked away. He looked angry and ashamed. Her heart ached for him. Instinctively, she wanted to protect him. As she stared at Michael, she felt an anger so intense it flowed through her like electricity.

"This seems to be my day for men to teach me lessons," she said as she turned to stare malevolently at Howard. She stood with her hand on the sleeve of her jacket. "School is over."

Her gaze unsettled Howard. His smile disappeared to be replaced by a haughty look as he shook his head. "I see you haven't learned your lesson."

His hand flicked up, and one of his men stepped forward to strike an open-handed blow across Michael's face, one that rocked his head back.

Her voice devoid of emotion warned him again. "End this now, Howard, and I'll let you walk away. If not, people are going to get hurt. One of those people is going to be you."

He looked uncertain for a moment then seemed to dismiss her threat. He started to raise his hand again. She flicked the knife from her sleeve. The blade smacked into the center of Howard's palm and buried itself to the hilt. He looked at one side of his hand and then the other. The knife protruded evenly on both sides.

He let out an ear-piercing scream.

Half of his security team rushed toward Howard to protect him while the other three men dropped Michael to the floor and rushed Bai. Ducking under the first man's grasp, she kicked the back of his knee and forced him into a kneeling position. She took a quick step back to use the kneeling man as an obstacle to the other two men facing her before leaping onto his back and using him as a springboard, launching into the air to kick a second man in the face. Her shoe slapped his head hard enough to flip him to the ground.

The third man reached for her. From behind him, Michael swept her assailant's feet from under him. Bai turned in time to kick the man in the face to make sure he stayed down.

She took a quick look at Michael to make sure he was all right. He pointed behind her. Her first attacker lurched to his feet. She turned and clapped her hands over his ears. As he reached up to cover his ears, she reached inside his jacket to pull a gun from his shoulder holster then turned to train the automatic weapon on Howard, who whimpered as he held his bloody hand out in front of him.

Everyone froze. It took Howard a moment to realize Bai pointed a gun at him. He plopped into a chair with fear distorting his features. When one of the bodyguards started to reach for a gun, Bai shook her head and pulled back the hammer on her weapon while flicking off the safety. The bodyguard's hand slowly dropped back to his side.

"I've enjoyed the lesson, Howard," she said evenly. "We should do this again sometime soon."

He didn't appear to hear her. His head bowed over his bleeding hand as he mewled like a kitten.

Bai directed her comments at his bodyguards.

"We'll be leaving now. If I ever see any of you again, you'll be very sorry. If I hear you've tried to teach anyone else a lesson, I will find you and hurt you. That's a promise. As a sign I have no hard feelings, you can keep the knife. Michael, we're leaving now," she added for his benefit. "Say good-bye to the nice gentlemen."

Michael looked aside at the guard who'd slapped him. Before the guard could react, Michael punched him in the face, knocking him to the ground.

"Bye," he said before preceding her toward the exit. She walked backward with the gun still pointed at Howard. At the exit, she flicked on the safety, ejected the clip, and tossed the gun back into the room before pulling the door closed behind her.

No one followed. The two of them avoided the elevator and took the stairs.

She hesitated when they reached the street, turning to face Michael she asked, "How bad is the lip?"

He reached up to feel his mouth. "It'll be fine. Thanks."

"I'm sorry that happened."

He shook his head and smiled. "I should have been the one saving you. I feel like an idiot."

"Don't," she said. "You couldn't have known what you were getting into when you asked me out. My life is a mess."

He looked at the ground. "When I met you, I thought I could handle anything, Bai." His gaze lifted, and he tried, but failed, to smile. "I've learned that's no longer true. When you said we live in different worlds, I really didn't understand."

"You're a nice man, Michael. Forget this ever happened. Forget you ever met me."

He nodded and smiled. "I think you're going to be a hard woman to forget."

She patted his cheek affectionately. "You have my number. If Howard bothers you again, call me."

He nodded and smiled soberly before turning to walk away. She watched him go while thinking things might have been different if she'd met him ten years earlier. Then again, maybe not.

She'd never wanted anyone the way she'd wanted Jason. And that hadn't changed.

chapter 34

The drive to Healdsburg the next morning gave Bai time to think. Mostly, it gave her time to put together a plausible story for Elizabeth. She mentally tried out a number of scenarios. Nothing held together. After an hour of trying, she decided to tell her the truth—but not the whole truth.

The family had just finished lunch when she arrived. The triad soldiers looked a little heavier than the last time she'd seen them. Coleta's cooking was broadening their waistlines along with their taste in Mexican food. The entire house smelled like roasting meat, sweet spices, and baking bread.

She found everyone in the kitchen helping with cleanup. Jia threw her arms around Bai to hug her while Dan held back. She could see the hurt on her child's face. Alicia nodded a restrained greeting.

Bai smiled. "I have an announcement. I'm no longer dating Howard Kwan. I have no intention of marrying him."

Dan grinned and ran to throw her arms around her mother. Bai laughed as she hugged her daughter. She'd managed to make at least one person in her life very happy. The stormy look on Elizabeth's face informed her she'd managed to make another person in her life very unhappy.

"May I have a word with you alone, Bai?" Elizabeth asked.

"Certainly," she acceded soberly and turned to walk into the living room.

Elizabeth followed her and confronted her when she stopped. "What do you mean you're no longer dating Howard? I thought you were doing marvelously. His mother said he'd taken you shopping. What happened?"

"It's a long and ugly story. The end result is that I don't think Howard wants to marry me. Not after I stabbed him."

"You stabbed him?!"

"I warned him first. He wouldn't listen."

"There are other ways to end a relationship. How badly is he hurt?"

"I suspect he'll be signing his name with his left hand for a while."

"Why on earth would you stab him?"

"You really don't know him, Elizabeth. I met a young man for drinks. When I saw Howard for dinner the next night, he had that young man held down by his bodyguards so I could watch them beat him. Howard said he was teaching me a lesson—that people should know their stations in life."

Elizabeth looked stunned. "Was this young man all right?"

"Yes, he's fine, but that doesn't excuse Howard's behavior."

Elizabeth grew silent a moment before replying. "No. I agree. I'd hoped Howard might be a good match for you, but I can see I was mistaken." Her eyes met Bai's gaze steadily. "I trust your judgment. You did the right thing."

She put her arms around Elizabeth and hugged her. "I can't say that I'm sorry for stabbing Howard, but I'm sorry if I disappointed you."

"You haven't disappointed me in the least," Elizabeth replied hurriedly, though her dejected expression suggested otherwise.

Bai decided it was a good time to change the subject. "Will you be going to the spa with us?"

"Of course," she replied. "I insisted Coleta come with us as well. We've all been working far too hard lately. We need an afternoon of relaxation."

"What about Lee?"

"He's coming too, not that he's keen on a spa day. He'll go anywhere just to get out of the house. You might want to take him back to the city with you. He's starting to get irritable and restless."

"I'll talk to him and then to Dan. She'll have a better idea of whether he's ready to leave the nest."

"She's done really well." Elizabeth said, referring to Dan's role as a nursemaid.

"I know. I'm proud of her. My little girl is growing up."

"Which reminds me," Elizabeth confided. "There's an older boy at the stables who Alicia feels is showing too much interest in Jia. She says Jia is very naive about boys and fears he may be up to no good. I didn't want to say anything for fear Jia may have a crush on him. You know how foolish young girls can be, and she's still very fragile. I feared if I were to caution her, she'd just become more determined in her pursuit of romance. I've seen this happen before."

"Are you referring to me and Jason?"

"I knew you'd understand," Elizabeth said sweetly.

Bai accepted the rebuke.

"Young love can be a trying experience for everyone involved," she replied. "I'll ask Dan and Alicia to keep an eye on Jia. I know how she feels; I won't interfere with her romance unless I absolutely have to. Anything else I should know?"

"Alicia's a lovely girl, and smart, but very reserved. When I talk to her about returning to school or her plans for the future, she retreats into her room. I'm not sure what to make of her."

"Give her time," Bai said. "She's been abused. Her father was a gang member. She doesn't know what happened to her mother. Her only family was the gang, and they were neither kind nor gentle. I'm happy to say one of her tormenters has moved on."

"As in, left town?"

"I suspect he's gone a bit farther," Bai replied while avoiding eye contact.

Elizabeth lifted her eyebrows in silent appraisal but didn't appear shocked by the revelation.

"I'll talk to Alicia," Bai continued. "I suspect she's still trying to make up her mind whether or not to give this family a chance."

"We must seem an odd bunch to an outsider," Elizabeth mused.

"I used to think the same thing. Recently, I've come to realize perhaps we're not the most dysfunctional family in the world. When I think about the Kwans and how badly they treat one another, I'm left feeling grateful for the family I've got. We may not always agree with each other, but we've always loved and protected one another."

Elizabeth looked chastened. Bai quickly backtracked. "I didn't mean to imply your sister is a bad person."

"I don't think you need to," Elizabeth replied sadly. "Jade was single-minded even as a child. Her determination to acquire wealth became an obsession. I thought she would eventually realize there's more to life than money." She let out a deep sigh. "I guess I was wrong. I think I've been wrong about a lot of things."

Elizabeth wiped tears from her eyes as she continued. "When you became pregnant with Dan," she said in a soft voice, "you were little more than a child. I never told you, but I was selfishly pleased when you fought to keep your baby. Dan is as dear to me as you and Jason, but I often wonder if I didn't take advantage of you."

"What's this all about?" Bai asked, wondering where the conversation was headed.

"You missed college, and parties, and the adventure of living on your own. I robbed you of your youth. I've never told you how sorry I am."

Bai put her arms around the older woman. "You have nothing to be sorry for. I love my life. I love my daughter. And I love my family. And, if you hadn't told me, I wouldn't have known my youth had ended." She paused in thought. "Lee's the same age I am. I wonder if he knows he's no longer young."

Elizabeth sniffed and spilled tears while gently rapping Bai on the shoulder with her clenched fist. Bai captured the errant hand and held it tightly while drawing Elizabeth closer, holding her as Elizabeth cried while wondering what she'd ever done to deserve so much love.

chapter 35

Spa day might have been more appropriately labeled torture day. Bai found herself stripped and scrubbed from head to toe as a small army of gloved professionals exfoliated, nourished, and oiled her skin. Hot towels and cold packs got intermittently applied to either shrink or to plump various parts of her anatomy. Tiny fish nibbled on her toes while a woman with delicate hands removed the cuticles from her fingers.

The experience lasted the entire afternoon. By the time they'd finished, it was time for Bai to return to the city. Despite Dan's objections, Lee insisted on accompanying Bai. After his things were loaded into the MINI Cooper for the trip home, the rest of the family gathered to see them off.

Bai drew Alicia aside to speak with her. "I wanted to thank you for looking after Jia."

"You don't have to thank me," Alicia replied. "Anyone can see she's damaged goods."

"I'm sorry I haven't been around more. I'll be back tomorrow, and we can talk."

Alicia shrugged. "You don't have to worry about me. Life here is good. The Corazons are nice people. Dan and Jia are fun."

"Is there anything you need? I feel like I've been neglecting you. I hope you understand."

"You need to worry about yourself," Alicia advised her in a hushed voice. "Rafe doesn't like to lose. He might come after you when he can't find me."

Bai rested her hand on Alicia's shoulder. "You don't have to worry about Rafe. I heard he went up against Hector, and it went badly for both of them. He's gone."

Bai had sanitized Rafe's demise. She didn't feel the need to burden the girl with the truth.

Alicia brightened at the news. "Maybe now the nightmares will stop. I want to forget the last year like it never happened. With him gone, maybe I can start over." The girl took a deep breath and continued. "The truth is . . . I don't want to go back to the city."

Once she started to talk, the words came out in a rush. "I've talked to the Corazons, and they said I could stay with them. Their children are grown. They have room for me, and they said I could stay here if I got your permission. I could go to school here where nobody knows me and work in the orchards with Mr. Corazon. He said he'd teach me."

Alicia's plans took Bai by surprise. Putting her own feelings aside, she considered what was best for the girl.

"I'll talk to the Corazons, Alicia. If that's what you really want, I'm sure we can make arrangements."

Bai put her palm on Alicia's cheek and smiled. The girl looked a little embarrassed by the gesture but didn't draw away.

"I don't mean to hurt your feelings," Alicia said. "I just feel more comfortable here with the Corazons."

Bai could understand how unfamiliar Alicia might find a home where the inhabitants spoke another language and followed different customs. She'd hoped Alicia would overcome those differences, but those expectations may have been unrealistic and selfish. Alicia had enough problems without Bai's adding to them.

"Don't worry about me," Bai replied. "If you're happy here, then this is where you belong. Follow your heart, Alicia, but know that I'm here if you need me."

Alicia smiled and thanked her before stepping back to join Jia and Dan.

Bai walked to the car and stepped into the driver's seat. Already sitting next to her on the passenger side, Lee squirmed restlessly. She started the engine and waved farewell as they spun around the driveway. As they rolled down the long drive, Lee let out a long sigh of relief.

"Are you that happy to be leaving?" she asked.

He turned to look at her with a smile. "Country life isn't for everyone. I yearn for the smell of diesel and the clamor of traffic. I want the fog and drizzle to dampen my spirit. I want sushi delivered to my door. Like a jilted lover, I yearn for my love—the city."

"You've only been away a couple of days."

"It seems much longer. I've found that time passes very slowly when you're surrounded by nature. So what happened between you and Howard?" he asked, changing the subject.

"He tried to teach me a lesson I didn't have any interest in learning. Push came to shove, and I put a knife in his hand."

He chuckled. "I just knew you were having fun without me."

"I should have listened to Jason. He told me something was wrong with Howard."

"He also told you that Naugahyde came from naugas. That was when you were nine. He had you running all over the neighborhood collecting money to save the baby naugas."

She smiled at the memory. "I was pretty gullible at nine. I've grown up since then."

"You're still gullible," he replied. "You've just gotten bigger. That's part of your charm."

"How are you feeling?" she asked in a more serious vein.

He paused before answering. His mood became somber. "I feel like I've been shot in the back."

She glanced aside to see his grave expression. "This is me you're talking to. I know when something is wrong. What else is going on?"

He seemed reluctant to answer her. His words came out hesitantly. "I feel mortal." His head tilted back against the headrest, and he closed his eyes. "For the first time in my life, I'm facing the aspect of nonexistence—the world without me. I find the prospect frightening."

"What are you going to do about it?"

His eyes opened, and he turned to her. "What do you mean?"

"You've been shot, Lee. I think it might help if you talked to someone about it."

"I'm talking to you," he said brusquely.

"I mean a professional, someone who specializes in treating traumatic experiences."

"You mean a shrink."

"Yes, a psychiatrist."

"I'll think about it."

"I'm going to nag you."

"I know. I'm surprised you've waited this long."

She glanced at him and smiled. "I'll go with you, if you want. Maybe we can get a discount."

The thought seemed to please him. He returned her smile.

They made it across the Golden Gate and home without any delays in traffic. Pleading fatigue, Lee went directly to his apartment. She suspected he needed time alone after spending several days surrounded by teenage girls.

After a light dinner, Bai followed his example and went to bed early. She awakened to find Lee sitting in a chair next to her bed.

"What are you doing here? What time is it?" she asked groggily.

"It's around ten o'clock."

"In the morning?"

"No. At night."

"I just got to sleep. Why did you wake me?"

"I was bored and decided to investigate the whereabouts of my phone, the one I'd dropped into Wen Liu's trunk. I'd expected to find it in Daly City under lock and key in the police tow yard where her car, by all rights, should be. Imagine my surprise when the map showed my phone had taken a detour to the Berkeley Hills."

Suddenly interested, she sat up in bed. "You're saying her car didn't get impounded?"

"That would appear to be the case. If I had to take a guess, I'd say someone took the car before the police could tow it away."

"Someone like Daniel Chen?"

"If I were to guess," he said while leaning back to admire his newly manicured nails.

"Why don't you make us some coffee?"

"The coffee is already made."

She got out of bed to walk to the closet, while Lee got up and retreated to the kitchen. Donning a red silk robe with intertwined dragons embroidered in gold on both front and back, she joined Lee at the kitchen counter where he sat sipping coffee. A steaming pot and an empty cup rested on the counter next to him.

As she poured coffee, she asked, "Have you made any more progress on deciphering the files on Wen Liu's phone?"

He looked at her and frowned.

"Not really. The files I've already managed to access don't have the same level of encryption. There's a strong possibility each file has its own key, which would mean my having to unlock one file at a time—a very long and tedious process. I suspect most of the information stored on her phone is also time-sensitive. Secrets tend to have a short shelf life."

"Then don't bother trying to access the files," she said. "Give me back the phone. It might be of more value to someone else."

"You're thinking of Chen?" Lee asked.

"Yes. The phone has little value to us. Perhaps we can trade it for something else."

"What?"

"Information. I'm hoping with the right incentive Chen will tell me what he knows of Wen Liu's murder, the tan man, and how all of it relates to the drug heist in the SOMA."

"If you're going after Chen, I'm going with you."

"No, you're not!" she stated. "You're barely able to walk. I'm sorry, but you'd only get in the way."

"You can't go alone. Chen may be a killer."

"I'm not Chen's enemy. He has no reason to harm me. He told me himself he owes me one."

Lee didn't look convinced. "I still don't like it."

"Trust me," she said with a note of determination. "I can do this on my own."

chapter 36

Bai drove her MINI Cooper to Berkeley and parked the car in the same set-aside where Lee had parked his Cadillac on their previous visit. She wanted to approach the house from the rear and look around before making her presence known.

Also, parking her car on the street below the house would make the vehicle less conspicuous. It seemed likely the police would periodically monitor the house for signs of occupation. Chen was still considered a person of interest in a cop killing, not to mention the little matter of two bodies having been found in his office.

She crossed the street quickly and made her way up the dark winding path while trying to make as little noise as possible. Night sounds surrounded her. Frogs croaked and crickets chirped a spring-time serenade. Light mist fogged the trees to keep the atmosphere chilly. The branches and leaves she brushed aside left a moist trail on the sleeves of her leather jacket.

She stopped at the edge of the glade nearest the garage to survey the dark house. No car was in sight. The place appeared deserted. She stood motionless and silent while considering her options. Now that she'd arrived, she didn't feel nearly as confident as she'd professed to Lee.

As she looked at the dark and forbidding house, it occurred to her that one of her options was to turn around and go home. She could forget she'd ever laid eyes on Daniel Chen, forget her compulsion to find out why Wen Liu was murdered, and give up finding the money or drugs from the heist in the Mission District. Her confidence wavered.

Steeling her resolve, she didn't give herself the chance to chicken out. Breaking from the cover of the trees, she marched up the drive in plain sight of anyone in the house to step onto the porch and ring the bell. Her stomach knotted in apprehension. Balling her fists, she willed her hands to stop shaking.

She waited, but no one answered.

Taking her phone from her jacket pocket, she looked again at the GPS coordinates of Wen's car. Her phone app insisted the car was nearby. She glanced at the attached garage, but there were no windows to give her a view of the interior. She had no way to confirm the car's presence.

Convinced her phone wasn't lying to her, she rang the doorbell again and kept on ringing it, pressing her thumb against the button repeatedly. Several minutes passed as she doggedly refused to give up.

When the door sprang open, she jumped back in surprise.

Daniel Chen stood in the doorway pointing a gun at her. He scowled at her and flicked the barrel of his gun to indicate she should join him inside. After she walked into the house, he shut the door behind her with a thump. The house smelled musty and acrid.

Without speaking, he motioned for Bai to walk toward the back of the house. She preceded him down a dark hallway to a large modern kitchen. Following her into the room, Chen pushed against a wood panel, and a thick hidden door sprang open. He motioned with the gun for her to enter. She walked through the portal and down a set of metal stairs.

At the bottom of the stairs was another door. Chen leaned past her to open the door by pressing his thumb against a bio-sensor. Pushing her from behind, he ushered her through the doorway.

Bright incandescent lights dazzled her vision. Blinking to focus her eyes, she took in a large room holding racks of guns, a wall of electronic equipment with flat-panel monitors, a bunk bed, and a utility kitchen. Images on the flat screens shifted from one view to another, displaying the rooms in the house as well as the grounds outside the home. It became obvious to Bai the house had dozens of hidden cameras. She hadn't detected even one.

Chen's voice was inquisitive. "How did you find me?"

She held up her phone. "I used GPS on Wen Liu's car."

"Impossible," he replied. "I disabled the GPS on the vehicle."

She smiled. "My friend put a phone in the trunk of her car."

Chen frowned at her. "You're a resourceful woman. What do you want?"

"What is this place?" she asked.

"This is a safe house. At least I thought it was until you rang my doorbell. I'll ask one more time," he said in a threatening manner. "What do you want?"

"I want to give you this," she replied, pulling Wen's phone from her pocket and holding it out for him.

"Why are you giving me a phone?"

"It's Wen's phone."

He reached out and took it from her.

"I don't really need it. I have duplicates of all the data she carried."

He looked at her with a bemused expression then held up the phone. "Then again, it's probably best this doesn't find its way into wrong hands. Thanks, but you shouldn't have come here."

"You've been here the entire time, haven't you? You were here when we questioned Wen. You saw her leave. Why didn't you stop her?"

The question seemed to take him by surprise. When he answered, his voice sounded defensive. "We assumed you were sent to find *me*. I'd been warned someone was looking for me. Wen was doing her job, what she'd been trained to do. She led you away from me. We didn't realize we'd both been targeted." His face became taut, and for a moment his eyes lost focus. When his attention returned to Bai, he said, "I don't believe you came here to point out my mistakes. What is it you really want?"

"I want answers. I want to know why the tan man killed Wen and why he shot my partner. I want to know what you have to do with the heist in the Mission District and why two men were killed in your office."

He scoffed. "Why should I tell you anything?"

"Boobs said you were a good man. I believe he's a good judge of character."

"Who?"

"Jefferson Boob," she said in exasperation, "the man who owns the gym where you fight."

Chen shook his head. "I don't have any idea what you're talking about."

His remark brought her thoughts to an abrupt halt.

"Are you saying you don't know Jefferson Boob?"

He nodded. "That's exactly what I'm saying."

The revelation turned her state of mind upside down. She thought back to the discussions she'd had with Boobs and the stories he'd told her. Suddenly, a new perspective on the situation opened up. After a moment of reflection, she sighed with the realization she'd been conned from the very beginning.

"Is there something wrong?" Chen asked at her prolonged silence.

"There's a lot wrong," she replied. "It turns out I've been collecting money for baby naugas again." When she'd gathered her thoughts, she asked, "Why did the tan man kill Wen? Why did he shoot my partner?"

His face clouded over with a dark expression. "You hired him to kill Wen."

Her eyes got big. "I didn't hire him. I swear I didn't."

He looked momentarily taken aback by her startled expression. Then he smiled. "Not you. *Yu* . . . Kwan Yu."

"Jade Kwan?"

He nodded as she recalled the word he'd uttered in her office while watching the video of the tan man. Chen had spoken Chinese; she'd listened in English. She felt like giving herself a head slap.

Instead she asked, "Why would Jade Kwan want Wen Liu dead?"

He smirked. "Howard Kwan sold Wen information about his brother's gambling debts and didn't want anyone to know he'd betrayed his family. To be safe, he told his mother Wen had provided the information, assuming Yu would have her killed in reprisal. With Wen out of the way, Howard assumed there would be no way his betrayal could come back to haunt him."

"Why would Howard sell information about his brother's gambling debts?"

"To discredit his brother and take the presidency. But if his mother were to find out he'd given away a casino to sabotage his brother, he'd face serious repercussions. Of course, neither of them knew Wen was an MSS agent. As her handler, I had knowledge of all her dealings."

"Are you absolutely sure the tan man works for Jade Kwan?"

He shrugged. "At one time, he was a government agent. He may or may not have retired before starting a charter flight business in the Far East. His clients seem to be mostly warlords in Afghanistan and northern Pakistan, but he's not particular about whom or what he carries on his aircraft. Of late, he's been doing work on behalf of Kwan Yu. She was trafficking drugs through a casino. They used his chartered planes to distribute the drugs."

"Do you have any idea why the tan man would shoot my partner?"

He frowned. "You ask a lot of questions."

She waited, unwilling to give up until she had the answers she'd come looking for.

He shrugged and walked across the room to pull aside a screen. "Why don't you ask him?"

The tan man sat strapped to a captain's chair with duct tape wound around his ankles, wrists, and waist. He looked a little gray beneath his brown skin. A number of his teeth and fingernails lay on the floor at his feet. Several of his toes had been smashed to bloody pulps. Burn marks marred his skin.

Chen gestured at his captive. "Let me introduce you to Ryan Elliott, or the 'tan man,' as you call him."

The shock of seeing the tan man so near and so bloodied left her momentarily frozen.

Shaking off the shock, she asked, "How long have you had him here, torturing him?"

"Since yesterday," Chen answered diffidently. "To be honest, I don't think he has any more secrets to tell. At this point, I'm just taking revenge. Wen was my friend, my lover. I was thinking of flaying him next. What do you think?"

Despite her hatred for the tan man, she couldn't condone torture. The sight repelled her.

"I don't think you're enjoying this nearly as much as you pretend.

Otherwise, you wouldn't have bothered showing him to me. You want me to tell you it's all right to stop now."

He looked at her and sighed dramatically. "I fear you may be right. Should I put a bullet in his head?"

"No. Please," she begged. "I think he's had enough."

Chen barked a brittle laugh. "Your sympathy is wasted on him. He wouldn't show you the same consideration. Wen opened her door for him because she trusted him to abide by the rules. He didn't show her any mercy."

"What rules?"

His face quickly shut down, and the anger he'd let her witness vanished in an instant.

He ignored her questions and said brusquely, "Ask him about your friend. You don't have much time."

A croaking voice interrupted. "That man is an enemy agent."

She turned to look at what was left of Ryan Elliott. His head listed, but he was conscious.

She walked over to stand before him then dropped onto her haunches so he could see her face. "I may be able to save you if you tell me the truth."

His head came up to stare at her with one eye. The other eye remained swollen shut. "You're one of them."

"One of who?" she asked.

"Commies," he spat.

"I'm not a commie," she said in denial. "I'm a Democrat. Some might argue the distinction. Nonetheless, if you help me, I may be able to help you."

"Water," he said, licking his lips.

She looked around at Chen, who nodded impatiently and pointed at a small stainless steel sink. She stood to fill a glass sitting in the sink then helped Elliott drink. Most of the liquid sloshed down his chin to fall in his lap.

When he'd had his drink, he rasped, "What do you want?"

"Why did you shoot my partner in the back?"

"Who's your partner?" he said tiredly.

"This was several days ago—a Chinese man who was following you on Sansome Street."

"He followed me."

"You shot him because he followed you?"

"I thought he was one of them," Elliott said with a nod in Chen's direction.

Bai shook her head in dismay. "You shot him because he's Chinese?"

Elliott didn't offer a rebuttal. She stood, stunned by his reasoning. In her mind, every action required a rational motive. She stared down at her nemesis while trying, and failing, to understand him. Finally, she gave up.

chapter 37

Chen's voice interrupted Bai's dismay. "I seem to have another visitor. This place has become entirely too popular."

Chen watched a screen that showed Jason standing in the dark living room while staring into the camera. "Whoever he is, he's very good. He shouldn't have been able to detect that camera in the light, let alone the dark. Who do you suppose he might be?"

"He's with me," Bai replied.

Chen turned to her. "If that's the case, I suggest you join him. Very shortly this house will be an inferno. If you hurry, you'll live to miss the fun."

He reached behind him while keeping his gun on her. The door to the stairwell sprang open as he flicked the gun barrel to hurry her along. She took the hint and moved toward the door.

Ryan Elliott's raspy voice hailed her. "What about me?!"

She stopped and turned.

Before she could make another move, Chen fired two bullets into Elliott. She whipped around to stare at Chen. His face showed no emotion.

"Leave now if you want to live," he said, turning the gun on her. "I've repaid the favor, so now we're even. If you come looking for me again, I'll kill you."

Bai bolted for the door to take the steps two at a time. Her breath came in rapid, shallow gulps as she swallowed her fear.

Pushing open the hidden door in the kitchen, she ran toward the front of the house. Jason met her at the entry. She'd never been so glad to see him.

"What's happening, Bai?"

"No time to talk," she blurted. "Run!"

She grabbed his hand and pulled him toward the door. He followed her reluctantly as she twined her fingers in his and ran.

They sprinted across the lawn behind the house, ignoring wet branches as they scrambled through bushes to reach the flagstone trail. Her feet flew down the path. When they reached her car at the bottom of the hill, she pushed her keys into Jason's hand then ran around to the passenger side. Jason got in and started the car as she jumped into the seat next to him. He put the car in gear and drove down the narrow lane.

"Can you tell me why we're in such a hurry?" he asked.

A boom sounded behind them, and flames shot into the night sky. Jason looked into the rearview mirror but kept driving. "I guess that answers my question."

"Did you drive here?" she asked.

"No. Lee dropped me off then went back to the city. He's in no condition to even be driving. He insisted I come out here and save you. The idea seems a little silly now."

She put her hand on his, the one shifting gears. "Thanks."

"Do you want to tell me what this is all about?"

She spoke rapid fire, the adrenalin in her system still making her jumpy. "I met with Daniel Chen. He says he's an MSS agent. I'm not sure what that means. Ryan Elliott, the tan man, said Chen was a Communist. Chen killed Elliott, just shot him twice! Bam! Bam! Crazy! Crazy! Crazy!"

"Slow down and take a deep breath, Bai. You're safe now."

She drew a deep breath and felt a tremor run through her. Panic still pushed her heart into her throat as she swallowed her dread.

Bai felt Jason's hand tense on the shifter as he said, "The Ministry of State Services is not an agency to mess with, Bai. They're very good at what they do."

"What, exactly, do they do?"

"They're an intelligence agency, probably the largest in the world. They gather information and remove anyone who gets in their way. They report directly to the Central Party of the People's Republic."

She gripped Jason's hand harder.

"Are you sure you're all right?" he asked.

"I think so. Everything happened so fast."

She trembled, and Jason glanced at her, feeling her fear through the hand resting on his.

"Did you say Ryan Elliott?"

"Yes, that was the tan man's name."

"I've heard the name mentioned before. He worked with the Kwans. It was rumored he had CIA connections."

"That's what Chen told me. He said Jade Kwan had Elliott kill Wen Liu. Chen was Wen's handler, and her lover."

Jason nodded. "Chen was right to kill Elliott."

"How was he right?"

"If someone murdered you in cold blood, Bai, I wouldn't rest until I'd killed them. Chen did what he had to do."

"Revenge won't ease his grief," she said in a quiet voice.

"No," he agreed, "but it will ease his guilt. He was her handler, her protector. His failure to keep her safe will haunt him."

"You talk as if you know him?"

He glanced aside at her, his face a hard mask. "I think we might have a lot in common."

"Meaning me, I suppose. You think of me as someone you need to protect?"

"Yes," he replied. His voice conveyed frustration. "Why do you do it, Bai? Why do you put yourself at risk? Most of the people you look for don't even want to be found."

The question wasn't one she hadn't asked herself a number of times. Her reasons for being a *souxun* were convoluted, sometimes difficult even for her to figure out.

"I feel like I'm doing something good for someone, making a small positive difference in the world. If I can find a lost child or a sibling separated from loved ones by forces beyond their control, I've brought some joy into the world. And people aren't always lost. Sometimes they're abandoned. That pain needs to be addressed as well." She turned to look at his profile. "Those are all selfish reasons, I know. Most of the time, what I do makes me feel good and gives me a sense of accomplishment. Besides, I'm really good at finding people. I think it might be the only thing I'm really good at."

"You're a good mother," he reminded her.

She sighed. "I think Dan has done a good job of raising me. She's smarter than both of us put together. Did you know she's taking college courses now? I was lucky to make it through high school. Most teenagers just think their parents are dumb. Hers really are."

He smiled at her assessment. "You're being too hard on yourself."

They rode in silence as Jason efficiently chauffeured her through the town of Berkeley.

When she spoke her voice held a note of sorrow. "I still have some unfinished business. I've been such a fool."

He asked tentatively. "Is this about me?"

His question brought a reluctant smile to her lips. "No. All women are fools for the men they love. That's self-inflicted stupidity. In this case, I've been played by strangers. And that," she said, turning to look at him, "pisses me off."

"Who, other than me, has made a fool of you?"

"Until I'm sure of what happened, I'd rather not say."

"Can't you tell me what you think happened?"

She shook her head. "Not yet. I know how protective you are. Enough people have died because of my gullibility. I've left a trail of bodies in my search for Daniel Chen. I don't want any more blood on my hands."

He scowled but appeared to be resigned to her reticence. When they reached her home, he parked the car in front of her house behind his black BMW. He got out and walked around to the sidewalk to open her door. Handing the key to the MINI to her, he kissed her on the forehead.

"You're not coming up?" she asked.

"I have business."

"It's two in the morning. What kind of business do you have at two in the morning?"

He stared at her.

"Forget I asked. It's better not to know," she said.

She put her arms around his waist and held him. "Thank you for saving me."

"I didn't save you."

"It's the thought that counts."

He put his hands on her shoulders and turned her toward the steps of her building to send her on her way. She walked up the steps as he turned to reclaim his waiting car. She watched him drive away from inside the glass door then stepped into the elevator and pushed the button for the third floor.

Lee waited for her in the entryway of her apartment.

Wrapping an arm around her shoulders, he asked, "Did Jason find you?"

"No. I found him. Fix me a drink, and I'll tell you all about it."

Lee poured her a scotch neat and sat with her as she told him the story from beginning to end. His expression ran the gamut of emotions from surprise to anger as she related the secrets she'd uncovered.

When she'd finished, he asked, "What now?"

She frowned as she met his gaze. "Since I started looking for Daniel Chen, I've been stumbling around like a fool in the dark. I need to pull aside the curtain of lies and let the truth shine in. So, that's exactly what I'm going to do."

chapter 38

The next morning, while sitting in her car outside of Boobs's Gym, Bai called the house in Healdsburg to check on her family and to speak with Alicia.

When the girl answered, Bai said, "I want you to do something for me. I want you to call Boobs and ask him for money."

"Why?" Alicia asked with a note of concern.

"I'd rather you didn't know. The less you know the better. I just want you to tell Boobs that Rafe told you everything. You want $100,000, or you're going to the police. Do you think you can do that?"

"Sure, but what's this all about?"

"It's about murder, lies, and betrayal."

In a solemn voice the girl said, "*Sangre por sangre.*"

"Yes," Bai acknowledged, "blood for blood. Tell him you're running away and want to meet in an hour at the diner where you met me and Hector. Then hang up. If he calls back, don't answer. Leave the rest to me."

Alicia agreed to make the call. Bai gave her Boobs's phone number then closed the connection.

Lee sat in the passenger seat next to her. "I'm going in with you."

"I wouldn't think of leaving you behind. This is as much for your benefit as it is mine. After all, you're the one who got shot. Let's give Alicia five minutes to make the call then pay our respects."

They waited for the time to pass before exiting the car and walking down the alley to the door of the gym. Letting themselves in quietly, they walked to the back of the cavernous room and silently stepped up the metal treads to the loft office.

Lee went first, pushing the door open slowly.

Boobs had his back to them. He stood on the Murphy bed that had been pulled away from the wall. A suitcase lay on the bed. His arms reached up to a hole in the wall, where the upright bed had covered a wall safe, to grab stacks of money and drop them into the bag at his feet.

"Going somewhere, Boobs?" Lee asked.

Boobs started. Twisting around with a stunned expression on his face, he stared at them. Bai stepped around Lee to get a better look at what was taking place while Boobs stood frozen.

"This isn't what it looks like," Boobs said as a smile slowly made its way to his lips.

"It looks like a man stuffing money into a suitcase," Bai said levelly, putting her hands in her jacket pockets.

Boobs stared at her a moment then chuckled. "Well, then . . . maybe it is what it looks like. But I can explain."

"I'll bet you can," replied Lee, pulling his .32-caliber Tomcat from the holster on his shoulder.

"Whoa! Whoa! Whoa!" exclaimed Boobs, raising his hands and showing more teeth than a Venezuelan beauty queen. "You look like you're getting ready to shoot me with that thing, Lee."

"You must be clairvoyant," Lee declared. "That's exactly what I was thinking."

Boobs's smile tensed. "There's no need for gunplay, Lee. We're all adults here. We can settle our differences without resorting to violence."

Lee shook his head. "I don't know, Boobs. I'm finding the notion of shooting you pretty attractive. I'm still hurting from the two bullets I took in the back. I think I'd feel better if I had somebody to commiserate with."

Boobs's smile lost some of its luster. Lee motioned with his gun for him to step down from the bed. Obliging, Boobs made his way toward his desk on the other side of the room.

"Take a seat in one of those chairs in front of your desk," Lee said.

As he sat down slowly, Boobs never took his eyes off of Lee.

Bai stepped onto the flimsy mattress of the Murphy bed to take a closer look at the wall safe where the rest of the money was still stashed. Behind the money she could see brown bricks wrapped in plastic.

Turning back to look at Lee, she said, "The heroin is here, too."

She jumped off the bed to walk over and confront Boobs.

"I want to know if you and Kelly planned on involving me from the beginning."

Boobs looked from Lee to Bai. His eyes took on a calculated look before shaking his head.

"No." His voice sounded sorrowful. "I argued with Kelly when he came up with the idea of letting you do his legwork for him. I told him it was a bad idea, but he was getting heat from his people. His bosses came to him and said they needed to find this fella, Chen. They wanted to find him fast, and Kelly didn't have any idea where to look. That's when he came up with the idea of using you. He said you could find Chen for him, and we could sidetrack the investigation on the heist at the same time. Chen made the perfect fall guy, and the drug heist gave Kelly an excuse to use police resources to find him." Boobs blew out a puff of air in obvious disgust. "Kelly said it was a win-win situation. That man was just too lazy to do his own damn job."

"What part did Rafe play?" she asked.

Boobs looked at her and shook his head.

Lee cocked the hammer on his pistol. "Answer the lady."

Boobs frowned and hesitated before saying, "Rafe was our inside man with the Norteños. He wanted to move up in the organization, but Hector was keeping him down. We convinced him if he went along with our operation, he could deal with Hector and get rich. He wasn't too bright, but he was smart enough to give us the location and time when the drug meet was to take place. It was his job to keep an eye on the Norteños in case somebody caught on to our game."

"Like the two Norteños in Daniel Chen's office?" she asked.

Boobs squirmed in the chair. "Yeah," he said in a quiet voice. "Those two were starting to ask questions and piece things together. The heist went bad from the start. Nobody was supposed to get hurt, but Rafe went off like Rambo, spraying lead and shooting anybody who got in the way. Those two got suspicious."

Lee interrupted. "Why put their bodies in Chen's office?"

"Moving the bodies and planting money and drugs was Kelly's idea. He wanted to close the case, and he was good at rigging crime scenes. I suspect he'd had some practice."

Bai smiled wryly in the face of their cold-blooded calculations and said, "Then Kelly started to develop a conscience. A cop got killed in the heist. He started to lose it."

Boobs leaned back into the chair, no longer smiling. "He was always a drunk. After the job, he started drinking heavy. When he drank, he got sentimental. I thought I was going to have to take care of him, but then he did me a favor and shot himself."

"But Rafe wasn't so obliging," she said with a hint of anger in her voice. "You used me to kill Rafe."

Boobs shook his head and scowled. "When you came in here and asked for my help to take Rafe's girl away from him, I could see it was just a matter of time before you figured out what was what. The fact is, missy, you just don't know when to quit. I figured a little taste of Rafe would back you off, but you just kept on. The mistake I made was not letting Rafe kill you before I put a bullet in him. I've always had a soft spot for the ladies."

"That wasn't the only mistake you made," Lee said coldly.

Boobs met Lee's gaze and concern crossed his features.

"You wouldn't shoot an unarmed man, would you?"

Lee smiled. "It would be silly of me to give you a gun. You might shoot me back."

Bai put up a hand to interrupt Lee while asking a pointed question of Boobs. "Why did you kill Rafe?"

Boobs turned back to her with a look of distraction. Her question seemed to take a moment to penetrate his awareness.

"Rafe was a fool. He got Hector's job but still wasn't happy. He wanted his cut of the drugs and money. We agreed to wait a year before divvying up the haul, but he wanted to live the high life. If he'd started spending money, it wouldn't take long for somebody to put two and two together."

"And he was the only one left who could link you to the heist," Lee added.

Boobs shrugged. "That, too."

Bai asked. "Why did you do it, Boobs?"

He looked sad for a moment then bemused, as if the answer to her question was obvious.

"I turned sixty-five this year. All I've got to show for my life is a lease on a rundown gym that doesn't make enough money to pay the bills. I want to sit on a porch in the sun and drink rum punch. Maybe have a pretty girl take care of me. For that, I need money. What other choice did I have?"

Bai didn't answer.

After a moment of silence, Lee asked, "Can I shoot him now?"

Bai turned to Lee. "If it will make you feel better, go ahead."

Lee pressed the revolver against Boobs's forehead. To his credit, Boobs didn't flinch away. He stared down the short barrel of the revolver until Lee eased the hammer down with his thumb.

"You probably need killing, Boobs, but I'm not the man to do it," Lee said sadly. "Take your money and your drugs and run. Learn how to sleep with your eyes open. The Sinaloa cartel has a long reach."

Boobs's shoulders visibly relaxed as he settled back into the chair and let out a long sigh.

When he got his breath back, he asked, "I don't suppose I could interest you two in sharing some of that money. You can have the drugs. I don't want no part of them. Never did."

"The loot is all yours," Lee replied. "Enjoy yourself while you can."

Boobs didn't look pleased with Lee's decision, but he didn't waste any more time. Getting up hesitantly, he walked across the room to continue throwing money into the suitcase with his back to them.

Lee and Bai made their way out of the building as silently as they'd entered. Outside, Lee stopped on the sidewalk and turned to Bai. "Are you all right with letting him go?"

Bai shrugged. "Boobs will never be free. He'll be looking over his shoulder until someone catches up with him." She shook her head. "Besides, he helped me save Alicia. I owe him for that."

He put his arm around her shoulders. "I don't know about you," he said, "but I'm finding it increasingly difficult to tell the good guys from the bad guys."

cʰɑpter 39

The drive took only a few minutes. Midmorning traffic was light as they crossed the city and climbed Nob Hill. Stepping out under the portico of the Mark Hopkins Hotel, Bai waited for Lee as he tipped the valet.

When he joined her, he asked, "Do you want me to go up with you?"

"No," she replied. "If I'm not back in thirty minutes, call Jason. Then come looking for me."

"Do you think Jade Kwan is capable of holding you against your will?"

"Until yesterday, I wouldn't have thought so. Now I'm not sure what Jade Kwan is capable of. I'll just feel better knowing you're here if I need you."

"Be careful."

"I will be. I promise."

She took the elevator to the penthouse floor. When she stepped out of the lift, Jade's security entourage met her. They relieved her of her knife. She hadn't bothered carrying her gun. After searching her thoroughly, they escorted her into a formal dining room where Jade sat at the head of a long dark table. Howard sat on her right wearing a scowl and a bandage on his hand.

Smiling, Jade gestured for Bai to take a seat on her left, facing Howard.

When Bai was seated, Jade addressed her. "Howard would like to apologize for his boorish behavior. He knows now he was completely out of line. Don't you, Howard?"

Howard didn't look repentant. From his expression, Bai got the impression Howard wanted nothing more than to crush her like a bug. She smiled, and his face got red.

She turned to Jade. "I don't think Howard's really sorry. I think he's too petty and self-involved to feel much of anything. He's a bully and a coward. He uses money to push people around as if he were a spoiled child."

Jade managed to keep her smile in place, but just barely. "Don't say I didn't warn you, but I will admit that I underestimated his stupidity when it came to dealing with you. I don't suppose you'd be willing give him another chance?"

Bai barely managed to suppress a laugh. "I thought stabbing Howard was sufficient to end any question of a marriage. In hindsight, I guess I should have shot him."

Jade's voice took on a brittle quality. "I take it you've decided to decline Howard's offer of marriage."

Bai shook her head in dismay. "I believe you have more to worry about than Howard's nuptials."

Jade put her game face back in place. "What do you mean?"

"Ryan Elliott is dead."

Jade's eyes momentarily narrowed before she casually replied, "I don't know anyone by the name of Ryan Elliott."

"I think you do," Bai replied just as nonchalantly. "He murdered a woman by the name of Wen Liu. Before he died, he confessed he killed her at your request."

Jade's gaze bored into Bai as if trying to fathom the intent behind her words. Her voice, when she replied, remained firm. "I would think that would be a matter for the police."

"He didn't confess to the police."

"Then I have nothing to worry about, do I?"

Her question hung in the air between them. Bai didn't answer immediately. When she spoke, she asked, "Did you know that Howard sold Wen Liu the information on his brother's gambling debts?"

Howard jumped up from his seat across the table. "That's a lie!"

Jade slowly stood to look from Bai's steely gaze to her frightened son standing next to her. Jade's hand snapped out to slap Howard across the face. The sound of her hand hitting his cheek cracked in the quiet room.

"You fool!" she screamed as he cringed.

When the room went silent, Bai added, "And, did you know that Wen Liu was an agent of the MSS?"

Jade turned to stare at Bai in dismay before turning back to Howard.

"I didn't know," Howard pleaded.

Jade sat back down with a look of determination scribing her features. "We can salvage this," she said hurriedly as she stared at Bai with a calculating gaze. "Who else knows of this?"

Bai looked into Jade's eyes and saw murder. The woman was trying to determine if killing Bai would solve her problem. "Did I mention that Ryan Elliott confessed to Wen Liu's handler, who also works for the Ministry of State Services?"

The color drained from Jade's face. Howard stood by helplessly, fidgeting.

Bai didn't give Jade a chance to recover. "You staged the assault on Howard to draw the hotel security away from Wen Liu's room, didn't you? You used me as a diversion while Ryan Elliott carried out your orders."

Jade turned her head slowly to stare venomously at Bai. "What do you want?"

"The truth," Bai replied heatedly.

"You have it. Get out!"

Bai stared into Jade's eyes and could see she'd gotten what she came for. Standing, she walked out of the room and into the hallway to retrieve her knife. Taking the elevator down, the lift stopped several times to admit travelers and luggage. By the time she reached the lobby, she'd been jostled and crowded to the back of the lift. When she finally stepped into the busy atrium and spied Lee waiting for her, she walked over and took his arm to stroll out of the hotel.

They walked from under the portico and into the sun. A beautiful spring day greeted them.

She spread her arms wide while tilting her face toward the light, proclaiming, "Can you feel it, Lee? That's the truth shining down to chase away all the black karma."

"How interesting," he said blandly. "The truth feels exactly like sunshine."

Turning to look at him, she put her hands into her jacket pockets and found something that shouldn't have been there. She pulled the object out to stare blankly at the phone in her hand.

"You didn't tell me you'd gotten my phone back," Lee said, taking the cellphone from her.

Bai turned her head to look back at the hotel. "I'm as surprised as you are."

Lee followed her gaze. "What are you thinking?"

"I'm thinking a buttload of black karma is about to pay the Kwans a visit."

"What do you want to do?"

She smiled and shrugged as she turned to meet his gaze. "I've been taught to know my station in life. Who am I to interfere in the affairs of others?"

Lee put his phone into his jacket pocket as he mused, "I heard about this new breakfast place in the Marina that makes great waffles."

She nodded sympathetically. "A waffle would be nice."

"A bacon waffle would be better," he said thoughtfully.

She grinned and took his arm again. "I believe you're right. A bacon waffle would be better."

acknowledgments

Thanks to my editor Dan Mayer for caring enough to make me work harder. I'm grateful to my readers—Ellen Torgerson, Dennis Mangers, and Susan Socal—for their invaluable feedback. A special thanks to Alan Yoshimura of Yoshimura Auto Service.

about the author

Thatcher Robinson lives and writes in Northern California. He was previously employed as the chief operating officer of an Internet security firm that develops top-secret cyber-warfare materials for the military and various government agencies. Prior to that, he was a software specialist at IBM research laboratories in Research Triangle Park, North Carolina. *Black Karma* is Thatcher's second book, following his debut novel, *White Ginger*. To learn more about Thatcher, visit his website at www.thatcherrobinson.com.

Photo by Gerry McIntyre/
GMPdigital.com